The Secret Things

Books by

PEGGY TROTTER

Year of Jubilee
Reviving Jules

The Secret Things

Unchained Souls Series Book 1

PEGGY TROTTER

The Secret Things
© 2017 Peggy Trotter

Published by Ransomed-Ever-After Books
ALL RIGHT RESERVED No portion of this publication may be reproduced, copied, scanned, or duplicated in any form, whether printed, photocopied, stored on drives or other electronic devices, or any other methods, current or forthcoming, without written consent of the publisher. Short quotations may be used in reviews or articles.

This novel is a work of fiction. Names, characters, businesses, places, events and incidents are either the products of the author's imagination or used in a fictitious manner. Any resemblance to actual persons, living or dead, or actual events is purely coincidental.

First Edition, 2017
ISBN 13: 978-0-692-82648-5
ISBN 10: 0-692-82648-3
Library of Congress Control Number: 2017900103
Printed in the United States of America

All Scripture used with this work are from the New American Standard Bible © The Lockman Foundation, 1995.

Cover Illustration © 2017 by Zanne Davis
Edited by Nancy Clark

*To those who hold
secret scars and secret sins.*

The Lord heals and renews all.

"The secrets things belong unto the Lord our God, but the things revealed belong to us and to our sons forever, that we may observe all the words of this law."

Deuteronomy 29:29

Chapter One

The woman's cerulean eyes bugged. She tugged the screen door against her cheek, pinching her pale face like a vice. A wispy squeak exhaled from her parted lips. Brock Langston's itinerary drained through the soles of his feet into the tongue and groove porch floor.

Dead wife standing.

Mouth-drying emotion bloomed a hoard of imaginary hornets in his brain. He sucked the moist mountain air into his lifeless lungs and buckled his hand against the white doorframe of the front door. He stared at her and tried again. "Jenna?"

The pulse at his wrist throbbed as he gripped the frame. Her gaze flared a blue flame. A slight shake of her head was her only reply.

The vinyl siding collapsed under his suction-cupped fingers. One more time. "I'm your husband."

Her shuddering breath tripled into rhythm-moaned words. "A...unt...Ellen."

He wanted to grip her, shake her—no, truly he could barely resist cradling her close, clasping her tighter than ever before. Anything to knock the terror-mingled discombobulation from her face.

How long had he dreamed of her? Still dreamed of her. Those expansive innocent eyes, so tinged with confection one moment, coy and flirting the next. The blanched skin couldn't deny her delicate features. No, there could be no mistaking her. It was Jenna. *His Jenna.*

He scanned beyond her into the interior of the house. No one could have heard her mere breath of a call. Sanity revisited him like a puddle of warm mercury, calming the skull hornets, and he drove his fists into his pockets. Time for equilibrium. "It's me, Jenna. Brock."

The six-paneled door slammed, her screams reverberating through the walls of the home. Even her pounding feet echoed through to the porch. "Aunt Ellen!"

He spun and faced the darkening slope of the front yard. Smoky Mountain crickets chirruped about him in the dusk, and he fixated on the distant haze to ground his thought processes in this surreal place. Yet the gray mist only added to the hallucinatory atmosphere. *Be real, man.* It couldn't be her. His wife was wrapped in white satin, six feet under.

His shiny black car winked at him from the driveway. Haywood McCoy awaited his arrival in this jumble of dirt tracks. But the mountain man would lose no sleep if Brock failed to show. And right now, he couldn't care less about the interview. The magazine article's order of importance had tumbled to naught.

Exploring the curvy roads to locate an elusive destination darted from his brain. He turned to face the house. How could his deceased wife be here? Alive?

Well, he wasn't leaving until he found out. He jostled the change in his pocket to loosen his muscles and knocked again.

A nagging premise plowed a furrow across his brain. Not a flicker of recognition had appeared on Jenna's face. Only terror. Confusion. He scraped his short fingernails down the side of his cheek. Why hadn't she answered him?

The door screeched open, and an older, owl-faced woman peeked out. "Yes?"

Definitely not the person he wanted to see. Brock's brows bunched, peeking over the short, white-haired lady. The dimness of the interior impeded his attempt to catch sight of Jenna. His surveillance ceased when he met her weathered blue stare. Her features puckered into a frown. The smell of roast beef drifted from the interior and enveloped him. Darkness descended around him while insects popped against the porch light.

"May I speak to the woman who answered the door?" Good. His tone appeared relatively normal.

Her face pinched into stillness. "Well, I...I mean, she's..."

"Please." He feared spooking her. But he had no choice. "She's my wife."

The lady's breath snagged and she pressed a fist to her lips. "Oh, dear. Oh, my. Oh, glory. I—just a moment."

The door thudded shut once more, and Brock rubbed his temple. A simple conversation seemed like fording Lake Michigan. Carbon dioxide rushed from his lungs.

Jenna...alive. Why couldn't he quite take this all in? Three years buried, that's why. Brock swiped away a stray moth.

He paced the porch floor, pausing only to take unsteady breaths. At last the door opened, and a tall older gentleman, perhaps in his sixties, stepped out.

"Help ya?" He spoke in a slow deliberate way, the syllables alive with southern twang, reminding Brock he was deep in the mountains of Tennessee. His brown eyes, sharp as a cattle prod and wreathed with lines, perused Brock's face.

No point in not being direct. "I need to speak to the woman who answered the door. Jenna. She's my wife." He pulled the wallet from his back pocket. "Here. Our wedding picture."

"Uh-huh." The old man nodded, squinting a mere glance at the small photo and shifting to take in Brock's sleek car in the driveway. The man hooked his thumbs in his front pockets. "Reckon it's late. Probably better talk in the morning, don't ya think?"

"What? No." Brock yanked his hand through his hair. "Please. I need to speak to her."

The gangly man turned and grabbed the doorknob. "You call the town marshal in the morning. He'll know how to get ahold of us."

"But—"

The door slammed, and the light went out. Hope expired. Brock hammered his hand deep into his pocket. If he angered them, he'd never get close to her. With a restrained growl he strode toward his car.

He forced himself into the interior and backed down the rock drive onto the dirt road. While his thoughts rotated at warp speed, he punched the green phone button on the steering wheel. No signal. Who would he call anyway? His parents? His sister? Bro? Right now, voicing the events seemed impossible. He barely believed it himself. At the T, he racked his brain to retrace his way back to the small town of Mavey.

Memories of Jenna flooded his mind, and he clenched the wheel grips. Emotion strangled him. Whom he'd buried, he had no clue. But this was the least of his worries.

With a grunt, he turned left. For the next ninety minutes scenes of their life together converged in his brain as he navigated the winding roads back to his motel.

Jenna was alive. *Alive.*

Jerrica Rankin's fingers dug into her opposite sleeves, trying to make herself tighter, smaller. Her breathing came like a woman in transition labor, her heart an out-of-control bronco. Sweat doused her face.

This *could not* be happening.

She rocked, head down, on the edge of the bed and let her long straight hair brush forward, shutting out the world. Last act. Curtain closed.

Breathe in through your nose, out through your mouth. Shhh.

The man's dark stare haunted her. So probing. So petrifying.

"'Cease striving and know—'" Panic interrupted. Her fingers convulsed against the cotton material, turning into a thousand spiders. The deep yawned to her. The edge of blankness.

She fastened her gaze on the worn volume near her bed. "Jesus, Jesus."

Say it. Proclaim it.

"'Cease striving and know that I am God.'" The old adversary, panic, drifted further away.

"'He will never desert me, nor will He ever forsake me.'" More space gave her room.

"'Even though I walk through the valley of the shadow of death.'" Brevity ruled, but peace beckoned. Spiders became goose bumps.

"'Be anxious for nothing; but in everything by prayer and supplication with thanksgiving let your requests be made known to God. And the peace of God, which surpasses all comprehension, will guard your hearts and your minds in Christ Jesus.'"

Her tightened muscles uncoiled, and her two fingers crawled to her carotid. She anchored the wall of hair behind her ear and flicked a glance at the clock. One hundred and forty-two. Good. The rate of her pounding heart had slowed already.Jerrica surveyed the room, focusing on the pink log cabin quilt, her desk, the flat screen TV, the stacks of classic movies, and back to Uncle John's aged Bible. She was home. In her room. Levied in safety.

The knock at her door shot a cry from her throat. Safety? *Only a bogus illusion.*

"Honey, it's me. May I open the door?"

She pinched her eyelids closed briefly to still the new tremor. It was only Aunt Ellen. Had the visitor left? The abnormal breathing pattern set in again and in the darkness of her room, she grappled to control it. "Yes."

Her aunt popped her face through the crack and flicked on the light. Jerrica cringed. Aunt Ellen was wreathed in shiny placation, but her gray-streaked hair seemed awry. "You okay, dumpling?"

Jerrica sucked in her lips. The nicknames. More fake assurances. All was not well. The accelerator pedal pumped her adrenaline, and her heart lurched back to Indy 500 speed.

Her aunt blinked and edged the door wider, the false bright smile like a neon sign flashing danger. "I think we need to discuss something, lambiepie."

"Not now. Please, Aunt Ellen."

The older woman maneuvered through the door. She stood twiddling her fingers, Stooges style, before propping herself on the far bottom corner of the bed. Such a dear sweet soul. Always supporting. "Remember our prayer?"

The twitch below her left eye went viral and Jerrica pressed a finger to it.

"Well, sweetums, this may be the answer." Aunt Ellen folded her fumbling hands in her lap, her sing-song voice akin to a hundred cymbals.

Jerrica had never prayed for terror. But it always seemed to find her. And now it stood on her front porch. How she wished she could stay strong for Aunt Ellen. This lady had prayed over her, fed her, nursed her, tolerated all her freakish quirks.

But resisting the irrational fear was like holding a milk jug lid above her head in a drenching downpour and expecting not to get wet. Old enemy, numbness, bled through Jerrica's brain like hot lava. Burning, consuming, distorting. Blotting out everything.

Aunt Ellen patted the quilt, giving her a start. "John's downstairs talking to the visitor right now. Let me go check on things, and then maybe you could come down? Sure would be nice to clear things up."

That man. She shook her head, but Aunt Ellen had already turned to open the door.

"Be right back."

The door yawned open with a sinister creak after her departure. Always. Like a repetitive Frankenstein black and white talkie. Jerrica scrambled around the bed to shut out the imaginary Boris Karloff, glancing at the movie stack where the exact movie lay, mocking her. Then her aunt and uncle's voices drifted up the stairs and across the open balcony.

"Well, where is he, John?"

"Who?"

"Oh, you know good and well who. The man on the porch." Impatience stained her aunt's tones.

She leaned out the door as they disappeared below the open balcony.

"Sent him on his way."

"John Rankin, what were you thinking?"

Jerrica stepped from the room as their conversation grew softer. Uncle John probably hightailed it to his study beneath the stairs with her aunt in hot pursuit.

"Can't let in a perfect stranger at dusk, Mary Ellen."

A door closed below. Jerrica shot inside her room and pressed hers shut as well. Her fingers groped to twist the lock and flip off the light. In the darkness, she rested her forehead against the wood. Weak lightning flashed at the window. Storm coming.

That iconic silver screen laboratory thunderclap resounded in her brain. Curse that silly movie. Her bed transformed into the still operating table. When her fantasy Frankenstein elevated from the stainless steel surface, it was the stranger.

Only this was no movie. No remote control could turn it off. This was reality. She moaned, slid to the floor, and huddled in the corner.

Please, Lord. Please let this monster disappear.

Brock thumped again on the Police Station's door. He'd spent most of the night googling the tiny town of Mavey, studying the buildings, playing and re-playing what he'd say. Most people didn't stop in the town marshal's office to demand a meeting with their dead wife.

The tall, two-story brick building stood a block and a half east of Main Street, identical to the image on his phone. He stepped back. Age buckled the bricks, but, to the right, a concrete ramp updated the place. "Mavey Police Station" arced across the door's glass pane, indicating he'd reached the right place. Movement inside caught his eye. A compact, dark-headed woman strutted in small firm steps toward the door and flipped the dead bolt.

"Good morning." Her cheery voice rang out as she swung the door open. Her short figure turned and sauntered back the way she'd come. "Gonna be another scorcher today, huh?"

"Yes, uh—good morning."

"You must be lost." She smiled and waved a hand at him before disappearing behind a wall to the right. She reappeared behind a window and slid it open. "We get folks in here all the time needing directions to Gatlinburg or Pigeon Forge. I have some maps if you prefer?"

With a deep breath, he bellied up to the glass. This woman had no idea. "Sorry, no maps. Just need to talk to the town marshal."

She blinked and drew back. "I see. Do you have an appointment with Chief Rankin?"

Brock glanced around the small, empty waiting room. Was she kidding? "No."

She sat at her desk and picked up a pencil to tap it on a stack of papers. "What's this concerning?"

Weariness from lack of sleep and tension weighed on him. He exhaled audibly and leaned forward. "Please, it's urgent."

The woman's brow rose, and she tugged the front of her red suit jacket. "Name?"

"Brock Langston."

She wrote it on a scrap of paper. Then she proceeded to peck away at the computer. "Why don't you have a seat? I'll check and see if he has a slot in his agenda."

He spun and settled into an armless upholstered chair. He clasped his hands between his knees and stared at the warped, weathered floor covered in new carpeting. Agenda? The four empty chairs nearby merely stood to collect dust. If the town had a thousand residents, he'd be surprised. What could the marshal have on his schedule for the day?

While he took in the aging foyer, his mind shot back to the questions simmering in his brain for the last ten hours. For the umpteenth time he wondered how Jenna had arrived at such a place. Virtually the middle of nowhere.

And why hadn't she called? Texted, emailed? Anything? Even before the wedding they'd pledged to—the door in front of him opened. The irritating woman stood there, clad in her professional demeanor.

"He'll see you now."

Brock stood and strode to the door. Down the hall she opened a door to the left and swept her arm to the opening.

Behind a battered desk, the officer stood well over six feet tall. Red-headed with small patches of white above his ears, his grip made Brock feel sorry for anyone who stepped outside the law in this tiny hamlet.

A small wooden sign on the huge desk spelled out "Town Marshal." The man settled into his seat behind the desk. "Robert Rankin."

"Brock Langston. Thanks for seeing me."

The officer indicated a beat-up wooden chair. From the nicks and age, it must have survived Alexander the Great's Balkan Campaign as a battering ram. Brock nodded as he seated himself facing the huge oak desk.

"You've been one busy little camper." The older man slapped his desk. His stocky build made him an intimidating presence even though he pushed sixty.

"I'm sorry?"

"Gotta call from my brother last night, and my fax machine is stacked with documents this morning. That's more business than I generate in six months."

"Brother?"

A slow grin vined across his face. "I think you met him last night?"

Cold dread built a subfloor in his stomach. All in the family. "I see."

With a slow ease, the big man reached for a file on his helter-skelter desk and flipped it open. He slid on a pair of dark-rimmed glasses and squinted at the contents.

"I'll need a little information." He rotated, his sausage-like fingers hovering on his computer keyboard. "First of all, your wife's full name, including her maiden?"

Brock gripped the armrests and glanced to the lone window in the closed office. "Jenna Loralynn Price Langston."

The marshal's voice droned on. "And the last time you saw her?"

"Our wedding reception. Three years ago. We were married on her birthday."

"Uh-huh. Her age?" More tapping on that incessant keyboard.

He cocked his head to block out the noise and calculated. "Twenty-one."

Robert lowered his glasses and glared at him. "You were married on her eighteenth birthday?"

"Yes, sir." Brock ignored the long pause.

"Last known address?"

Brock shifted. "Uh, I'll have to check the exact address. She never lived in my house. I know it was in South Pinewood Mobile Home Park. My address is Seventh and Grand, Washington, Indiana."

An invisible thread snugged the sheriff's wiry eyebrows into a tuck above his nose. "Hmmm. Cause of death?"

Brock stared at the sterile white wall behind the desk. "Plane crash."

A squeak split the air as Robert leaned back in his chair. "Which one?"

Dread nailed in four-penny memories of agony. The frantic calls. The drive to Knoxville. Endless meetings with the police. Continuous layers of grief, thickening, sickening.

The funeral. The burial of random body parts. Acid reflux burned the back of his throat.

"You okay, son?"

Brock moved his jaw in a circle. "The Browning 707, north of Knoxville."

Robert let the chair fall level and rested his forearms on the desk. The man's glare latched onto him, and after a good long stare, he turned to input more information into the computer. "All right. Let's start here. I'll need both sets of parents' names, addresses, and phone numbers. I need a little time to organize these documents to verify them."

Brock leaned forward and clasped his knees. "My parents are not a problem. They run a construction business in Indianapolis. Jenna's father is dead. But her mother was institutionalized a week after the funeral."

The marshal nodded and flung the file closed. "Gonna take some time to follow these leads. I'll contact the Knoxville police and the folks in your hometown. Either way, Mr. Langston, this is one messy situation."

Brock hung his head and nearly crushed his molars. "Can I at least speak with her?"

Chief Rankin's head spasmed, and he shot a crooked smile. "Well, I got good news. Ellen's frying up chicken tonight, and we're invited. Five o'clock. Get your glad rags on. We got lots to talk about."

Chapter Two

Aunt Ellen might as well have served bailing twine for supper. Fear strangled Jerrica's throat, and the aromatic fried chicken went down like a wad of tacks. The family around her carried the conversation, a reality Jeopardy quiz show with this strange man as the solo contestant. He possessed double-portion patience, and she had to give him kudos for survival.

His features had dissolved from last night. Except for the haunted black eyes. Now in plain daylight, even without her peering too closely, it was apparent this man in no way resembled a monster constructed with cadaver parts.

She brushed a peek past him while he focused on his dinner. Not really a John Wayne, per se. Nor a wild, smoky James Dean. More a young Gregory Peck with a melancholy cloak of charismatic mystique wrapped about him. His head lifted and her gaze scatted away.

Uncle John pitchforked him with his stare. "You're a long way from home, boy. What brings you out here?"

"I'm doing a piece on a man who makes his own pottery from clay he digs right here in the mountains. He built his own kiln and lives like a mountain man. I was searching for his place and stopped here for directions."

Uncle John tilted his head back. "Ah, Haywood McCoy. What do you mean a 'piece'?"

"An article. I'm a writer."

Robert nodded, pausing at his worship of Aunt Ellen's chicken. "I'll verify his occupation. Spent most the afternoon chasing his background."

The heat of the outsider's regard seared Jerrica's cheek. She avoided eye contact and shifted in her seat like a bug on a specimen pin.

Uncle John cocked his head at his brother. "Anything funny come up?"

Robert laughed and spoke over half-chewed poultry. "Squeaky clean."

The dark stranger dug something from his pocket. "Here, I know all of you haven't seen this picture. Perhaps it'll give me some credibility."

Uncle Robert took the small photo in his hand and nodded. "This you?"

"Yes. And Jenna." His voice smoothed into salt flats as he shot a glance in Jerrica's direction. "That was the last day I saw her."

Uncle Robert handed the photograph to Aunt Ellen who wiped her hands on her napkin before poring over it.

She turned to Jerrica. "Oh, gracious."

Jerrica gripped the under supports of the table. Please. No sugarbowl, darling, or saccharin pinky toes. Aunt Ellen remained mum, tapping the photo against Jerrica's hand. Did she have to take it?

Rivulets of shivers dripped down her frame. Like looking at herself in a mirror to a fuller, happier time. The bride smiled, her cheek pressed to the stranger. The black tux stylishly disguised

Frankenstein into a handsome groom. Stitches across his cheek and double anodes decorating his neck would go a long way to tone down his attractiveness. Instead, anxiety reared its ugly head, sending those thoughts far away.

She gawked at her aunt. Only a whisper came. "It's not me. It can't be."

The side door in the kitchen burst open, and her cousin, Beth, came through in a rush and plopped her purse on the counter. Her hand flipped the sandy-colored braid over her shoulder. Pink scrubs covered her slightly heavy-set form.

"Hi, everyone. Sorry I'm late." Her full face brightened as she noticed the silver screen newcomer. She hurried around the table. For thirty-five, she sure could move. "You must be Brock Langston. I can't tell you what a pleasure it is to meet you. You're an answer to prayer, and that's for sure."

She pulled out a wooden captain's chair next to him at the table, and Aunt Ellen handed her a plate of chicken. A light laugh tumbled from her cousin. "I don't even know if I can eat."

Jerrica cringed. Even Beth was star struck. How she wished she could be a little more like her. The forever-single woman never paused to linger over what could have been, should have been, yada, yada. She simply embraced life in a grizzly hug, never fazed by any challenge. The perfect heroine.

Ugh. She and Beth. Complete opposites. Meanwhile, Jerrica burrowed inside her cage of fear.

"I want to know everything. What did I miss?" Beth's expression sparkled, her face a jar of fireflies. "Oh, how exciting."

A sob clawed its way up Jerrica's throat, clad in spurs. Oh, Beth. *Not you too.* She jumped from the chair and bolted from the room.

❧ ⸺ ☙

Brock stood and stared at the doorway. It took all his self-control not to sprint after her. He hadn't even said one word directly at her. She was so different. Why did she not speak to him?

The woman, who had seated herself next to him, lost some of her giddiness, and she turned to Ellen. "Mom, what's wrong?"

Ellen passed the photograph. The young woman studied the pic, her mouth springing open. "Oh, wow."

"Please sit, Mr. Langston. Where are my manners? This is our daughter, Beth. And as you've guessed, honey, this is Brock Langston. Apparently he stopped by last night for directions, but...ran into a little distraction." The aging woman fixed her attention on Brock. "Coffee?"

He plopped back in his vacated seat. "Yes, please."

Beth patted his hand. "Well, I for one am very pleased to meet you. You're a miracle. There's no other way to explain it."

"Beth..." John warned, crossing one lean leg over another.

"Dad, don't you see? We've finally received an answer after praying for three years. This man knows Jerrica. I mean—you do, don't you?"

Brock looked from Beth to Robert. "Jenna's my wife. Look, the marshal has our marriage license and Jenna's birth certificate. If you need more proof, I also have letters, photos, and other documents. I can have them immediately emailed or faxed straight to you."

Beth giggled. "Jenna? To hear her real name is amazing. Oh, and about the Internet. Sorry. We don't have it out here."

Brock tensed the muscles in his cheeks. "I see."

"A marriage license, you say? He get that taxied to you, Robert?" John withdrew a pipe from his pocket and tapped the stem on his bottom lip.

Beth snorted. "Not taxied, Dad. Faxed."

John loaded the tobacco into the bowl. "Faxed, taxied. It's all the same to me. What do you say, Robert?"

He nodded as he took the last bite of meat on his plate. "Yes, John. It's authentic. Ellen, you outdid yourself with that chicken."

"Thank you. My grandma's recipe. Perhaps we could finish our drinks in the living room?"

Everyone rose, and John led the way through the house. Ellen followed the crew with a tray of coffee and mugs.

Quilts, antiques, primitive knickknacks, and inspirational art crowded the living room like a flea market in downtown Gatlinburg. The white ceiling soared to a second story, and, on the left, an open wooden stairway led up to a spindled balcony. Brock's attention deliberated on the doors lining the second floor. Is that where Jenna hid?

He longed to stride up the stairs and confront her. Why was she being so difficult? He settled on the edge of the couch, and Beth plunked next to him.

"Here we are." Ellen Rankin stopped at the coffee table, edged over a large flower arrangement surrounded by a collection of carved angels, and set the coffee tray down. "Dear me, I have too much stuff."

"Amen." John, now seated in a burgundy recliner, puffed on his pipe. His eyes twinkled as he ogled the woman. "'My most brilliant achievement was my ability to be able to persuade my wife to marry me.'"

She waved a hand in dismissal and picked up the carafe. "Oh, go on with ya. This young man did not come here to hear all your memorized quotes. Although I've heard the quote enough to know that's Winston Churchill."

Robert chuckled from the wing chair across the room.

Brock's backbone solidified into iron and he cleared his throat. It was time to rip up the chitchat. "I buried my wife three years ago. And now, she's upstairs. I need to talk to her, Sir."

"First things first, young man. Why do you call me sir?"

The heat in Brock's veins congealed. What a crazy question. "It's a common address, I suppose."

Smoke rose above the older man's thinning hair, finely oiled. The striped, buttoned-down shirt threw him back several decades.

He appeared older than his age, yet still mentally, guillotine sharp. The man fixated on the far wall, his expression growing hazy. "Hmmm. 'I also found being called sir rather silly.'"

"Excuse me?" Brock jerked his head.

Beth leaned forward and whispered. "It's a quote. Ignore it."

John glanced at him. "Harold Pinter. Nobel Prize for Literature, 2005."

"I see." Did he? They were discussing literature while he waited to reconnect with a woman he thought was dead? He shoved down the roiling wad of impatience tossing in his gut.

John's lips pulled into a semblance of a smile. "Familiar with him?"

A "no, sir" jumped to Brock's lips, but he squelched it. Best to avoid that address. He could barely keep his seat. "I'm afraid not. Perhaps you don't understand my intention here."

A chuckle sounded from the gentleman next to him. "I assure you, son. I understand your predicament."

"Well, then—"

"Oh, Mother. Why did you get Dad started on those silly quotes?" Beth groused good-naturedly, settling into the cushions of the couch. "We'll never get him stopped now. Dad, please. We have more important things to discuss. Serious things."

John elevated a brow, and Brock gripped his hand into a fist. Quotes? They were discussing quotes?

"Please, John. Some folks find it quite boring." Ellen handed him a mug.

"'When people are bored, it is primarily with themselves.'"

Beth, next to Brock, gave him a nudge. "Eric Hoffer. I've heard that one since I was a girl."

The older woman skirted the coffee table to sit beside him with Beth on her other side. She patted his leg. "I'm sorry. I know you're puzzled beyond puzzled, and frankly we are too."

More placating words, no answers. "Enough! Why didn't she call? I buried her, do you all understand? She's my wife. Why can't I talk with her?"

Silence hovered and uneasiness palpitated through the room as if a wasp had bumbled into an allergist's office.

John plucked the pipe from his mouth. "It ain't about understanding, boy, it's about waiting."

Was this another insane quote? Ire catapulted in Brock's chest. "Look—"

"Och, John, be plain with the boy," Ellen whispered.

Brock blasted from his seat and edged his voice up a notch. "I wish *someone* would be plain."

Ellen stood and rubbed the front of her June Cleaver white apron and glanced about. "Oh, my."

"Look, I'm not disrespecting you." Brock splayed his fingers on his scalp. "I'm trying to find out about the woman who answered the door. Could someone please let me speak to her?"

John knocked on the arm of his recliner. "Sit down, son."

Brock scraped a hand at the nape of his neck. If he teed them off, he'd never get close to her. He eased back down on the edge of the cushions.

Robert leaned forward and held up a hand. "Now, Mr. Langston—Brock. There's some things you need to know."

Ellen nodded before collapsing back on the couch. "The fact is, she doesn't remember you."

"What?"

Any gaiety threaded through the room suddenly vacuumed out.

Beth drew a pillow into her lap and fingered the tassels hanging from the corner. "She's missing large chunks of memory. She honestly has no idea who you are. Not only that, she has no idea who she is."

Anger became a non-issue as he grappled with Beth's words. "She doesn't remember me?"

"No."

He stood and paced to the front door, where he'd first innocently rapped on the frame last night. His attention went to the balcony. He shrugged his hands. "How?"

The sympathy in Beth's expression branded him. "We don't really know."

"How'd she get here?"

She shrugged. No one else seemed to remember their communication skills. "She appeared in the yard, wandering. Burns all over, feverish. I believe she was in shock."

He snorted. "But you notified no one when you found her?"

Beth pointed to Robert. "Him. Robert ran her through the system. She didn't match any description for missing persons."

"So that's it. You adopted her in, gave her a random name, and forgot it? No one questioned her appearance? Hospital personnel? Anyone? Obviously not the marshal."

Like an air mattress, Beth deflated. "We didn't take her to the hospital."

Brock took a step forward. "Are you kidding me here?"

Robert stood. "Settle down. There's more to this."

Ellen rose. "She wasn't able, Brock. Please understand."

"Mom's right." Beth crossed herself with her arms, tears wetting her cheeks. "She was unstable. I mean mentally. When we tried to load her in the car, she became hysterical, like a wild creature. Tore open her burned skin. Bled everywhere."

"So you kept her. Like a stray kitten."

Ellen let out a breath before she spoke. "We were afraid to push her. She was so fragile. Still is."

Robert laid a hand on Brock's shoulder. "I investigated it quietly. Nothing turned up. And given the state of her health, we kept her here to heal."

"You gave up?" Brock fired a glare at Robert.

"We didn't give up." Beth grew still. "Putting her through the system would have been nothing short of cruel. We treaded carefully. Even now she has a terrible fear of new situations, new people. I believe Jerrica has agoraphobia and extreme anxiety attacks."

"But then, you really wouldn't know, would you? A doctor's never seen her."

"Yes, she has. I'm an RN in a Behavior Management clinic. I took pictures and videos and the nurse practitioner prescribed medication. Jerrica's talked to a counselor on numerous occasions by phone, but still won't step foot in any kind of medical office."

"Her name is Jenna. Where did you get this name if her memory is blank?"

"She came up with it," John's low voice cut in. "We kept her here to protect her."

"I'm her husband. You had no right." Brock lowered his voice.

Beth rose and planted her intense gaze on his. "She was suicidal."

Brock's roller coaster ride of emotions plunged to a new low. He rubbed his hands on his outer thighs. Jenna. *Suicidal.* The agony resting in their faces glared authentic. They'd watched it, balmed it, and saved her. And Jenna was alive. He pinched his nose on a hiss of an inhale and turned his back to pace a few feet.

Ellen's wispy tones fell on his stiff back. "She's become part of our family. Maybe we didn't make the right call. But there were no options. We lost our youngest daughter in a car accident shortly before Jerrica came. Gretchen was seventeen. I don't know if you're familiar with the Lord's grace, but we felt God brought Jerrica to us."

A big hand touched Brock's back. Robert.

No. It couldn't be so simple. Three years. Three *long* years he lived in agony trying to process and accept what had happened.

He shrugged off the hand of comfort and turned to face them. "No one found it odd that a complete stranger appeared and stayed to live with you?"

Ellen's hands clasped and unclasped. "People assumed she was family. She had no I.D."

He let a stream of breath expel from his lungs. *Focus on the positive.* Jenna was alive. These people, for whatever reason, had nursed her and seen to her needs.

Just probing his wife's tortured eyes told him she'd endured some kind of deep trial. For the first time since entering the house, a scrap of peace entered his heart. "I'm a Christian myself...it's a lot of strange things to work through."

John, the only one still seated, snorted, clutching his pipe. "I agree. Too coincidental."

Beth pressed her fists on her ample hips and scowled at John. "Dad, I can't believe you're saying such gibberish. Mom, what's the quote Dad always says about coincidences?"

The tightness in the air eased a tad.

The corner of Ellen's mouth quirked. "Oh, darling, I have no idea."

"Caught in your own net, Brother," Robert added.

Beth fixed a stern eye on her father. "Dad. Spill it."

John chomped his pipe stem, and a cloud of smoke rose from the bowl. He crossed his forearms in an X over his lap. "'Coincidences are spiritual puns.' G. K. Chesterton."

The younger woman gripped and flailed her fists. "Exactly the one. And I'll add a quote of my own. Romans 8:28. 'And we know all things work together for the good to them that love God, to them who are the called according to his purpose.'"

Beth, face wet and yet tranquil, approached Brock and patted his arm. "And my Author trumps all—God."

Three taps sounded on Jerrica's bedroom door. She pressed her forehead tighter against her kneecaps. Beth's signature knock. She usually allowed fifteen minutes to let Jerrica "get normal" as she called it. This time, however, Jerrica needed about three days. Or three months.

The doorknob turned, and Beth peeked around the door. She flipped on the light. Jerrica peeped at her. Her plump face was bright with hope, yet flushed. "May I come in?"

"Yes." A mere squeak. Offering more was not an option.

Beth entered, eased the door shut, and perched on the edge of the bed to peer at her. Much like Aunt Ellen had done yesterday.

Jerrica rubbed her upper arms. "You saw the picture?"

Beth nodded. "It's pretty convincing, don't you think?"

Dear Beth. Dear sweet Beth. How she'd supported her. Until now. "It's not me."

"How do you know?"

Oh, no. More talking. More counseling. Jerrica tugged her shins tighter. Becoming a small ball always helped. "It just can't be."

"Listen. I know this is horribly difficult. We've talked about how new situations and curve balls will knock you for a loop. But you can't pass this over." Beth rubbed at a piece of lint, and then raised her head to glower at her, conviction deeper than the ocean itself. "What if you really are this 'Jenna?' You've been praying for so long. Asking, seeking. How can you dismiss it instead of finding the truth?"

Whooshing swelled between Jerrica's ears. "No. I don't want to be this woman."

Beth snorted. "What are you talking about?"

Jerrica's breath came faster. How could Beth not see? A tremor snaked through her body. She snugged her lids closed. Tears squeezed through and rested on her cheek. "What kind of woman leaves her husband on their wedding day?"

Beth stood and rammed her hands into her smock pockets. "I don't know this woman either, but I do know you. And you are kind and loving. If you are this 'Jenna Langston,' you had a very good reason for leaving."

"Maybe he's sitting on the couch downstairs." Jerrica's eyes flared.

"Right there. That's the spark that keeps you fighting, Jerrica. The one that has you searching. You *need* to know. This guy might be the problem, but he might be the answer to getting it all back. If you give up before you try, you'll never know. And you can start by going downstairs."

Lapping her lips, and squeezing her forearms nervously, Jerrica eyed the door. Simple became impossible when breathing morphed into an inaccessible commodity.

The first step is always the hardest.

Beth's oft repeated mantra. Now hers. This would not be easy.

The occupants in the living room turned and raised their chins when Jerrica stepped from her bedroom door to the landing. The dark-haired stranger rose from the couch, his hands deep in his blue-jean pockets.

Aunt Ellen's fluttering hand covered her open mouth. Uncle John tapped his foot, calm as a sloth, while Robert relaxed against the big wing chair, an encouraging smile plastered to his face.

The Gregory Peck similarities spun up and vanished into a black hole. Too many people. And the monsters were back. Huge ones. Jerrica spun to fight her way back into the room, but Beth guarded the opening. A strangled cry escaped.

"Take a deep breath. Another one." Beth coached. "Imagine walking down the stairs. Everyone will greet you. There is no danger there. I'll be right behind you."

Her voice tumbled through a tunnel with a shimmer of orange sparks flickering on the outside. Jerrica's jackhammer heart appeared as a thundering rhinoceros, begging to charge from her chest.

"Think of all the things you've accomplished." The cooing continued. "You can do this, Jerrica. Fear is not an option. Faith is. Step out in faith."

Blasted faith. Cursed life. Ever pushing her closer to agony. Stop, stop, *stop*. She couldn't live forever in her jar of doubt and anger.

Jerrica glimpsed the crowded living room from her shimmering corner peripheral vision before targeting the first step. *Do this.* Beth followed, ever her gentle Jiminy Cricket, whispering wisdom, murmuring encouragement.

This man could be my husband.

She jerked to a stop, mid-flight, left leg aloft, fingers squeezing maple syrup from the wooden railings. Denied.

He's not. He's not.

A flush of hot spreading anesthesia crept into the crevices of Jerrica's brain. Her sight tinged red. Blankly she counted the episodes of her boiling, bleeding gray matter. One, first time in town. Two, first Sunday at church. Three, meeting Frankenstein husband.

Dumb all-nighter black and white Monster Movie bash. *Have you no sense?*

He's not my husband. Even the corpuscles in her skull shouted the phrase. The acid simmering in her stomach effervesced their agreement.

Beth leaned forward, and Jerrica stutter-stepped the narrow tread. Thank goodness she knew better than to touch her.

Her mentor murmured in her ear, "Remember, most of the time, the terrible situations we imagine—"

"Never come true." Exactly. *Snatch that thread of positivity.* Jerrica pinpointed on slowing her breathing and the next twelve inches.

At the foot of the stairs, her legs locked, the walls bowed toward her. Surely the white rabbit was due an appearance. Her freakishly minuscule coping mechanism flatlined. Abruptly.

The first step— Forget it.

She garbled a groan and lurched for the rocker.

If I can make it there, I might salvage a snippet of composure.

She half collapsed, half climbed the rocker and settled, her right hand gripping her shirt directly over her heart. Safe. Anchored.

She raised her head. Dark monster orbs shanghaied her sanity.

Chapter Three

Brock eyeballed her hungrily. His first real look at her, not just a torso above the kitchen table. Her hair had darkened, but of course, Jenna highlighted hers, giving her dishwater blond hair a lighter hue. From what little he'd seen in the kitchen, her amazing baby blues still stole his breath. Brighter than the aquamarine of the tropical ocean.

Her hair hung longer, however, and her body bordered on gaunt. Fear hung on her like a soiled, wet garment, weighing down her body and facial expression.

But her caged look distressed him the most. Dark circles rimmed her eyes and contrasted against her pale skin. He was the cause of her discomfort, he was sure, with his sudden appearance. His Adam's apple bobbed in the proverbial tub of water.

He longed to take her in his arms and ease her hurts, caress away the terror. His wife huddled a few feet away, and he couldn't touch her. Regret burned in his chest. With great restraint he managed to hold his seat.

"Jerrica," John's gentle baritone poked a hole in the tension in the air. "This man says he has a marriage license, and he's taxied it here to your Uncle Robert."

He paused a moment before he murmured to himself. "Whatever that means."

"Faxed, Dad," Beth reminded, pressing her lips together to stem a smile.

Brock's breath snagged when slight dimples dented Jenna's hollow cheeks. He remembered her dimples, the one on the right deeper than the left. His throat ached to blurt their entire relationship. To demand answers from her. But he swallowed and tried not to gawk.

"Fax, taxi, it's all the same to me." Uncle John fixated on his pipe stem.

"How about some dessert?" Ellen rang out, the syllables as falsely bright as a suspended interrogation bulb.

Jenna shook her head.

"None for me, either." Brock pulled his attention from his wife.

Jerrica picked at the hives blossoming on her arms. Rounded points of exposed nerves. How much longer could she sit here? Her heartbeat thundered through her head, the rushing sound all but blocking her aunt's next words.

"Well, if no one wants dessert, Jerrica, why don't you take Brock to the workshop and show him some of your projects?" Aunt Ellen's glance, akin to the Library of Congress, contained volumes.

The shake of her head negated that horrible plan. Had her aunt lost her mind? She could barely hear the conversation over the complete hysteria swirling inside her head.

"Yes, Jerrica," Beth broke in with uber optimism, "What a fabulous idea. It'll give you a chance to get to know Brock."

"You take him." Jerrica attempted murder with her glare.

Beth laughed. "I don't know diddlysquat about any of it. That's you and Dad's thing."

Jerrica targeted the dark-haired stranger on the couch, coffee cup in hand. His black fathomless eyes perused hers. A sheen of dark shadow outlined his finely groomed jaw. The gray buttoned-up shirt added a nuance of danger. She checked for Frankenstein-like thick heavy shoes, but only casual brown leather met her eye.

A groan shimmied up her throat. Give a tour or continue to sit here, her skin frying with the heat of everyone's surveillance, pulse jumping at every voice. Fine. Ask a beetle to spin a web. At least she could get up and release the pent-up tension. Her shoulders hunched in acceptance. "If you want."

Jerrica popped up. He rose too. Instant panic seized her. This was real, not some old iconic movie with a predictable ending.

She hurried from the room through the kitchen to the back door. Her hands shoved the screen door open. Her brain throbbed one message. *Escape.*

"Nice screen door you've got there," Brock grumbled behind her.

Perhaps it was rude to ignore the fact she'd slammed the door against his finely shaped nose. Her strange black humor sometimes rescued her, after all. But not now.

Jerrica skipped to a faster pace, panting with exertion, hands deep in her Levi's. She contemplated the breathtaking view, something which usually brought her a shred of serenity. Fed her tousled soul. The stranger who tailed her ruined her comforting routine. The steep slope added speed to her march across the lawn.

The evening mist had settled across the tops of the mountains, and the smoky blue haze snaking through the trees created a mysterious nuance. The goats and sheep greeted her with bleats behind the fencing to her right. *Goats to the left, sheep to the right.*

Normally she stopped and slathered affection on her favorite pets, but tonight she ignored them and hastened to the wooden barn. Beth's voice echoed in her brain. "'Caring for animals is therapeutic and helps improve confidence and trust.'"

She gritted her teeth. Nothing but psycho-bull at this point with terror striding behind her. Beyond the pen, the woods with a canopy of the leafed-out trees darkened the ground. Between the mist and the shadow, she could easily disappear. Like the invisible man.

Perhaps if she walked fast enough, she could bluff herself into believing it was a normal summer evening. The cicadas hummed with throbbing rhythm, the crickets carefully revealing the temperature in their chirrups.

Unfortunately in her make-believe meadow, the footsteps behind her added a chasing green demon. Belching sulfur. She barked a cough. How could she talk face to face with this stranger, let alone expose her private creations?

"What kind of work do you do?" he asked as she reached the weathered barn and groped inside the doorway for the light switch.

Light flooded the large addition to the main barn, revealing the tables and cement floor littered with wooden trash bins, laundry sorters, shelves, pie safes, hutches, cabinets, and wood cut-outs. Organized rows of paint bottles and supplies lined the counter along the back wall next to a primitive sink.

Shelves covered with hand sanders and other small tools stood to the left. She walked into the one place where she felt immune from the world, where she could express the core of her creativity.

Except part of the world stepped in, erasing her invulnerability and revealing her private efforts that might as well be part of her body. To divulge them invited rejection and dislike, and Jerrica knew she couldn't handle criticism of her work.

He strolled around the room glancing at the wooden items in various stages of completion. Her current project, a pie safe, sat on the low work table with an intricate primitive design of an American flag.

"Did you paint this?" He rubbed a hand against the smooth pine top.

At least his voice was richly timbered and not the clipped Mid-Atlantic language version of the old movies. Or the exaggerated drawn-out Brando tones. *Sayonara.* Perfect word for her guest. Rubbing her sweat-dripping hands down her jeans, she nodded.

He rubbed his chin as he examined her work. "It's beautiful."

Her face puckered, and she stepped nearer, still maintaining a good distance from him. "You think so?"

He turned then, and she resisted the urge to jump away.

"Of course. I remember meeting your old high school art teacher. He said you were the most talented student he'd ever had. You had a small art scholarship to go to college before—"

"I'm not that woman." Oh, glory. He really thought she was her. End scene. She tripped to the door and turned away, yet keeping him in view.

"Sorry." He took a breath and rubbed a hand across the back of his head. He shifted his weight but didn't come any closer. "Hasn't anyone ever told you how beautiful your work is?"

"No one's ever been out here but my family." She bit the inside of her cheeks and refused to meet his scrutiny. "I don't usually go into Gatlinburg when my uncle sells them."

He continued to ogle her, but she fixated on the cement floor. His voice came steady and low. "I wish I didn't make you so nervous."

"Everybody makes me nervous." She turned and crossed the floor to the counter of paints. There was so much she could be doing instead of wasting time with this man. She propped herself upon the stool and grabbed the small dowels to piece a wooden bear together. Her hands wobbled so much she could hardly join them.

He sauntered across the floor to the stool next to hers. "May I sit here?"

"I suppose." Her shoulders stiffened as he settled himself. Too close.

"Do you cut all these wood items yourself?"

She shrugged. "Some. But Uncle John does most of it. I'm...a little afraid of the saws. Mostly I put them together and paint them."

"Interesting." He picked up a dowel attached to a leg and rotated it in his hands. Well-formed, smooth hands. She pasted her glance to her task.

"Country items made by 'real,'" she inserted air quotation marks with her fingers, "mountain people are in high demand here in the Smokies."

She paused a moment to pull their signature tag from a small cubbyhole in front of her. "Rankin Mountain Crafts. Uncle John says some folks would sell their left nostril for this stuff."

Her lips pressed together to stem a nervous sort of giddiness but still curved upward into a tiny smile nonetheless, and their gazes locked. Loss mingled with hope resided in the deepness of his pupils. *Look away.*

Brock chuckled. "Sounds painful."

Despite her apprehension, a giggle popped out. She covered her mouth with her hand.

"Actually, I have several bins of similar stuff."

She bunched her forehead. "You do this stuff, too?"

He cleared his throat and glanced away. "Not exactly. They're my wife's."

Present tense. She frowned at him and gritted her teeth. Dark wit lost its stranglehold. If he thought he was going to convince her she was this "wife" of his, he was sadly awry. Her tone froze over. "I see."

"You sell much?"

She yanked at the tub containing the bear heads and grabbed one. *Stay in the here.* "Enough to keep us working. Uncle John's cousin owns a shop in Gatlinburg. He has a website, too. We keep him supplied. Sometimes we deliver the heavier stuff."

Silence foamed in the shop like a washing machine with a gallon of detergent. She wanted to ask him how his wife died, how he so conveniently stopped at her house, but she couldn't be so bold. Besides, did she care? She sympathized, in a way, to have lost his wife. Still—

"Do you think I'm your husband?"

Jerrica slid the arm over the dowel before losing her coordination again. "No."

He exhaled. "It's crazy. So far-fetched, I know. I keep expecting to wake up in a dark hotel room."

He paused at her glare. "Don't you recognize anything about me?"

Normality tilted. She sprang from the stool and knocked it to the concrete floor. The crash sent her heart speeding ever faster. She spun and skittered across the room and paused at the doorway. Terror shoved audacity to the forefront.

"You can't come in here and, and...claim me like a lost puppy or something." Her voice rang out in a strange pitch. "I don't know you because I've never seen you before. So please, *leave.*"

She threw the door open and fled.

❦ ⋯⋯ ❧

Brock shoved his hands into the pockets of his jeans and jangled his change. He'd handled that well. Or not. Jenna had never been so flighty. Or morose. It cast a sliver of doubt. Wouldn't she recognize something about him? If it weren't for the fact she was the spitting image of his wife, he'd—what? Leave? Fat chance.

Despite a shard of doubt, he knew this woman was Jenna. And he'd prove it and win her back. He righted the fallen stool and strode to the door, taking one last look at the works of art lining the walls of the room. Trauma might have stifled her identity, but the items in this room stacked one more brick of proof in his favor. If only she wasn't so resistant. If only she could remember some small snatch of their life together.

When he arrived at the back door of the house minutes later, he got sympathetic looks from Ellen and Beth who washed dishes in the kitchen.

"She ran, huh?" Beth questioned.

He nodded.

"Well, that's normal," Beth began, "and this could be an all-nighter."

Brock's head jerked. "An all-nighter? Out there? Aren't you worried for her safety?"

"Sure. One night, Dad searched for her until three in the morning. Found her down by the dry creek bed throwing pebbles. You remember, Mom? She was pretending to skip rocks across water."

Ellen smiled. "That was the night after her attempt to visit town. What a doozy."

"Well, isn't it dangerous? I mean there has to be wild animals on the prowl. This is a pretty remote stretch of land."

"Yes, well, Jerrica knows the area well. Uncle John eliminates any cougars or coyotes that get too close. She knows where all the abandoned cabins are. But still, you're right. It is potentially dangerous. And she knows the risk. We pray." Ellen brought a mug to her lips. "Here, why don't you sit and have a cup of coffee?"

He shrugged. "I wish she'd talk to me."

Ellen plopped a large cup on the table and motioned to a seat.

Brock settled at the kitchen table. "I don't mean to sound disrespectful, but is Jenna...I mean, Jerrica, mentally deficient?"

Beth's laugh tinged with sorrow. "Oooh, you really worked to make it sound polite, huh?"

Her face grew serious. "No, on a regular day, she behaves like you or me. She doesn't talk to strangers, as you can tell, and she has many irrational fears. But then you have to get in her head."

She opened a cabinet and slid a clean plate on a stack. "She can't remember anything about her past, so she is constantly doing and trying new things. Things you or I did as young toddlers, who don't think about consequences. Kids are kids.

Jerrica, on the other hand, is an intelligent grown-up who knows nothing about her background and nothing about what to expect. She's improved a great deal because she's learning to trust."

Ellen turned from the sink and her voice dropped to a whisper. "What was she like before?"

"Fun, quirky, creative. At times she was very open and lively. At other times, secretive."

Ellen smiled. "I'm afraid she hasn't changed much, then. Except, I suppose she's more somber. Had you known each other long? Goodness, it's strange to ask such questions about someone who's been living with you for so long."

"We knew each other for a while but got serious about six months before we married." He paused to gather his thoughts. "It doesn't seem long, but we were in constant communication with one another and spent most every day together."

Ellen set the last cast iron pan over a flame on the stove to dry it and then wiped her hands on a towel. She let a hand settle on her hip. "I guess a person could best see her personality when she's with the neighbor girl. She adores Katie. She's six now, the last in a pack of six.

The child gets ignored a lot, being the youngest and given the fact those folks don't put much care on their children. Jerrica treats her like a sister. That girl spends the entire day here and sometimes even the night."

Ellen stared at the corner of the ceiling as she talked. "Katie will try anything too, which helps Jerrica with her fears. Beth, remember the day Katie climbed on the barn roof with a big beach umbrella?"

Beth nodded. "I think their love of Mary Poppins inspired that."

"Well, perhaps. But all Katie managed to do was catapult into breaking her arm. Jerrica had spotted her down the road. That was the first successful trip into town and first successful trip to the hospital. Jerrica did it for Katie. I guess she needed an important enough reason."

Brock looked out the screen door at the darkness. "Listen. I don't know how to tell you this, but Jenna's mother has schizophrenia."

Gasps drew his attention back to the women. "She's been in the state institution for nearly three years."

Beth whispered. "I never thought about her family. I mean..."

She pulled a face at Brock. "I'm sorry. *You* would be her family. How rude I'm being. Forgive me."

He waved a hand at her. "It's not to be helped at this point."

A long pause stretched before Beth spoke again. "I still believe Jerrica is within normal behavior patterns. I think once she recovers some of her memory, she'll lose some of these fears and work through her phobias."

Brock nodded, but doubts converged. His presence demanded Jenna do a great deal of adjusting. If he could only get her to recall a few memories of their times together, it might unravel the whole garment of her life. Yet, what if she never remembered a single thing? How could he continue to remain married to a complete stranger who only thwarted his every attempt at reconciliation?

～ ⸱⸱⸱⸱⸱⸱ ～

Jerrica entered the dark cabin and fumbled on the shelf until her hands found a box. Inside she located a candle and matches. With practiced ease, she affixed the candle into the holder on the shelf and struck the match. The flame threw the room into shadows, and she sighed, the bunched-up stress in her shoulders easing.

A bench stood at the far corner, but her scrutiny traveled to the bunk beds on her left. After lighting the wick, she sank onto the bottom cot, still gripping the wooden box. Her fingers sought the last item inside a secret drawer. A simple silver wedding band joined to a diamond solitaire.

She lifted it, and the metal shimmered in the candlelight. Even in late May, the band chilled her fingers. The large stone caught the light, shooting a rainbow across the wooden-beamed ceiling. Her one possession she'd owned when she'd stumbled into the Rankins' yard three years ago.

Weeks passed before they were able to remove it from her burnt, swollen hand. How easy it had been to ignore the symbol of wedded nuptials. Merely hide it in the cabin. Out of sight, out of mind. Like her disappearing acts.

Not so much the stranger who ascertained a personal link with her. Who wished to rip apart every shred of normalcy she'd constructed as padding around her. She swallowed and pressed the ring set back into its compartment and shut it. *Snap*.

Dread mounted in her chest. She *had* been married to someone, hadn't she? Memories of the early days flooded her brain. The pain, the bleeding, the burns, the uncontrollable anxiety, the strangers who'd taken her in. The searing tug of the ring scraping across her raw finger. Yes. She remembered these things. But before that, nothing but a blank, black chalkboard. Fear spiraled within her. How could she know what was real? What was true?

She squeezed her lids shut, and she sucked in a shuddering breath, panting to calm herself. An owl's hoots diverted her thoughts and occupied her mind for a moment. Most people would be frightened of her surroundings, but she was more frightened of what lived inside her.

"God, *God*, I don't know what you're doing here. I'm supposed to trust you. Uncle John says you know everything. Why would you not let me remember if I had a husband?" Her voice broke on the last syllables. "Why God?"

Humorless one-liners fled. Old movie scenes abandoned her. She gasped for air and clutched her chest. Terror pressed on her from every direction. The panic attack sent the room into spin cycle. She covered her face and drew into a trembling fetal ball on the dusty cot.

"I can't do this. Please send him away. Oh God, please. It's too hard. I can't. I *cannot* do this. I'm not this man's wife."

Through her full-blown misery she barely registered the footsteps outside.

Chapter Four

J errica focused on the sounds she heard outside. Foot falls, slow, soft in four-beat time. Then feather-light taps followed. Not human. Envisioning the caramel-colored doe with her spotted little one, bedded under the yellow poplar north of the cabin, soothed the throes of gripping terror. Several times during the spring, she'd hovered at the shuttered window and peeked at the pair. Now? Pure Divine distraction.

Her breathing slowed and her heart trotted to a normal speed. She rose and inched toward the window, pausing to locate the deer outside. Sweat trickled down the sides of her face. She eased the shutters open. A hinge's screech split the air, and the pair dashed off. Jerrica jerked the wood panels open, and the white triangular tails disappeared into the woods, their bodies slapping against the thick foliage. The darkness settled back into nocturnal tranquility. My, the peace steeped her bones in oil.

Her pupils dilated to stare deep into the overgrowth, the moon dappling the ground in eerie, pale patches. A mist snaked through the canopy of the trees, and her lungs filled with the moist, cool air. The tang of damp evergreen further calmed her tight nerves. It was so very still. So remote. So safe.

The hoot owl echoed through the woods once more as she closed the shutters and locked them. Such a shame to have missed her four-footed friends. Next time she came to the cabin, she'd bring some of Uncle John's lubricant to silence that squeak.

She turned from the window and walked to the plastic tub where Aunt Ellen kept a quilt and pillow. It made no sense to feel safe here. Katherine Hepburn and the Fondas would understand, having experienced it in *On Golden Pond*. Or at least their onscreen personas. Most people hated the bugs, the dirt, the snakes. Yet the tranquility comforted her soul. Made things simple again. And golden.

She spread the blanket over the cot, blew out the candle, and lay down, punching the pillow. The sounds of the forest surrounded her. Maybe there were no loons echoing in the distance surrounding Golden Pond, but the bugs buzzed, the crickets chirped, and the leaves rustled a lullaby in the slight breeze.

The hoot owl chimed in like a grandfather clock, keeping his own time. Moonlight seeped into the cabin like a comforting nightlight. Her eyes adjusted to the dimness, and she relaxed into the soft scented quilt. *Just like when she camped as a child.*

Jerrica jerked to a sitting position. She'd camped as a child? This new memory ricocheted inside her brain like a steel sphere in a pinball machine. Her eyes ransacked the room, now an illusion of long ago.

A campfire...and she, in a sleeping bag.

Yes. The firelight, the smell of smoke, the shadows of the trees, and she—giggling. With...who? She clamped her hands to her head. *With who?*

But the image faded and the reminiscent tail of recall slithered into the fog of amnesia. Her brain filled with what could only be termed as warm goo, and then a lightning flash—*snap*. A whip of laceration lashed across her brain.

She gasped and uncovered her face, her widened eyes searching the interior. Rhythmic pain oozed into her head, the reverberations gaining strength.

A flicker of blurry vision throbbed in her lower line of sight. Oh, no. Not this. She panted in forced tempo, tracking the pulsating rainbow across her line of vision. With muttered prayers, she willed the aura to disappear, leaving her vision untouched. Fifteen agonizing minutes marched by until the frightening visual abnormality vanished out of sight. Like her memory.

She took a deep breath and rubbed her temples. Her own aurora borealis, steeped in trepidation. She glanced about, thankful to see clearly. The moonlight danced shadows throughout the room, mute with the stillness of the forest.

It'd been months since she'd remembered anything new. Now this. Ugh. A million chainsaws churned agony through her skull. She rotated her head slowly and massaged the back of her neck. Was it significant this memory materialized within twenty-four hours after the arrival of this stranger?

Beth's behavioral analyses had invaded her brain. She groaned. Yet, she couldn't wait to tell her what she'd recalled. Beth had been such a cornerstone for her. What would Jerrica have done without her?

She exhaled, snuggled into the soft quilt, and rubbed her left ring finger to quiet the cadence in her head. Thankfully, the pulsating blur hadn't made a reappearance. Her body began to relax in her little cocoon. The smell of fabric softener rose to her nostrils, and a smile tugged at her lips.

Sweet Aunt Ellen. Always taking care of everyone. Strangers once, the Rankins had truly become her family. The only one she knew. Her face scrunched. But what if there were another family? Her real family? Strangers. Like Brock.

His face invaded her thoughts. Those black brooding eyes, so filled with anguish and grief, yet sparked with hope. The shock on his face when she'd answered the door had been real. Probably as real as the terror on her own.

She chewed her lip. It was a shame this man had lost his wife, but it wasn't her responsibility to be his fill-in. She yawned, lulled by the insect chorus about her. Yes, he'd soon realize it was all a misunderstanding. How terrible to break his heart again.

By seven o'clock the next morning Brock rose and dressed in a simple red polo and khakis. With the sketchy Wi-Fi, he stepped outside. He wandered the grassy slope next to the motel, holding his phone in four directions, trying to get a strong enough signal. He cocked his head and scowled at the tree cover. The beauty of the area struck him still.

His eyes traveled to the line of trees on the other side of the road, bursting with late spring vitality. This place had embraced Jenna—*Jerrica*. He had to call her by her name of choice, even though it felt so wrong. What he wouldn't give to pack her up, load her into his car, and drive away. Back to the way things should have been a trio of years ago. A new marriage and a new life. A groan escaped his lips. That didn't appear to be happening anytime soon.

He studied the tree trunks. She was out there, literally. Somewhere. Her acquired family had just brushed this situation off. He'd hardly closed his eyes obsessing about it all night. Of course the stiff motel mattress hadn't helped his quest for sleep. Nor the musty smell.

What to do first? He growled and tossed the change in his pocket. Go back to the Marshall's office or head straight for the Rankins' house? Could he even find their house again?

He grunted. Apparently it proved to be a day massed with guttural sounds. With another groan of frustration, he shoved the cell phone into his pocket. There were too many mountains and too many trees. A person could literally lose themselves up here.

Brock let out a stream of air from between his lips and locked his arms into a snug *X* at his chest. Isn't that exactly what Jenna had done?

Deciding to take his chances at the Rankins, he fetched his wallet, made reservations for the next couple of days, and then loaded up in his car. At least daylight assisted navigation on the curvy, winding roads.

Ellen, dressed in a long floral muumuu, greeted him from the porch where she sat on the swing reading. "Come in, come in." Her tinkling laugh was so like her daughter's. "And how are you this fine day?"

He could definitely be better. Like if Jenna would actually recognize him. "Fine."

"You're just in time. Won't be long before the whole crew will be up."

She snorted as she escorted him into the kitchen. "Ock, everyone needs a good cup of coffee fresh in the morning."

He couldn't protest that thought. She scurried about the kitchen to lay a mug before him.

"Now help yourself. You know where the cream and sugar is, though my memory tells me now you take it black. Anyways, I'll be back. I gotta get my work clothes on, and I'll be back in a whipstitch."

Brock sipped his coffee, wondering how Ellen could be so relaxed knowing Jerrica had spent the night in the woods. He glanced toward the window in the back door. What kind of animals made their homes in those woods? Bears for sure. Cougars? Bobcats? He shoved away from the table and rose, pacing to the back door.

Ellen scurried back into the kitchen and pulled an apron from a peg near the stove. "I trust you had a restful night?"

Brock cleared his throat as he stepped around the big kitchen table. "As comfortable as anyone could make it."

"Let me fix you some breakfast. Some oatmeal or eggs?"

Brock straightened his belt. "No, I couldn't. Right now I just want to get the air cleared so Jenna and I can hit the road for home."

"Well, you might not like this, but you're going to have to wait for John. He and his brother will work together to get the situation righted." She paused as she pulled a package of bacon from the fridge. "John's very concerned about Jerrica. He just wants to be sure everything checks out, you know?"

He nodded. Couldn't blame the old man. They'd adopted her as one of their own.

"Here, more coffee?" Ellen pulled out the wooden captain's chair with a blue plaid cushion.

Brock contained a groan, circled the table, and lowered himself into the seat. "Have you seen her?"

She tipped the beaten metal coffee pot into the large mug in front of him. "I heard the door around five-thirty. She's still in bed."

He let out a gust of air and his shoulders relaxed. *Thank God.* He stirred the thick brew. "John still asleep as well?"

"My dear husband is down at the workshop. He'll be in any moment."

The dark coffee burnt his tongue. "I'm having trouble finding a signal for my phone."

Ellen's laugh chimed through the room. "Yeah, Beth gets so irate. She usually gets in her car and drives towards Jones Cove Road before she gets one."

The door squeaked open, and John stepped through. He rested a hand on his wife's shoulder before making his way to a seat next to Brock. "Just the man I want to see."

Brock forced a smile. "Good morning, Mr. Rankin."

John shook his head as Ellen plopped a mug of coffee in front of him. "Naw, John will do fine."

Ellen eyed Brock. "Yes, please don't stir him up. We'll be listening to quotes all morning."

"'A woman works from sun to sun but—'"

"'A man's work is never done.'" She snorted. "Only you've got that one backwards."

John tipped his head back and guffawed, reaching over and slapping Brock's shoulder. Ellen giggled and pulled an egg carton from the refrigerator. John cupped his hands around his mug. He turned his shrewd eyes on Brock. "Reckon you're anxious to be on your way."

Brock nodded.

The back door swung open and Beth entered, carrying a basketful of large brown eggs—the largest Brock had ever seen. She swung a bucket full of milk to the counter.

"Hello, everyone. Dad, I milked the goats and left the majority in the separator to cool. So you've got a good batch of cheese to make up today. And here's the morning eggs in case anyone stops to buy some." She smiled at Brock. You're up and ready to hit it this morning."

"Yes, I'm quite ready." Hint, hint.

Beth looked back at him with one eyebrow elevated. "It wouldn't be in your best interest to rush things."

She placed the wire basket of eggs in the sink and turned on the water.

He stood and leaned against the counter. "Do you raise ostriches or what? Because if you don't, these are the biggest chicken eggs I've ever seen."

Brock picked up an egg that was a least twice the size of a large store egg.

She laughed. "No, no ostriches. We haven't the money for that. Although some folks over in the next county have an ostrich ranch. These, believe it or not, came from a normal chicken. A fat

White Rock to be exact. Except the big white ones on the bottom. Those are duck eggs."

"Duck eggs, too? Huh."

"They're much richer than chicken eggs. Mother uses them in some of her recipes."

"Giant chicken eggs are odd enough, but duck eggs?" He weighed a large white egg in his palm.

Beth giggled as she placed the clean eggs in Styrofoam cartons. "You've given yourself away. Now I know you weren't raised on a farm. What kind of writing do you do?"

He set the egg down carefully before answering. "I write a lot of different things. Articles, biographies, novels. Sometimes I write what my publisher wants me to write. Sometimes not."

"Interesting." Beth moved to the refrigerator and stacked the containers on the bottom shelf, already laden with several egg cartons. "Jerrica devours books. She'll read one in a day. Or walk through the woods with a book in her hand. I guess she gets tired of sitting. And when she's not reading, she adores old movies. She's a story nut, I guess."

Ellen turned and showed Beth two big, ripe tomatoes. "I've been waiting for these to ripen. John started them in the cold frame. Earliest I ever plucked one off the vine. I can't wait to make BLT's for dinner."

She flanked the table and placed her prize tomatoes on the window sill. "Has anyone seen Jerrica this morning?"

Brock leaned against the sink, glad the conversation had turned back to his wife.

Beth glanced at her mother as she strained the milk. "No, but I'll go encourage her."

After sticking the three Mason jars of milk into the refrigerator, Beth disappeared through the door.

"Reckon I'll need a shower." John leaned back and began to fill his pipe as if he had no intention of leaving anytime soon. Everything seemed to be in slow motion here. He pointed the stem in Brock's direction. "I guess you know you're going to have to do this gradual-like. Jerrica...she's not like other folk. You may have to stay a few days. Maybe a couple of weeks."

An instant protest jumped to Brock's mouth, but John held up his hand. "Son, I know you're all fired up to get yourself here and there, but if you want to get to understand Jerrica, if you really believe she's your wife, and you love her, well, you'll put in the time."

Brock crossed his arms and peered through the cheerful yellow curtains at the window behind him. The old man had a point. How to get that much time off was the big question.

John puffed on his pipe before continuing. "'It takes less time to do a thing right, than it does to explain why you did it wrong—'"

"Henry Wadsworth Longfellow." Brock cut in with a quiet voice.

John gave a slow smile and exhaled a puff of smoke. "You might be okay yet."

Chapter Five

Jerrica gasped as she sat up in bed. The sunlight tinged rosy through her pink curtains. She pressed a hand to her chest, glancing around the familiar room. That's right. She'd returned to the house shortly before sunrise. After a glance at the clock, she swung her legs to the floor. It was late. But then, it was Saturday. No hurry. Had she missed breakfast? Or a certain stranger?

Uncle John would be disappointed she'd fled to the cabin. She squeezed her hands together. They all worried when she bugged out. Goose bumps broke out on her arms and she rubbed the bumpy flesh. If they could only understand how completely terrifying this whole scenario was. Worse than any old horror flick. Not just terrifying. Petrifying. No, horrifying. No, not even that explained it. It was...There were not words strong enough to describe it.

She took a cleansing breath and wandered to the window. Through the lacy sheers the sun shone, but she shivered, anticipating laying eyes on him. The outsider who wanted to tear her world apart.

A headache nagged the back of her head while she dressed in record speed. She perched on the end of the bed. Now what? The scent of bacon filtered up the stairway and into her room. Well, that answered one question. Aunt Ellen had started breakfast.

A knock on the door tore a gasp from her. Then Beth's head peeked through the crack. Her face was plastered with a big smile. Jerrica couldn't still the quiver that rippled through her. The stranger must be downstairs. Beth's wide grin gave it away.

"Hey, Sunshine. Ready to start the day?"

Those goose bumps bloomed into hives on her arms. "I'm not a child, Beth."

Her cousin, self-appointed shrink, pushed her plump form through the narrow door opening and parked her hands on her hips. "I realize that. Just trying to get a little positive energy going this morning."

Jerrica chafed her thumbnail against one particular bump. "Well, get that outsider to leave, and I'll leap about spreading joy and gladness at every footstep."

Beth pulled a mock frown. "Sarcasm. Hmmm. Haven't heard that one today."

Jerrica moaned and shrank against her pillows. "Please don't make me go down there."

Beth plopped on the corner of the bed and reached for her hand. Jerrica snatched it away. Beth lowered her voice. "This is what we prayed for, remember?"

She scrambled to her feet. Rage thundered to the forefront. "I didn't pray for some pitiful guy to come here and...change my entire world."

Beth fixed her with a firm stare, her voice calm. "No, but we prayed for answers, and you're not giving this a chance."

Her uninvited adversary, panic, rose up to clamp her windpipe. Breathing optional. Waves of irrational fears washed over Jerrica, growing like a mythical magical beanstalk. Even her eyeballs beat the same tripping rhythm of her heart. Pulsing zigzag lines with rainbow auras throbbed across her line of vision. Oh, no. Not again.

She closed her eyes, pressed herself against the louvered closet doors, and sank to the floor. This time the thundering pain tromped through her brain, each stroke increasing in pain.

"Work through it." Beth's hushed voice grounded her.

She spoke through clamped teeth as tears worked their way through her lids. "It's not fair, Beth. None of this."

"You have to face your fears. Running away doesn't solve your problems."

Why did she preach at her at such a time? Why couldn't she just show some scrap of understanding?

"Sometimes…I hate you, Beth." Jerrica gasped and clutched her head. How she loathed herself. The pain and pressure increased. "Sometimes I hate everything."

Beth rose and went to the door. Despite Jerrica's flashing blurred vision she could make out Beth's face, wreathed in a gentle smile. "I know. Wouldn't it be nice to stop hating?"

Her cousin slipped through the door and Jerrica dissolved into tears.

Brock paced the sloped yard. This was not working. He couldn't bear to leave, yet Jerrica had not put in an appearance, and it neared lunchtime. John had finally disappeared into the bowels of the house, presumably to shower and begin a morning of making cheese. *Cheese.* High heaven, wouldn't getting Jenna's future aligned bump up in front of the need to make a batch of cheese?

The front door opened and Beth stepped out. "Hi."

He paused, jamming his hands in his pockets. "Look, maybe I oughta just come back later."

She stepped down the stairs and walked the sidewalk to the mailbox. "Later is relative to this situation."

He joined her at the road. "I guess I'm just too impatient."

Beth pulled several envelopes from the back of the black mailbox and slapped them against her palm. She paused under the silver maple fingering the breeze and gave a small smile. "My father's right, Brock. This could take some time. Are you willing to spend weeks here? In the Smokies? Even then, there is no guarantee she'll accept all of this and agree to go with you. For that matter, there's no guarantee my father will let her."

He gritted his teeth. "I'm not leaving without my wife."

She paused and searched his face. Finally she nodded. "I don't blame you. I don't know you well, but you appear to be someone who would be good for Jerrica. She needs someone who is dependable and will go to any lengths to see her recover."

With a stifled harrumph, he swiped away the sweat that gathered at his brow. "I just wish she'd remember something."

"Listen. She's spent for the day. She took a load of ibuprofen for a migraine and will probably nap most of the afternoon. Honestly, she's shell-shocked and hasn't had time to re-boot herself. Why don't you head back into town? Tomorrow's church. Be here by nine and you can join us."

Resistance swelled in his gut but he pressed it down. "I suppose your father would say some sage quote here about Rome not being built in a day?"

A soft laugh rumbled from Beth. "Ugh. So true. But you know, they had to make some progress on Rome each day. I suppose it's the same with Jerrica."

Brock took a deep breath. "I hope I'm making progress."

She turned, headed to the house, and then paused at the steps. "You're not alone, Brock Langston. I hope you'll pardon me while I take my father's route and leave you with a quote. 'If God is for you, who can be against you?'"

He set his hands in his pockets and scanned the roofline before he nodded. "You're right. I'll see you at nine tomorrow morning."

Beth gave a sad sort of smile and turned to disappear into the house. The slam of the front door sounded so final. The noise he made was more of a whoosh, cheeks expelling frustration and disgruntlement. *Frusgruntlement.*

Brock pivoted and approached his car. With the car door hanging open, he laid a hand upon the hot roof and gazed off into the distance. True, Rome wasn't built in a day, but at least the people remembered what had gone on the day before.

He seated himself in the low leather seat and gripped the steering wheel. *It's up to you, God. I can wear out my hammer here and accomplish absolutely nil. You are the maker of everything. Only you can see this through.*

He started the car and steered it down the mountain, heart as heavy as a travertine colosseum.

Jerrica tiptoed down the stairs. The light slanting through the living room curtains indicated a late afternoon. The nap had refreshed her and eradicated most of the pounding in her head. Now she nursed an ache in her soul. How could she have been a screaming shrew to her adopted cousin?

She needed to find Beth while at the same time avoid Brock. A shiver ran through her body as if chilled, and she massaged her upper arms. She ran her tongue over her dry lips. Saliva MIA. Fear was a callous sergeant.

At the foot of the stairs she caught sight of Aunt Ellen working on one of her crocheted projects. "Oh, hello, dear. Looking for someone?"

Jerrica nodded. "Beth."

Aunt Ellen stood and stretched her backbone. "Oh, honey, she's done gone to work. Is there something I can help you with?"

Jerrica shook her head and tears rushed to her eyes. "I owe her another apology."

"Well, come to the kitchen with me and have some lemonade."

They entered and Jerrica slumped into a chair. Aunt Ellen pulled a glass pitcher from the fridge and poured a couple of glasses full, the circles of citrus swirling among the ice chunks. Her aunt brought them to the table and laid one in front of her.

"I was horrible to her." Jerrica sniffed. "Why do I have to be so afraid? Can't I just be normal?"

Aunt Ellen's laugh percolated through the room. "Darling, ain't none of us normal."

Jerrica swiped at the moisture hovering on her eyelids. "I'm always apologizing to Beth. And she's helped me so much. She doesn't deserve the grief I give her."

Aunt Ellen eased herself into a chair and laid her hand over Jerrica's. "She's a good egg, and she understands more than anyone what you're going through."

Jerrica took a sip from her glass. "Is Uncle John going to send him away?"

Aunt Ellen grinned and patted her hand. "I don't expect so. All his records check out. He's clean as far as the law is concerned. Robert's verified his address, his vocation. Everything is as he's told us. I sense he's a very caring person, a Christian. That goes a long way for me."

Jerrica anchored her gaze on the widening water drops on her glass, and her stomach constricted. Finally she rose.

"I'm going to the workshop," she murmured and left the table, letting the screen bang.

"But you haven't had anything to eat," Ellen protested, following her to the door.

Jerrica shoved her hands in her pockets. Her life had suddenly gotten out of hand after three years of trying to focus it. The Rankins were so kind. Now everything was being torn apart.

Katie suddenly whooshed by on an old bike. "Hi, Jerrica. Going to the shop?"

Jerrica couldn't help but pull a weary smile at the child. As usual her little neighbor girl's bangs were too long, and her face and hair were filthy. Her clothes looked as if they were never washed, dingy and stained. Then Jerrica looked down. Bare feet as usual.

"Aren't you ever going to wear those shoes I gave you?" Jerrica chided.

"No way. I'm saving them for first grade. I gotta keep them clean." Katie stretched her face long and raised her brows to emphasize the point.

"Well, it's a long summer without any shoes. Got your brother's bike again today, I see."

Katie shrugged. "I just took it. They all went down to the creek to swim without me."

"Your mother is going to skin you."

Katie screwed up her face. She was small for six. Amazing she could ride a bike that large.

"She won't care what I do as long as I do it outside." Katie shrugged. "She don't like us around much. Besides, she's still in bed."

No news flash for Jerrica. Katie's parents didn't supervise their children much at all and took very poor care of them. Apparently they made them, had them, and then tossed them outside. Jerrica leaned forward and brushed the dirty blond hair from the child's face. Those big blue eyes turned up to her.

Haunted, seeking eyes. Much like her own. She so wished she could snatch her up, toss her in a bathtub, and dress her in some cute little clothes. Like a little Princess, Shirley Temple-style. Maybe fix her hair and nails, and just love the stuffing out of her. She seemed so neglected.

"So ya going to the shop or not?" Her eyes gleamed with excitement.

"Yes, and you may come too," she said, anticipating her next question and careful to use proper grammar. Who knew how the poor child would survive first grade? Jerrica tried to insert as much correct English as she could when they were together.

"Cool beans," Katie straddled the sissy bar, kicked the ground, and coasted to the workshop.

Jerrica sauntered down the slope, and Katie threw her bike to the ground near the barn. She came running back to meet her, jumping around like a goat kid.

"Can I do the bears and rabbits like I did yesterday? I really like those bunnies. They're really cute. Will you teach me to paint them like you do?"

"Well, I guess," Jerrica laughed. Her shoulders relaxed. She could almost imagine a normal day, spent with Katie. Before Brock had shoved down her carefully constructed walls of security. She grimaced at the child's grubby paws. "But you will definitely have to wash your hands first."

Inside, after two not-so-careful washings, Katie went right to business. She knew where all the pieces were and how to construct them. Before Jerrica was even ready to paint, Katie had put together a bear.

"Look, this is the best one I ever done." Katie beamed.

"I've ever done," Jerrica corrected and smiled. "Besides, you always say that."

She sighed. If only being with other people were as comfortable as being with Katie. This six-year-old took her as she was, no questions, no strange looks, no psychoanalysis. Just simple acceptance.

"What's a matter?" Katie asked, still peering at the bear in her hand.

"Nothing really." Jerrica sighed again as she mixed a batch of paint.

"Yeah, huh." Katie persisted. "You only do that breathing thing when something ain't right. You scared again?"

"Isn't right,' she corrected automatically. "I just wish sometimes that I wasn't afraid to do things."

"You mean like going to town and stuff?"

Jerrica gave a short laugh. "Yeah, that stuff."

"Well, maybe when you get bigger, you won't be scared." She nodded with childlike logic.

Jerrica pulled her lips to the side. "I don't know how much bigger I can get."

Katie jumped off the stool, came to the bench where Jerrica sat, and laid her hand on Jerrica's leg. She turned big sincere eyes on her.

"Sometimes I gotta do things I don't wanta. My brothers try to be the boss of me all the time. They tell me if I don't listen, they'll throw me in the cow poo. One time they put me in this old car in the woods 'cause I wouldn't do what they said, and they left me there by myself. I was only four then."

"What did you do?"

"I cried a whole bunch at first. But they never came back to get me, so I started to figger how to get outa there. I couldn't get the door open so I rolled the window down. It was super hard. That car was really old and rusty. And I crawled out, just like that. The next day I kicked Delbert real hard 'cause it was his idea."

Jerrica smiled and touched Katie's little pert nose. "Poor Delbert. Weren't you afraid?"

"Yeah." Katie put her hands on Jerrica's cheeks and patted. "But I didn't give up. Like when I had to learn to tie my shoes."

Jerrica's stomach flopped and tears rushed to her eyes. *God, don't let me give up.* She searched the sweet innocent gaze peering up at her. If a small child could overcome a difficult hurdle, surely she could too. A hankering to wrap her arms about the girl grabbed her, and Jerrica caught her breath. She leaned forward and clamped Katie against her. For the first time in three years, she'd embraced another human.

"Bringing in the sheaves, bringing in the sheaves, we will come rejoicing, bringing in the sheaves."

The old hymn eddied about Jerrica's ears, old Maudielou Spivey pumping at the organ with her thin claw-like hands. Even from the last pew she could see the woman's rapt face, not bothering to look at the notes in front of her. Probably couldn't read them anyhow. Nor needed to. Aged chords branded on her very soul.

Jerrica's gaze drifted up to the hand-carved wooden cross near the ceiling of the church. Solomon Oliver's handiwork, Uncle John had told her. How this church had become a lifeline to her. It had given her a legacy of sorts to replace the one she couldn't remember. Why, old Solomon's grave lay in the church yard, his concrete stone worn with age to the point that his death date of 1884 had nearly been eradicated.

Although it gave her some sense of centeredness to know the long history of the structure and the ones who had come before, the graveyard made her shiver. Blame the hokey *Frankenstein* movie. What kind of anxiety-ridden nut watched old horror flicks? Nothing like putting out a forest fire with gasoline dropped from the Hindenburg. Wow. What a gaslight paradox.

Only you can prevent forest fires.

She tugged her brain from her dark sarcasm. The organ went to a different key, forcing her thoughts back to reality. So many tidbits of information about this church and community made this place home. Had made her feel like she belonged.

Now, the man beside her erased all the comfort this place had bestowed upon her soul. Brock didn't hesitate at the old hymns like some newcomers did. He'd belted the notes right out, his rich baritone instantly melding with the other voices, the powers that be accepting him as part of this place.

She exhaled a trembling breath. Only he also strove to carve out a place next to her. Trying to change her whole life. *Be* her whole life.

Distress sent shudders up her throat that threatened to interrupt the music. She pivoted into the outside aisle and hurried to the door. She simply had to have fresh air, escape the tight walls that echoed back his voice of praise. When she gained the outer door, she slumped through it, setting her hands on her hips, inhaling the clean mountain air.

Knowing he'd be right behind her, she avoided the cemetery on the left, stumbled behind the church, and settled on a step of the old entry into the baptistery. No one ever used the door anymore, and Jerrica settled on the ancient block of concrete, weathered with time and footsteps of parishioners long departed.

She breathed in slowly, trying to calm her heart. Sweat broke across her forehead. It wasn't even ten o'clock yet, and the early summer heat had already moved in. Thankfully the elevation kept some of it at bay.

She picked up a stick and scraped it across the age-old cement. Did Maudielou remember a time when the congregation had used this step? What about old Solomon? The turn in thoughts calmed the speeding of her heart, but the man who popped around the corner did little to ease her nerves.

"You okay?"

She bit the inside of her cheeks, resisting the retort that skittered up her throat. She still owed Beth an apology for her ogre behavior from yesterday. It was bad enough to snap at her family, but this stranger was another thing entirely.

She stood and scrambled away, shrugging. Oh, how she wished he'd leave. "I guess."

He slid his hands into his pockets and nodded. "I'm probably not helping either."

Her eyes caught his, and she ran her tongue across her lips. Like always, Sergeant Fear had hoarded all the moisture in her mouth.

Brock raised his hands and gave a small grin, cocking his head to the side. "You don't have to say it, it's written on your face."

Despite the heat, her jaw convulsed with a chill. She cut her gaze into the woods.

"I'm not leaving until I get some answers here. You know that, right?"

She squinted at him. Oh, yeah. That seemed obvious. "Yes."

He squatted to pick up a small acorn, pulled off the top, and tossed the pieces in the gully beyond. "I don't suppose we could call some sort of truce?"

Sure. A truce. Why not? Did the man really think it was so easy? Her skin crawled with a colony of writhing bees with him at twenty paces.

"I mean, I'm not going to snatch you up and drag you away from here."

"Then what do you want?"

He took a few steps closer, and Jerrica cast a desperate glance toward the steep slope, considering the idea of running into the woods.

"You know what I want."

She pressed her fingernails into the damp wood siding of the church. "I'm not her, and I'm tired of saying it."

He nodded. "I know."

"We should get back inside." She backed away a few steps when he eased forward and lowered himself on the step. With a turn of her head, she could now see the worn tombstones on the top of the hill. Perhaps silver screen Victor was digging up old Solomon for body parts. No escape that way.

"I suppose we should."

Silence lengthened between them. The birds chirped overhead, the cicadas buzzed in the distance. The sun dappled her clenched arms. The smell of damp grass filled her nose. Finally he turned his head, and she met his gaze.

"Don't you even want to know?"

His eyes were deep, with all kinds of jumbled emotions. But haunted pain made itself plain. She caught her breath. Her own eyes revealed the same in her mirror every day. She struggled to stifle the empathy that rose inside her. "No."

His voice dropped to velvet and she couldn't look away. "Can't you remember one little thing? Our engagement, our wedding?"

The bottom dropped from Jerrica's emotions. Oh, he was clever, and he could sure draw her in with his enigmatic eyes and handsome face. Her breathing turned to pants and she back-treaded toward the gully. "I know what you're trying to do. You're trying to make me remember things that never existed. You think my mind's so weak you can convince me of anything. Well, you can't."

"Wait, we're just talking."

She swung her head violently. "No. I don't remember you because you never were. I would remember my husband. Of all things," her voice dropped to a mumble, "I would remember my spouse."

Reality stabbed at her. *The rings.* A wedding set with no origin in her memory. With a strangled cry she pressed a fist to her mouth.

"Jenna, just listen."

"I'm not Jenna," she screamed.

He rose from the step. "Okay, calm down."

"I won't. You must leave." She back peddled from him. "I'm begging you, please just go."

She spun and rushed headlong into the undergrowth, a cry ripping from her and the brush grabbing at her clothes.

∽ ⋯⋯ ∾

Brock made his way down the gulch to follow her until he heard his name behind him. Beth stood up on the knoll next to the church. With a shake of his head he made his way back to her.

"What happened? We could hear screaming in the sanctuary."

He rasped his hand through his hair. "I'm sorry. I thought I could help."

Beth shrugged. "Don't worry about it."

"Look, I'm going after her."

She gave a short laugh. "I wouldn't bother. She knows the way home."

His brows scrunched. "Are you kidding me? We're miles from your house."

"Miles around the mountains, but cutting through is much shorter."

He turned his gaze back to the trees. "I'm going."

Beth rolled her eyes and crossed her arms across her chest. "Great. We haven't organized a search for a lost hiker in a long time."

Brock stared hard at her. "I have to try."

A smile creased her face as she nodded. "Yes, I suppose you do. At least I'll know the general area to search if you don't show up."

He raised one brow. "Gee, thanks a lot."

"Go on, ya goof. If she gets too far ahead of you, you'll never catch her."

Brock didn't need any more encouragement. He swiped the perspiration from his neck and nodded. "Wish I'd worn my tennis shoes."

"Is she worth it?"

Brock didn't hesitate. "Yes."

She smiled. "You're about three mountains shy of our place. You'll cross a stream midway. Stay to the south side, keep in the shadow."

"Right. See ya soon." He took off down the gully once more.

Beth's voice trailed to his ears as he approached the trees. "I hope so."

At first it was easy to follow. Branches were broken here and there like the Jolly Green Giant's breadcrumbs through the forest. Then his eyes had to search for pressed soil, grass, and weeds. His calves began to ache from the slant of the ground. He set his eyes to the trunks of the trees ahead, marked one in his mind that seemed to be at the same elevation, and then headed for it.

He soon came to a downward slope where it was plain her footprints had slid down the grade. Hopefully that was mountain one. He increased his speed and ignored the pain as he headed up another incline. The brush thickened here, making it hard to distinguish the way ahead, but the faint rush of water indicated the stream lay ahead. Thankful to have reached the next milestone, he pushed himself into a jog. The slick bottoms of his black dress shoes had zero traction, and the slope of the terrain worked against too much speed.

He broke through the brush near the stream just in time to see her edge into the shallow water flowing over a rock formation. He couldn't stem the grateful humph that slid from his mouth. *Thank you, Lord.* No search party today. However, now he'd have to face her wrath.

Perhaps if he trailed back far enough, he could avoid that, and merely shadow her to the house. Surely by the time she arrived back home, she would've mellowed a bit. He snorted. *Don't bet on it.* He wasn't on her list of favorite people.

She gained the other side and paused to put her shoes back on. Then she stood and continued on her way. He hesitated a moment longer, waiting for her to disappear into the undergrowth. It wouldn't be hard to get another visual on her. Her yellow sundress made her easy to spot.

He slipped his shoes and socks from his feet and stepped into the frigid mountain stream. The rocks were slippery with flowing moss, so to steady himself, he grasped a jagged rock jutting above his head. She'd made this look like cake.

The flowing sound of water made it difficult to catch the crunching noises of her return, and he scrambled to make it across before she spotted him. His left foot gave on the moss below, and he lost his balance. To avoid a complete belly whop on the rocks, he sidestepped into the pool below.

He plunged into the water, thigh deep, his feet screaming from the landing on uneven stone below. Only the waistband of his black dress pants remained dry. He let out a gasp at the shock of cold water. The brush parted in front of him and there she stood, face blotched with tears.

A giggle spurted from her mouth, and she slapped a hand against her face to cover it. A grin worked its way across his face. Water spattered his shirt and his legs ached from the chill. One way to cool the pain in his lower legs. "Hey."

She swiped the tears on her cheeks while fighting to keep the mirth from showing on her face. He'd plunge into icy water a thousand times to see her face brighten. Her dimples rose to the occasion, and Brock couldn't tear his eyes away. Dimples vs. ice water. Dimples, hands down.

He gave a grin. "Go ahead. Laugh. If my teeth would stop chattering long enough, I'd laugh too."

A small smile broke over her face, and he let his eyes trail her. He stopped short when he recognized blood dripping down her left leg. "You're bleeding."

Chapter Six

H e stuffed his socks into the interior of his shoes and pitched them to the bank. Then he clambered from the rocky pool while the rush of water tugged at him. He managed to add a layer of mud to the bottoms of his dress pants, but that wasn't his main concern. "Are you all right?"

She sniffed, the smile disappearing from her face while distrust once more took residence. "I fell. It's nothing."

He dipped his handkerchief into the stream and approached her gingerly. "You could sit there."

She eyed him. Then shook her head.

"It'll get on your skirt."

Jerrica's gaze darted down and he pushed the advantage. "It won't take a moment."

"I don't need your help."

"Okay, here. You do it." He tossed the handkerchief onto a dry rock nearby. She glanced around before picking it up and perching herself on the small boulder. With a quick swipe she cleaned the flow of red from ankle to knee. Then she eased the dress hem up several inches. Bright red blood coursed from a deep scrape on her knee.

"Wow. Are you okay?"

"It looks worse than it is. The water from the stream set it to bleeding again." She grimaced when she laid the cold compress on her knee.

"It's bad enough. Are you sure you can walk?"

She shrugged, dabbing at the wound as blood continued to pour out. "I'll be fine."

He grabbed one of his socks and removed his pocketknife. "What you need is some continued pressure."

With a flick of his wrist, he sliced off the bottom of his sock. "Here."

She flinched as he moved closer but allowed him to kneel next to her. He cradled her foot in his hand and slid the sock sleeve up her leg to secure the wet handkerchief over the wound.

She had beautiful legs. Smooth, shapely, delicate. He restrained a groan. What a time for that thought to cross his mind. Yet touching her skin was intoxicating. "Hope you can stifle your disgust for my dirty sock. At least it should staunch the bleeding."

She parked her gaze on the top of his dark head as he adjusted the elastic black band to lay flat against her skin. Why she trusted him to doctor her, she had no clue. But his hands were firm and sure as he slid the stretchy section of his sock up to her knee. It perfectly fit around her joint, keeping the clean wet hanky pressed against her skin.

He grinned as he collided with her gaze. "How's that for first aid? They'll be begging me to join one of those survivor shows on TV."

A jumble of emotions danced inside her. "Uhhh, thank you."

"How's it feel?"

"Fine. Sorry about your sock."

His grin widened. "Well, don't be disappointed later when I cancel the sock puppet show."

A snort burst from her. "I'm sorry to miss that. I've never seen a puppet show."

The grin on his face faded, and for a moment, her stomach gripped. What did she know about her past? His face stiffened, and she ran her eyes over the handsome planes of his features. Her knight could never be mistaken as some ugly ogre.

And that was part of the problem. The man could charm bears to river dance with a mere tilt of his head and a crooked smile. She blinked and pulled her gaze away. So he wasn't Frankenstein's monster. What did it matter if he was striking? He was a stranger. An unwanted stranger.

Squashing the trail of her thoughts, she stepped out with purpose. She supposed she couldn't just rush off and leave him, as if her knee would allow that speed. He slipped his shoes on and then his hand lighted on her elbow. She jerked away, paused, and pinned him with her eyes. Her heart tripped a faster beat. Fear and a light batch of attraction fought in her midsection.

The disappointment that lit his face shamed her. He'd been such a rescuing gentleman, yet allowing him to touch her was out of the question.

"I just want to help."

She worried her bottom lip, drawing his gaze. Perhaps imagining him with sock puppets on his hands would allay her unease. She pressed her lips together to waylay a grin.

He stepped up beside her but didn't touch her again. "I'm afraid you're going to have to guide me out of here. I'm not sure I can find my way back."

He was right. Puppets or no, he'd never find his way out of the mountains without her. With an exhaled breath, she turned and led the way, skirting thickets and tall trees. She reached up and grabbed a hanging grape vine and sent it swinging.

"You ever run across any dangerous animals?"

She shrugged. "A bear or two. I keep my distance."

They walked for a while in silence, until Jerrica cut up the mountain. Brock followed without question. She gestured toward the left. Here was the perfect opportunity for them to part ways. "If you want to head back to the house, keep going that way."

"What do you mean? Where are you going?"

She hurried up the slope, ignoring the twinge in her knee. Rats. It would be quite a challenge to leave him today. He came abreast of her and laid his hand beneath her elbow. Although it humiliated her to accept his help, it made going up the steep slope easier.

Their breathing increased as they struggled up the steep incline until the land finally came to a ledge. She huffed for a moment, gathering the oxygen into her lungs. Her partner did the same, wiping sweat from his forehead. Here's where she could lose him.

"Now what?"

She indicated the small hole in the rock face of the mountain. He took a couple of steps forward before turning his gaze toward her.

"You kidding me?" His brows descended and he searched her face. "That opening is barely big enough for us to crawl in."

"I told you to head back that way." She dropped to her knees.

Perhaps she hadn't thought this through. Her knee already throbbed. Yet she knew she could hunker through without using her wounded joint. His hand on her arm stopped her.

"You're going in there? In the dark?"

"Go back, Brock." *Back to where you came from.* She ducked and entered the dark tunnel. From the scuffle behind her, he followed close behind.

Jerrica knew just where she was going, despite the darkness. Once through, she rose and took a deep breath of the dank air.

"Where are you?" His voice echoed through the short tunnel.

She felt her way along the wall and located the rock alcove where she kept her flashlights. Her fingers fumbled through the choices, choosing one. Then she froze against the wall.

"Jerrica?"

With the snatch of light from the small entrance, she could just barely make out his squatted form. He fumbled in his pocket for a moment and then flicked on his cell phone light. "I'm not leaving until I find you."

Great. There was no ditching him. First he'd invaded the workshop, now her cave. She clicked on the flashlight. His gaze locked on her location against the wall.

"Hiding from me, weren't you?"

"I suppose."

He stood and cleared his throat as he took in the fifteen foot square cavern with the tiny beam of the LED light. "Look, I know you don't want me in your life. But I'm not going anywhere. Can't we just establish a cease-fire for now? At least until you guide me through this cave?"

"You could just go back."

A low chuckle greeted her. "I'm not going to do that."

She blinked at him in the low light. "Fine. A cease-fire."

The limestone ceiling sparkled in the beams of the flashlights while the smell of wet stone filled her nostrils. Her gaze worked its way back to him.

He still stared at her. "You're amazing, you know that?"

Remorse filled her as she bent to locate another flashlight for him. She was anything but amazing. Fearful, yes, crazy even. Definitely not amazing. "I don't know what you're talking about."

"Not many people would have enough guts to gallivant all over the mountains and then squirm through that small hole."

"I have like fourteen flashlights by the entrance, plus a lighter and a lantern. I don't think that's too brave. Here, this one is stronger." She flung it at him.

He managed to catch it and flicked it on. "Still, you had to crawl through that dark tunnel for the first time, and that takes some guts."

He would never say such a thing, if he only knew how afraid she was. Of everything. Literally everything. This place was her way of escape. Eluding people had become her main occupation. Over the last three years, she'd always convinced herself that nothing could touch her in the hills or deep in this cavern.

Her tongue ran over her dry lips while he continued to search the surrounding stone walls with his flashlight. Now, this stranger invaded yet another one of her private retreats.

She flicked the beam across the room to the columns of stalactites meeting stalagmites in a long skinny hourglass shape which framed the corridor that would bring them to the exit. Then she flicked the beam up. Thin white soda straws hung from the lowered ceiling near the columns. Dripping sounds echoed through the large room.

She sighed at the incredible things her Creator had thought to array here in majesty in the bowels of the earth. Despite her fluctuating reality, God's creation remained still, glorious, colossal, yet healing. Being in God's earth simply quieted her soul. "It's peaceful here. Safe. Come on."

He followed her through the stone columns that parted to allow a natural walkway. The formations around him proved fascinating, liquid stone frozen in shining globs of magnificent color and shape. She continued to walk at a good clip, dodging the stone creations. The cave opened into a larger cavern.

"Look, cave bacon." She pointed the beam toward a flowing curtain of rock that glowed a red-brown, resembling its namesake. "And here's some rimstone. There's blind cave fish in there."

He brought himself to a stop behind her and ran his flashlight around the ripples of rock on the floor of the cave. A small shallow pool glowed in his light while the small white fish darted away from their echoes.

"Interesting. You must have studied about caves."

She turned and continued, flanking the rimrock. "A little."

The trail led to the left, and Brock wondered exactly where they were going. A person could easily lose themselves in the passageways of the cave. The cool air that had felt so good on entry, chilled his skin, yet she kept leading farther and farther into the deep labyrinth of the cave.

"Do you think we ought to turn back?"

"Huh? Oh, no. We're almost there."

The glittering limestone columns narrowed, and Jerrica turned sideways to maneuver between them. She flashed a beam upwards. "Watch your head."

He surveyed the low ceiling and ducked. "Thanks."

The wet floor dropped and then opened into a wide corridor. Jerrica paused in the middle and flashed her beam around the room. "Look."

Here the ground appeared dryer. Her light traced the edge of the slanted ceiling accessible by climbing the flowstone formations revealing names and dates. "See this? These people burnt their names into the rock with candles. And here's the tins they used buried in rock."

Brock trained his beam on the names. Frank Dawkins and Homer Glasson, 1874. William and Norma, 1914. Others littered the rounded room.

She spoke in hushed awe. "Can you imagine? We're in the area where these people were more than a hundred years ago. She flicked her beam across the room. "See Cora Struhl? Her tombstone is in the church yard."

He studied her before nodding. "Makes you wonder about their lives."

Silence grew between them until she spoke. "Yes."

He stepped closer and lowered his voice. "But what about your own? Don't you wonder about that?"

She scrambled away, her light growing dimmer as she hurried down the pathway. He jogged to catch up and gripped her arm, their flashlights flinging dancing beams about the walls.

"Stop, Jerrica."

She wrenched from him. "Some cease-fire. I led you through the cave and all you can do is grab me?"

He swiped a hand across the back of his neck. "I'm sorry. I just want to discuss this."

Her sniffs filled the cavity of the earth, and her voice dropped to a whisper. "Please...I can't do this."

She pivoted and ran. He followed as the tunnel's size decreased. Finally he ducked into the sunlight and gratefully inhaled a fresh breath of air. The bright sun caused him to squint and blink away tears. When his vision cleared, he was greeted by the sight of Jerrica scaling the slope towards the workshop.

Somehow they'd ended up just below the barn. Thankful to have his bearings, he strode toward her fleeing form. She disappeared into the house with a slam of the door. He rubbed the back of his neck and retreated to the front porch to wait for the rest of the crew and pray.

Chapter Seven

"**Y**ou ditched us the other night, didn't ya?" Uncle John eyed Jerrica as he piled a second helping of mashed potatoes on his plate. "If you only knew how your old Uncle John worries for you out there."

Jerrica glanced up from the roll she was mangling. Sunday dinner had lost its appeal long ago. Her eyes jumped over to Brock at the table. "I tried, Uncle John."

Uncle John nodded. "You spend the night at the cabin?"

She fixed her eyes on her plate. The heat of everyone's stares fried her skin into rinds. "Uh-huh."

Aunt Ellen cut in the conversation. "Well, Brock, I'm so pleased you joined us for church this morning. I just wished you would have both made it through the service. Such a good sermon."

"Yes, ma'am. Thanks for inviting me."

Jerrica knew him well enough already to recognize a stiffness in his voice. Aunt Ellen's voice curtailed any more thoughts.

"I've been giving a lot of consideration as to your accommodations. Now, John keeps his eyes on a couple of rental cabins, but they're so expensive. Especially during the summer. I think it'd be best just to stay here with us. We have an extra room upstairs."

Jerrica held her breath. Was she kidding? Her stomach knotted, Boy Scout style.

"Oh, Ellen, I appreciate the invitation, but I've got a room at the motel in Mavey."

"Pshaw, darling, that's not a comfortable place to stay for a spell." Aunt Ellen held her hands up. "No, no. Don't you think about going anywhere else. You need to be here. You stay as long as you want."

Jerrica's eyes flicked from Aunt Ellen to Uncle John, and lastly to Brock, but he was nodding at her aunt. Her mouth parted. *Somebody say something to reject this plan.*

"I appreciate that. It'll make more sense to stay here. Thank you."

Jerrica gripped the seams of her jeans. Unwelcome shards of panic filled her head.

Aunt Ellen rose. "Not a problem. We've got plenty of room. Now, I best get a plate fixed for Beth before we get all this mess put up."

Jerrica jumped up and scurried around to collect the dishes from the table. She turned on the faucet at the sink, rinsed the dishes, and plopped them into the dishwasher. Her hands quavered, and she clutched the slippery plate tighter.

"Here, I'll be glad to help." Brock slid from his chair and picked up his plate and glass.

He brushed Jerrica's arm and a glass slipped from her hand. The crash froze everyone in the room.

"Oh, dear." Aunt Ellen's delicate hand fluttered to her throat.

Tears rushed to Jerrica's eyes as she surveyed the floor.

"Son, might be best for you to let the ladies take care of it." Uncle John stood, his calm voice doing little to settle the tension in the room.

Jerrica, her face a burning caldron, took the broom from her aunt and knelt to gather the heap of fragments. How clumsy could she be? Turning on the Three Stooges would be a lesson of dexterity next to her fumbles.

"I'm so sorry." He shuffled towards the door. "Well, thank you for the dinner. It was very good. I have some writing to do, if you'll excuse me."

Uncle John's tall form sauntered after him, and they both disappeared through the door. Jerrica's cheeks puffed full with a rush of air, and she wiped her face. Aunt Ellen squatted next to her and patted her arm. "Now, don't worry, pumpkin. It's just a glass."

Jerrica took a huge gulp of air and swept the pieces into the dustpan. "I wish that were true, Aunt Ellen."

Her aunt gripped Jerrica's hands fastened around the broom handle and dustpan, forcing Jerrica's eyes up to hers. "Listen, why don't you let your old aunt take care of this? It sounds like Brock's gone to the porch. Go and make some conversation."

"Aunt El—"

"No." Her aunt reached up and patted her cheek. "You can't ignore him forever, child."

Jerrica rose and stumbled toward the door. Once in the darkened living room, she paused and laid an unsteady hand on her midriff. Katie's story of being trapped inside the car replayed in her mind. She rolled the window down. Such a simple thing.

Jerrica shivered. Had Katie felt like she was suffocating? Like the whole world pushed at her, touching her, prodding her? She blinked and stared at the carpet loops at her feet. It was time to roll the window down.

The first step is always the hardest. "'When I am afraid, I will put my trust in You.'"

Her foot took the first awful step, and she eased the front door open. Brock sat with his laptop on the glider at the far end of the porch, and he glanced up when she edged through the screen door. With the sun settled behind the western tree line, the porch was comfortably shaded, and a slight breeze provided the air-conditioning. The scent of Aunt Ellen's rosebushes tickled her nose. She licked her lips, shrugged, and whispered. "Mind if I sit?"

Brock set aside his computer and indicated the white wicker chair next to him. "Not at all."

Jerrica crossed her arms tightly and ignored his invitation. The morning's clash still weighed on her mind.

A chuckle rumbled from her companion. "You're not really just going to stand by the door, are you?"

Her face puckered. He probably thought her juvenile. Sometimes she felt like a juvenile. Even Katie spouted wisdom that surpassed her own. Swallowing reluctance, she made her way to the chair. My, this smacked too intimate. He gave a lop-sided smile, and she glanced away.

"Nice afternoon." He settled back against the slats.

"Yes."

The birds chorused about them, and Jerrica rubbed the dimpled goose flesh on her upper arms.

"You like it out here, don't you?"

"Yes."

Another chuckle rumbled forth, and she fixed her eyes on him. "Could I get more than just a 'yes'?"

Feeling bold from the anger that simmered, she searched his face. His handsome features lit with a grin, and gentleness sprang from his dark eyes. She pulled her gaze away. Once passed the panic he invoked, he seemed likeable.

"How's your knee?"

His eyes dropped to her knee, encased in a pair of worn jeans. She'd all but forgotten about it. "Fine."

That one-word reply wasn't really fair, she supposed. The fact remained that she didn't *want* to like him, cease-fire or no. He represented the unknown. Or an intruder. Her eyes closed for a moment and then opened, once more disgusted with herself. Okay. So conversation. Like normal folks.

"Your wife," she began, "how did you meet her?"

His brows elevated. "Ah. We met at church camp, actually."

Jerrica shifted her face to his. "Aren't you…older?"

Brock laughed. "Yes, I'm four years older than my wife. I was a counselor with a buddy of mine, and I first met her when she was just fifteen."

Her mouth dropped open. A cradle robber? Perhaps he wasn't as likeable as he seemed.

He held up his hands. "It's not what you think. That's the first time I laid eyes on her. Other than she being a camper and I a counselor, nothing else entered my mind at that point. She was cute and flirty in a junior high sort of way. But that was it. I returned to counsel the next three years, and by the time she was seventeen, well, we started to talk. Later we started an on-line relationship."

He shrugged. "She helped edit my first manuscript which later published. I graduated from IU and got a job at the newspaper in her hometown. We hung out together at church, and her mom encouraged us to continue dating, despite our age differences. And it wasn't long before I proposed."

Brock looked away from her. It was difficult to talk about her in third person when she occupied the chair next to him. He wanted nothing more than to hold her and caress her soft skin. Jerrica, clad in a white, short-sleeved top and jeans, fastened her eyes to the concrete floor. Brock worked his throat in several swallows. Perhaps sock puppets would lighten the mood.

Shock waves still rippled through him at the sight of her. She was actually here. Alive. Her long blond hair fell forward, hiding her face from him, and his heart squeezed. He longed to swipe it from her face and witness love in her eyes. He glanced away. Even if he could get close to her, love would not radiate from Jerrica's gaze. He was nothing more than an intruder.

A car approached, turned in the driveway, and rolled to a stop. Beth got out and came up the walk, sporting a wide smile. "Howdy, all. Nice afternoon for sitting out."

Jerrica stood. "I need to water the goats."

Beth grinned. "If you wait a couple of minutes, I'll help you."

Jerrica rushed to the door. "No, I got it."

Brock crossed his arms as she slipped inside. "Hey, Beth."

Beth trudged across the yard, lugging her purse, and lifted her long skirt to navigate the steps. She grinned as she settled into the chair Jerrica had vacated. "Having a talk, were we?"

Brock snorted. "I talked. She said nothing."

She nodded and stretched her neck back. "That sounds about right. I see you made it through the cave. Did you make any other inroads?"

He shook his head. "I'm not sure how this is going to work. She barely acknowledges my presence, let alone start a real conversation with her. And when I do, she's fearful or angry."

"Time, my friend, time. And I know we're leading up to her leaving with you. She couldn't have left three years ago, but now, with God's help, I think she can."

He stared at her. "You believe me, then?"

Beth studied his face, her usual merry eyes serious. "I do. I think we all do, even my dad, for all his sputterings. It's just a little hard to embrace. Jerrica's not the only one who needs a little time."

She gathered her bag and rose. "As much as I hate to leave your engaging personality, I must eat something."

He waved as she moved toward the door. She paused. "I'll talk with her, but it's a process that won't happen overnight. Rome, my friend."

Brock's face stiffened. "What if it doesn't happen at all?"

Beth smiled. "That's not going to happen."

The door shut behind her and Brock crossed his arms. He wished he could be so confident.

An hour and a half later Jerrica opened the barn door, and the goats hustled out. She cleaned the milking stands, swept the floor, and wandered toward the workshop. Light flooded the large space when she flipped on the light, and she bellied up to the sink to wash her hands. She needed to finish lettering one of her signs. Thankful for a familiar distraction, she gathered the needed paints and brushes and bent over her creation.

She was so focused that when Beth's voice sounded from the door, her arm twitched, knocking over a navy bottle of paint, splattering it across the concrete floor. She buried her head in her arms. Nervous quivers shot through her like shivers.

"Wow, you're on a tight leash." Beth grabbed some paper towels from the dispenser and bent to wipe it up.

Jerrica grabbed a rag and moistened it before she dropped to her knees next to her. A sob bubbled from her throat.

"Let it go, Jerrica. It's just paint."

Jerrica threw the rag down. "It's not about paint, Beth."

Beth looked up. "I know. I'm sorry."

Jerrica scrubbed a hand at the moisture flowing down her cheeks. "No, I'm the one who owes the apology. I shouldn't have acted like a jerk last night. You were just trying to help me. I don't hate you. I love you."

Beth nodded. "I know."

She thrust herself toward the towel and swiped up the spill. "What happens now, Beth? This...Brock guy can't stay here forever. I don't understand why Uncle John doesn't send him on his way."

Beth stood and threw the soaked towels in the trash. "You're right. I'm sure if a handsome man came to my door, insisting he was my long lost husband I didn't even know I had, I wouldn't bother talking to him either."

Jerrica froze as she met her eyes. Beth parked her hands on her hips as she stared Jerrica down. "You're not the only person involved in this situation."

Jerrica turned from her and folded the soiled rag. "He's lying."

"Excuse me if I don't trust your memory."

"I can't believe you said that," she whispered.

"I'm sorry," Beth wobbled her head back and forth, "but I don't really see you trying."

Jerrica sat back on her heels and placed her hand against her throbbing temple. "I talked to him."

"Yelled more like." Beth tapped her foot. "You need to prepare yourself. There's going to be changes. I'm not sure how big yet, but something has to give. You may even have to...leave."

Jerrica jumped to her feet, bulged eyes making her head ache. "I can't," she choked. "You know I can't!"

Beth blinked momentarily. "I just want you to ponder it, so if this comes up, you can keep yourself normal."

"Oh, Beth, there's no way." Nausea rocked Jerrica's stomach. She flung the rag on the counter and strode to the door. "This conversation is over."

Jerrica threw the door open and began to sprint.

"You can't run from the truth, Jerrica." Beth's words floated to her in the late-afternoon light.

Jerrica spent the evening ensconced in her bed. Sympathetic Aunt Ellen brought a snack and crooned, fluffing pillows and such. When she read the thermometer, she had that look. Completely normal. And for the rest of the evening that's exactly what Jerrica tried to remain as she battled the queasiness in her stomach—completely normal.

The sun cascaded into her room by the time she woke the next day. She showered, dressed, and straightened her room. Aunt Ellen brought a tray of blueberry muffins and juice. In the safe confines of her room, nothing tasted so good.

Wait. Was he gone? A wild hope lit her heart. Perhaps...her demeanor lifted. Yes, perhaps he'd left which was why her aunt hadn't forced her to come downstairs. But as she opened her door, her cheerfulness turned dour. Two men's voices floated up to her. He was still very here.

"Good morning, Jerrica. Feeling better?" Uncle John said as she stepped into the living room.

Jerrica centered her vision on her uncle. "Yes."

"Good." He stared at the ceiling and tapped the pipe stem against his teeth. "We've got to talk, you and I."

"Okay."

"Let's go to the den."

Brock stood as they took leave, and Jerrica ignored him, determinedly setting her course for the study. She sat in the big recliner while her uncle parked himself behind his huge desk. Something was afoot. Only the most serious of discussions took place in the den.

"Well, I know you've been wondering. But I want you to tell me one thing before we get started. What do you want to do?"

"What do you mean?" she whispered.

"Brock has some pretty solid evidence you are his wife. What do you want to do?"

Her mind spun. What did she want to do? "I...want the fear to go away. I want him to go away."

Uncle John nodded. "If he leaves, the fear will still be here."

Jerrica studied her hands. "I know. What do you think I should do?"

Uncle John leaned on the desk. His wizened dark eyes fixed on hers. "I made a lot of calls yesterday. I talked with Brock's pastor, his lawyer, his co-workers, the local police, and a Christian counselor who's a member of his church. He's highly thought of, and most claimed he's grieved too long for his wife."

Jerrica trembled. He was going to tell her something terrible. Something that would tear her world into worthless snippets.

"The counselor I spoke with tended to think you needed to go back to familiar things." Uncle John leaned back in his chair. "Three years is a long time, and I reckon those memories could stay hidden forever. But if it were me, I'd sure want to know."

Jerrica lifted her head to focus on Uncle John as her brain reconfigured into abstract sculpture. She blinked several times before she spoke. "What are you saying?"

Her uncle leaned forward. "I think you should go back with Brock."

Chapter Eight

Jerrica didn't remember leaving her uncle's study or recall climbing the stairs to her room. She only knew she'd sat cross-legged on her bed for a very long time. Staring.

Her brain awakened like from a horrible nightmare. The brass clock revealed late afternoon and her stomach rumbled. A tray with watery tea and cheese crackers rested beside the clock. Had she eaten today?

She did remember the plans forged earlier. All Brock's documents presented very strong evidence to prove she was Jenna Langston. Uncle John suggested taking two weeks to prepare for a trip that would take her *home,* a completely alien place. Perfect plot for a vintage movie. Not for reality. Do not attempt this stunt.

She covered her face with her hands. They waited to see if she could maintain her mental stability. As Beth always put it, time to "get normal." Audition for a starring role, per say. Fact was, it'd take longer than a couple of weeks to get normal about this.

No matter what they said, she knew she couldn't be *Jenna.*

～ ······ ～

Two weeks. The elation that coursed through Brock as he visualized taking his wife home waned a bit when he'd seen his wife exit John's study. Nothing but a shell-shocked hull, Jerrica had navigated up the stairs, oblivious to external stimuli. Recovering his wife was not going to be easy. She'd fight him all the way. He prayed she'd emerge from her stupor.

He glanced into the rearview mirror as he backed into a slot at the local police station. John volunteered to join him, but Brock declined. Having some time to himself away from everyone refreshed him.

Robert Rankin greeted him as he swung into the main office and motioned him back to his office. Brock nodded at his secretary, went on back, and seated himself in the same chair he'd occupied on the last visit. He drummed his fingers as he waited, and soon the big man strode through, flinging the door shut behind him. He stopped at his chair and put out a big hand.

"Brock."

"Marshal."

He settled into the seat with a groan. "I've been looking forward to this all afternoon. My feet are barking."

A corner of Brock's mouth curved up. Robert lugged a thick file from his right hand drawer and parked his glasses on his thick nose. Was that his file?

"All right. First of all, all your documents check out, and the originals are enroute." At Brock's nod he continued. "We need to exhume the body in your wife's grave. Lots of legal smeegle. I'll have to go through the county sheriff in Sevierville. It's out of our jurisdiction, so we have to get a court order. with your permission, of course."

He pulled a form from a pile and placed it in front of him. "We also need permission to question Jerri—Jenna's mother."

Brock shook his head. "I don't think that's a good idea. She's refused to see me for some time. The doctors told me she has schizophrenia and suffers with delusions. On the last visit, she spent most of the time warning me about the evil images formed in the fat of the T-bone steaks at a local grocery store."

Robert's face elongated. "You kidding me?"

Brock adjusted his body in the hard seat. "I wish I were. Before she was hospitalized, she made the pastor a blueberry pie, with detergent as filling."

"Ummm. I see." Robert turned toward the computer screen and pulled his chair in. He clicked the keys for a couple of moments and then glanced at him. "I've eliminated her as a source of inquiry. Now, getting Jenna's paperwork to verify she's alive will take some time. Working out of this small town office will also cause some delays. You're welcome to go to Sevierville if you think it'll speed the process."

Brock scrubbed at the shadow of stubbles on his chin. "I'm here for a couple of weeks anyway. I'd rather you handle it."

The big man raised a finger. "We got a lead on the person who may have inadvertently given Jenna a ride from outside of Knoxville to just south of Mavey. He'd hauled a horse to a buyer and then pulled the empty trailer home. Once home, he discovered blood smeared in a pocket of straw near the back. Said he even called the guy to make sure the horse hadn't shown signs of injury. He'd reported it to me at the time, but I'd shelved it as unsolved."

Brock's stomach dropped, and he fixed his eyes on the window. How had she done it? Where was she going?

"You okay?" The marshal's voice jolted him.

Brock cleared his throat and flicked his eyes back to him. "Yeah, just thinking about her hitchhiking here."

Robert nodded, a grim glint in his eye. "The Lord surely watched over her, didn't He?"

Brock set his teeth and clasped his hands.

The man behind the desk eyed him. "Listen. Although I believe what you're saying, the federal government is going to need hard proof."

Brock adjusted in the hard seat. "Like what?"

Robert knit his hands on the desk and leaned forward. "Dental matches, fingerprint matches, things like this."

"That's no problem."

The marshal let out a short laugh. "Then you don't know your wife very well. I'm not sure you and three wrestlers could drag her into either establishment to begin the process."

Brock stood. He just couldn't bear to sit any longer. He paced the small area behind his chair and rubbed his stiff neck.

"I know this is difficult, but we need to tread carefully. You're trying to reestablish a relationship with a woman who doesn't know you. And from what my brother has told me, who's resentful and fearful of you."

Brock's fists drove into his pockets as he stopped and pinned the marshal with pained eyes. "He's right."

"Okay. That means the rest of us will have to step up and get it done. With proof we can start recovering her identity on a federal level." He cleared his throat. "I hate to say my brother is still in denial as well, even though you have all the documents, pictures, and chain of events laid out to prove otherwise. But I have a little plan that'll provide evidence to prove she is who you say she is."

Brock approached the desk with pinched brows and settled his body back into the chair. "What plan?"

Robert crossed his arms and leaned back in his squeaky chair. "It ain't pretty, but it's foolproof. You game?"

A dove fluttered at the window, and its signature cry lured his eyes to the window. He blinked at the strong sunshine. Getting Jenna alone might be the key to rebuild what they had. Maybe she'd remember if she returned to familiar places. Isn't that what Uncle John had suggested? Brock leaned forward and gripped the edge of the marshal's desk. His eyes narrowed as he nodded. "Let's do it."

Jerrica flicked her gaze across the dinner table to Uncle Robert. What was he doing here? He never ate dinner with them through the week. She narrowed her eyes and studied him. Something was afoot for she could practically touch it in the air. Her eyes returned to the beef and homemade noodles in her plate, and her stomach tossed.

"Are you feeling all right, my dear?" Aunt Ellen asked.

Jerrica glanced up and caught several gazes resting on her. It was just too quiet, the conversation too stilted. "I'm fine."

"Do you not like the noodles?"

She worried her lip. Aunt Ellen had spent the afternoon mixing and rolling out the fresh noodles, and she was reluctant to indicate the fault may lie with her cooking. "No, they're great."

Aunt Ellen scooted out her chair. "Dumplin,' let me make you some hot tea."

Oh, boy. The pet name thing. Something percolated. "No, I'm okay."

Her aunt scurried about the kitchen as if she hadn't spoken. Jerrica clenched her teeth. She was one straw short of fleeing to the cabin.

"See Katie today?" Uncle John offered, holding a noodle-laden fork aloft.

"No."

The silence elongated until the microwave beeped. Aunt Ellen opened the door and pulled the cup out. Her aunt always thought a cup of hot tea fixed everything.

"You get things ironed out with your editor?" Uncle John addressed Brock.

Jerrica cut her eyes to his handsome face. Shaved clean each morning, he bore a shadow of dark stubble by evening. His black eyes, darker than a moonless night, seemed to smolder as he flicked his gaze briefly to hers.

"No. He's madder than a wet hen."

"Is that right?" Uncle John said.

"Are you going to have to leave?" Her voice burst from her, lightened with hope. Eating ceased, and all eyes turned to hers, most with disappointed stares. Brock's throbbed with...pain? She dropped her eyes and the skin on her face suffused with the heat of a thousand suns. "I mean—"

Aunt Ellen saved her with a cup of tea and laid it next to her plate. "Oh, sweet pea, have a sip."

Jerrica swallowed a scalding gulp. Her throat screamed as she forced the hot liquid down her gullet. Her watery eyes caught Uncle Robert staring at her.

Brock cleared his throat. "Yes, well, he's understandably upset. I should've sent in the article on Haywood McCoy four days ago. By some miracle, he agreed to give me an extension."

Jerrica refused to look up. The tea did taste good, and the heat calmed her frayed nerves. Sweat broke across her forehead as she blew on a teaspoon of liquid before sipping it down.

"I'm taking him out to McCoy's next week, John, and I expect you to ride along."

Uncle John snorted. "I'll not be getting out of the car."

Brock glanced from brother to brother. "I can go myself. That's what I'd planned to begin with."

A mocking glint lit Robert's eye, and he crossed his thick arms across his barrel chest. "Is that right? Well, let me tell you a couple of things about Haywood McCoy. You won't find his place without a local guiding you to it, and then when you do find it, you'll wish you hadn't."

Brock stuck his hands under his armpits and studied the big man. "Because..."

"You'll have to take him, Robert." John growled. "He'll be shot full of holes in a matter of seconds."

Jerrica's eyelids drooped. She took a sharp breath to rouse herself. The lack of sleep exhausted her. She blew on another spoonful of tea.

Her uncle laid his napkin down and leaned back in his chair. "I reckon I can come along, providing you carry that pistol of yours."

Aunt Ellen patted her hand and Jerrica widened her eyes. Wow, she was so lethargic. Aunt Ellen gave a kind smile. Jerrica closed her eyes, clutched the tea cup, and drained the rest. A bang sounded from the table, and Jerrica's eyes jerked open. Had she slammed the mug down?

She blinked at the occupants around the table. All of them were staring expectantly. Was there something wrong? Perhaps if she just rested a second she'd feel better. She laid her cheek upon her forearm. Her eyes fluttered closed and then open.

"Night, princess."

Uncle Robert's eyes narrowed, and she tried to make sense of it from her sideways view. In slow motion he parked his hand on Brock's shoulder. The marshal's voice floated in from far away. "If you're legit, I'll die righting this situation. If anything comes up that don't smell right, Glory help you."

The conversation around her continued to reverberate in mumbled syllables. Shadows wedged in. Someone patted her back, and she tried to revive, but the sleep tunnel approached. She chugged in full steam. Fuzzy wooziness claimed her and her body relaxed into sleep.

Jerrica sucked in a lungful of air and rose to a sitting position in the center of her bed. Her hands clutched the quilt on either side of her body as she swung her head around, searching the room. All appeared normal, and she worked to slow her breathing.

No sunlight shone through the window, and she glanced at the clock. It was the middle of the night. How had she ended up in bed? Hadn't she been at the table? And there'd been tea. And her Uncle Robert saying odd things. Her brow puckered as she replayed the last moments of conscience over and over in her brain.

Yes. So, how.... She opened her mouth and stretched her jaw. Why did her mouth hurt? Her jaw worked in a circle to ease the odd feeling. Her tongue prodded a particularly tender spot. About here, cheesy music would fill the background of this make-believe movie she found herself in. Something dramatic. Though she couldn't quite wrap her head around why this story line might need climactic music.

She flung the quilt off her legs, swung to the floor, and padded to the window. Through the lacy sheers the moon's silver light highlighted the mist creeping through the woods. She knelt and pushed the window up. A cricket chorus surrounded her in an even buzz, and the cool wet air settled on her arms as she leaned on the sash. Honeysuckle flavored the air.

Was she suddenly forgetting spans of time? She pressed her head against the screen as tears rose. Tears. Right on time. That would be the screenplay's next personal direction for the heroine. She swiped at the moisture on her cheek and shoved the comparison away, real dread stapling her gut.

God, what's happening to me?

❧ ⋯⋯ ☙

Robert's truck rumbled to a bumpy stop on the steep slope. Gravity slid Brock out of the backseat of the truck to the rocky soil, and he wondered how John would manage to climb out on the other side of the vehicle. But John slid out the driver's side and was soon standing next to him.

Brock glanced around. Scrub brush covered the rocky areas, and pine and deciduous trees populated the remaining ground. Not a house in sight.

John jumped into the trailer with Robert, and they backed the four-wheelers down the ramps in quick order. Brock eyed the small vehicle he'd borrowed from Beth. Somehow riding the four-wheeler up the steep slope didn't strike him as a necessary way to die today.

Nevertheless, he swung aboard and tested the throttle, satisfied with the rev of the engine. Maybe the engine had more power than it appeared. Beth was no small girl.

The marshal came abreast with a shotgun slung over his shoulder. "Ready?"

With a grim nod Brock pulled out tentatively, falling to the rear of the little trio. They zigzagged the slope through the trees, following a faint trail, and Brock tightened his hold on the grips as they climbed while a sensation of pressure squeezed his ear canals. The steep incline made him clench the body of the vehicle with his legs, shooting an odd glance down the mountain. He sure hoped he didn't' roll back to the truck. He opened his jaws to pop his ears clear.

Some twenty agonizing minutes later, Robert pulled to a stop on a relatively flat section, and Brock followed suit next to John. He stretched his aching body, thankful for the break. A shot rang out, and all three men dove for cover.

Brock seized the weeds around his head and pulled himself behind a mulberry tree. "What was that?"

Robert's short chuckle caught him off guard. "That, is Haywood McCoy."

John and Brock maneuvered to where Robert lay prone, peering through a bush.

"He gives a right neighborly welcome, doesn't he?" John muttered.

Robert wriggled the shotgun's strap from around his arm, aimed it into the treetops in the distance, and fired. The deafening blast rang in Brock's ears, and every muscle in his body coiled. What in heavens had he gotten himself into?

"Get off my land," a guttural bark demanded.

Robert worked his forearms beneath him and rose up a bit. "Haywood McCoy. This is Robert Rankin, marshal of the town of Mavey. If you don't stand down with that scattergun of yours, I'll handcuff you and toss your hind end in my jail."

Brock peered through the undergrowth as the silence stretched. Footsteps came stomping through the woods, and a figure cradling a long gun appeared in the distance.

Robert bunched his body and rose. "Haywood."

"Marshal."

"Got me a reporter who says he was supposed to meet you a couple of days past."

"Izat so?"

"Yep."

Brock glanced to John, but he made no indication to rise.

The long-haired hunched figure snorted. "Don't like to be stood up."

Robert pushed through the bushes. "I understand, I understand. I don't like to be shot at."

The man let the gun drop to his side and struck a relaxed pose. "Just trying to protect my property, Officer."

Brock shifted to a squatting position and then rose, sheltered behind the tree. John stood beside him and dusted his trousers.

"The man's crazy," he muttered lowly.

Robert was nearly on the stranger. "Well, it's not likely you need to murder three men to insure the safety of your property. You remember Brock Langston?"

The hippie nodded in assent, and the marshal motioned them to step out. Brock took a deep breath. If he survived this little incident, he surely had enough fodder to write a dozen articles.

The compact man squinted at him, shotgun snuzzled against his grizzled cheek. "You was supposed to be here last week."

Brock nodded and held out his hand. "I apologize for missing our appointment."

The mountain potter screwed up one eye and spat at the kidneyleaf buttercup at his feet. Ignoring Brock's proffered hand, the man pivoted and marched up the slope.

The marshal snorted. "I think that means, come on in."

Or don't let the screen hit ya on the way out. Brock's money was on the second interpretation. Despite his doubts, he followed Robert up after the odd character, Uncle John puttering on behind.

They climbed until they reached a plateau, a natural ledge on the far side. A small shack stood to the right, and an open roofed-in building without sides stood to the left. A teenaged boy cradling a firearm stood sentry. McCoy headed for the ledge.

The three of them created a half circle about him. Brock cleared his throat, to break the silence. "Thanks for agreeing to meet me. If you don't mind, I'll just get started."

The potter rumbled. "On with it."

Right nice fellow. "Okay. How long have you lived here?"

The answers came in mutters, akin to deciphering the yips of wild wolf pups gathered around a wad of fresh meat. The young sentry didn't move, even when they approached to examine the homemade kiln, the buckets of red clay, and the various greenware resting on a primitive shelf. Brock made efficient use of his time, not wanting to overstay their rude welcome.

With a blue homemade mug in Brock's hand, they turned to make their way down the hill. McCoy motioned with his shotgun for the boy to follow them. "Make sures the genteelmen find their mode of transportation, Delbert."

"Make sure that scattergun don't fill us with holes, neither," Uncle John muttered low enough for only Brock and Robert to hear. "Needs a good course in gun safety, I'd wager."

Robert gave a short, quiet laugh. "Oh, I think our friend is well versed in weapons, dear brother."

Brock's feet slid over a layer of old acorns, and he caught himself with his hand. The long-haired, dirty teenager's features

never flickered. The boy stood beside a large tree as they boarded their four-wheelers. Brock threw up a wave before revving the engine. But the kid had disappeared.

Chapter Nine

"**Y**ou be good to my girl," Uncle John admonished Brock lowly as he loaded Jenna's suitcase into the trunk of his car. He glanced up to see if they were still out of hearing range of Jerrica.

John continued. "You go slow now. If you have to stop and get a couple of rooms at a hotel tonight, all the better."

"I've been here for nearly three weeks. I really need to—"

"I know," John held up his hand, "it's only a seven hour drive, but it's late afternoon. This may be the only remembrance of kindness and understanding she knows from you."

Brock's heart sank as he peered at her huddled form on the porch swing. Ellen and Beth chatted cheerfully, trying their best to make a positive break. What if Jerrica never remembered anything?

They stood and walked toward the driveway. Jenna's tears and wild eyes caused his gut to mash. They hadn't even hit the road yet, and she was nearly hysterical. Beth leaned forward and whispered into her ear. An earful of encouragement, Brock hoped.

Beth opened the car door to settle Jerrica in the passenger seat when Katie came up the drive at a full run. The child was as grungy as ever except for her shoes.

"Look. I wore 'em. Jes for you." Katie motioned to her shoes. "What'cha cryin' for, Jerrica?"

His wife gave a weak smile. "I'm just sad about leaving."

"Don't be sad." Katie stuck one hand deep in her tattered jean shorts. "Here, this is my favorite rock. You can have it."

"Oh, I couldn't." A rogue whimper betrayed her emotions.

"Sure ya can. I got lots of favorites."

Smiling through tears Jerrica took the treasured stone, a smooth white quartz.

Katie hugged her, grime and all. "See ya later."

Jerrica lowered her head and the curtain of hair shielded her expression. With lots of persuasion and repeated goodbyes, she at last remained seated in the car. Brock put the car in reverse and backed down the driveway.

Several miles down the road she hunched in the same position, arms crossed, knees up, head down. Although she wasn't frantic, Brock could tell she was constantly weeping as she kept wiping her face. He handed her the box of tissues Beth had insisted he bring. Good ole' Dr. Beth.

"I'm really sorry this is so hard for you, Jenna."

"I'm not Jenna." A cat's hiss followed.

Okay. Everyone knew she was Jenna but her, apparently. Brock gripped the steering wheel. A marriage license, wedding pictures, federal red tape in motion. Even John now had proof. Brock had known the moment he'd laid eyes on her, but Robert's secret plan had convinced his brother beyond a shadow of a doubt.

Aunt Ellen's tea had knocked her out cold, and a local dentist had x-rayed her teeth. They matched her childhood dental records to a 'T.' How he wished he could share the caper. The positive ID.

But who knew how she would react to such an underhanded plan? So for the sake of making the trip easier, he'd go along with her.

"Fine. Jerrica."

She was very still for a few moments. He gave a start when she screamed.

"Pull over, Pull over."

Brock had barely done so before she bounded from the car and retched in the ditch. He closed his eyes and clenched his teeth. The woman was violently ill before they had gone ten miles from home. He walked around the car and handed the box of tissues to her. He reached to steady her as she staggered back to the car. She jumped from him as if she'd been touched by an electrical current.

With a sigh Brock shut her door, strode back around the vehicle, and slid into the driver's seat. "Are you all right?"

Back in her usual position she nodded, and Brock pulled the car out on the road. "You know, if we talk, it might make the trip go a little faster."

She didn't respond. Maybe faster wasn't better. Isn't that what Uncle John had suggested? But it'd help to get her mind off her fear. "So, do you like to read much?"

Silence.

Jerrica squeezed her eyes closed, trying to ignore the road passing beneath them which took her farther and farther away. Brrr-rump. Brrr-rump. Her breath trended shallow and her heart sped up. None of this made sense. Why was she being forced to live with a virtual stranger? How could her family do this to her?

Anxiety built a fortress in her midriff. Soon the twisted throbbing in her vision would punch in, towing the debilitating headaches. Maybe he was right. She needed something to take her mind off the distance they were now putting between her and her beloved home. "Wha?"

"Reading? Do you do much reading?"

"Um..." she grappled to gather her thoughts in her dizzy head. "Yes."

"Any particular kind?"

"Suspense. I like suspense mysteries."

"Great. I'm in to a little mystery myself."

She cast a hard sideways glance at him. Was he making a pun out of the whole situation? Did he think her hysteria was a joke?

He caught her look. "No, I mean I write them. Not all the time. But right now I'm in the middle of a series."

She glared at him, too unsettled to filter the undisguised disbelief.

"It's true," he said, giving her a half smile.

"What have you written?" Her tone sounded accusing, but she didn't care.

"Well, you may not have heard of them, but I have a few Christian mystery series. Let's see, there's the Last Rights and the Black Thread series, and now I'm working on The Frozen Pendulum series. I'm on the third book."

Her vision seemed to spin and a strange rumble set up shop in her head. She thumped the dashboard with her hands. "Stop. Stop the car."

Brock immediately drew the vehicle to the side of the road. She leaped from the car and rushed to the trunk. He got out, tissue box in hand.

The man looked totally baffled. "Is there a problem?"

She motioned to the trunk and forced out words. "Open it."

Wordlessly he clicked the key fob and popped the trunk lid. She dug through her belongings and brought out a heavy box. She lifted the lid and exposed the contents. "I have every single one of them."

A discovering sort of grunt emitted from him as he pulled one from the box. "Well, how about that?"

She pulled another from the box. The dark cover revealed Langston Roe across the top. Close, but no banana. He had to be lying.

"You didn't write all those." She stomped away and got back in the car.

The trunk slammed shut and Brock came back to the driver's seat. He put the key into the ignition but turned to stare at her. "I can see you don't believe me. So test me. Ask me something about one of the characters."

Jerrica bit her lip, "Who was Liza married to in the first series?"

He grinned. "Liza wasn't married to anyone. She was the maid and an old spinster. I got that mold from an old aunt of mine. Surely you can do better than that?"

"What was the fourth title in the Black Thread series?" she challenged.

"Um...let's see, that would be *Winding the Bobbin*. Quaint title, wouldn't you agree?"

She looked at him, his face alight with a small grin. Her heart stuttered. Could he really have written all of her favorite books? "Why didn't you let Chenelle shoot Ramsey?"

He shook his head. "What good would that have done? It would have made her a murderer. I can't have the heroine committing murder just for revenge. She had to be bigger than that."

She breathed aloud. "Yes, I guess. But I hated Ramsey. He made her live in fear of losing her daughter when he knew the birth certificate was behind the face of the old grandfather clock."

Brock's lips twitched to the side. "Do you know where I got the idea of the clock?"

Jerrica eyed him, mesmerized by the quiet sound of his voice. "No."

"From your grandfather's clock that sits in the hallway."

Jerrica's eyes froze into a glare. Her face throbbed as if he had just slapped her, and she was painfully aware it registered on her face. She turned away and bowed her head to shut him out with her hair.

"Hey, I'm sorry." His groan was audible. "I want you to remember so badly. Maybe once we get home and visit your mother—"

"My mother is dead." Her head shot up. She sat hushed, her mouth agape. Her mother was dead. She knew this truth with an unexplainable certainty. The prick of hot tears seared behind her closed lids.

"No, Jerrica," Brock said gently. "She's not."

She turned toward him and whispered. "I know she's dead. I never remembered before now, but I'm certain she's passed."

Like learning of her mother's death for the first time, Jerrica's breath dissolved from her lungs, and she groaned, gasping for air. Only she couldn't stop. Hyper. Ventilating.

Brock reached into the glove compartment and pulled out a plastic department store sack and covered her mouth with the opening. "Breathe into the bag."

Everything grew fuzzy, and she lowered her head between her knees. Through her fog she heard Brock's steady calm voice. Slowly the dizziness dissipated, and Jerrica was left with a pounding headache. As she began to adjust to the surroundings, she realized Brock had his arms wrapped around her.

"How are you feeling?" he mumbled softly.

Tears trickled down her face. "My mother's dead."

Jerrica wept and Brock's arms closed around her.

Holding her was torturous heaven.

"It's all right," he whispered against her hair.

How could she believe her mother was dead? The woman had given permission for them to date, pushed it really, and attended their wedding. Right now, Jerrica's mother was ensconced in her protected wing, nurses and aides seeing to her needs. His wife had to be mistaken.

Slowly Jerrica got ahold of her emotions and pulled from him. He cleared his throat and tried to keep his thoughts from the tender moment they'd shared as he steered the car back onto the road. They'd soon hit the interstate. Jerrica covered herself with a velour blanket, turned toward the door, and grew still. He didn't dare flip on the radio, and the car gobbled up the miles.

The sky had darkened by the time he pulled into Lexington, so he decided to yield to John's advice. He drove into a popular chain hotel's parking lot and perused it. It looked brand new.

"Where are we?" she muttered sleepily.

"A hotel."

She bolted upright, her eyes wide. "What for?"

Fear elevated her voice, and he studied her. "I thought we could stay here tonight and get up tomorrow and finish the journey.

"No."

Hadn't her uncle given the sage advice to take things slowly? "What do you mean?"

"I can't stay in a hotel."

Brock nodded. "Okay, look. I know this is all very difficult for you, leaving and everything, but we left quite late in the afternoon so unless we stay here, we won't get back until after midnight. I thought if we took the trip a little more leisurely, it would help you adjust."

He gripped the steering wheel and turned his gaze out the windshield. "Please, just tell me what you want to do."

Her voice came in a whisper. "I don't think I can sleep in a room by myself, and I don't think I can stay in a room with you either."

Well, that was honest. Brock gave an audible breath as he mulled this over in his mind. *Slow down, Langston. She needs a lot of understanding and compassion.* "I think we could possibly get adjoining rooms. That way if you need anything, you only have to open the door."

She blinked at him and then cast a glance back at the huge be-windowed building. "I can't ride the elevator."

"I'll get one on the bottom floor."

Her gaze swung back to him, and she searched his face. Finally she relaxed a bit. "Okay."

Brock left the car and Jerrica shivered. *Help me, Lord, she prayed. I'm being so unreasonable, but I just can't seem to help it.* His lithe body strode toward the entrance, and through the large glass front, she watched as he spoke with the woman at the front desk. A few minutes passed, and he emerged through the clear doors.

He stooped to her window and she lowered it. His dark eyes swept her face. "They have adjoining rooms on the third floor."

She caught her breath.

"They have stairs." He raised his brows in question.

Stairs? Three flights of stairs? She wrung her hands together and felt the warmth of his stare. His face seemed very close. "I'll try."

Brock helped her from the car, and they met the bellhop who took their bags and led them to the elevator. Jerrica turned her wide eyes on Brock, and he cleared his throat.

"My companion and I will be taking the stairs. We'll meet you there."

"Very well, sir," he returned with a courteous smile.

Brock stepped away from the elevator and held the door to the stairs. She swallowed as she stared at the enclosed area. It was very tight. With a deep breath she stepped through and gave a start as the door behind them thudded shut with an echoing crash. The sound was deafening. Hello, hives.

He stepped up on the first step while she panted. "Ready?"

Screaming no, would only frighten herself more with the horrid echoes. "I…"

His hand reached out, palm up. "You can do it."

Who are you, Brock Langston? Hero or zero? He nodded assurance. Okay, she'd go with hero. She slid her hand into his larger one. He squeezed it with gentle encouragement, and they climbed the stairway together.

Inside one of the rooms, Brock tipped the bellboy and then guided Jerrica to the adjoining door. "See, through this door is your room."

She walked in and looked around. The room was a mirror image of the one they'd just walked through. Her eyes took in the bed, end tables, dresser, a larger table, and a cushioned wing chair. The opened blinds beckoned her to the window, and she moved closer. The ground plunged below her. "Oh, my."

"Here, let me close those."

She perched on the bed and held her arms against her lurching stomach. "You think I'm crazy, don't you?"

What a stupid statement. Even crazy recognized crazy.

He walked over slowly and sat on the bed, leaving a comfortable space between them. "No, Jerrica. I think you are a woman who's survived in the only manner you could."

She stared at the knobs on the air conditioning unit just below the curtains. "What, through fear?"

"Yes."

End dramatic scene. End. *End*. Groan. Her default mode of escaping reality only seemed like a childish game. A shudder discombobulated her breathing, and a lone tear slipped down her cheek. Raw truth rushed from her lips. "I'm tired of being afraid."

He reached his hand up and swiped the tear away, his voice like a breeze across a meadow. "I know."

Chapter Ten

Odd sensations radiated from Brock's touch. The air conditioning kicked on, drawing her eyes from her companion. A rumble came from the vicinity of Jerrica's stomach.

"I'm hungry." She laid a hand to her belly. "I think."

He nodded and smiled. "Yeah, me too. We could go downstairs and eat."

She wiped her hands across her cheeks and inhaled. He said that like it was so simple. Easy breezy, lemon squeezy.

"Or we could eat up here."

"That would be so expensive." And so inconsiderate, she added to herself. *The first step is the hardest.* She closed her eyes and clutched the white rock in her pocket. *All right, Katie. I'm going to roll down the window.*

"It really doesn't matter to me. However you feel most comfortable."

She glanced sideways at him. Such kindness. He was exerting a great deal of understanding with her sheer lunacy. Perhaps he did qualify as top scholar in the hero category. On a burst of boldness, she stood. "Let's eat downstairs."

He smiled, and Jerrica felt a warming sensation begin in her middle. Hero. Handsome hero.

He nodded. "Sounds perfect. I'll leave you to freshen up."

Brock exited, closing the door behind him. Jerrica glanced at the wadded sweatpants she wore. This would not do. She quickly unzipped the suitcase and pulled on a long floral dress with simple white sandals. She carefully put her scarred arm through the three-quarter sleeve sky blue sweater that matched the dress.

The garment had been a going-away present from Beth. A new church dress, she'd said. "Sure to bring out your summer tan and gorgeous eyes." She assessed herself in the mirror. Well, it could be worse.

She perched at the end of the bed, nervous, but not panicked, despite the fact she was on the third floor. A knock sounded on the adjoining door and she jumped. She opened the door a crack and caught the startled look registered on Brock's face. His eyes grew wide and glistened.

"What?" she asked.

"Nothing." He checked his watch and then adjusted his belt.

"What's the matter?"

His Adam's apple did a few calisthenics. "Jenna loved blue. It was her favorite color."

He turned and walked toward the desk in his room with his hands in his pockets. Jerrica had been so occupied with her own grief and fear she'd never stopped and thought what Brock might be feeling. He was, after all, taking a big chance.

A shudder of an odd sort of compassion rippled through her. She followed him into his room. "I'm...sorry, Brock. I never really thought about how difficult this must be for you." She stopped a few paces from him. "I guess it's just as tough on you as it is for me. I'll change."

"No." His eyes met hers in the mirror. "You're beautiful."

Jerrica caught her breath and felt her cheeks grow warm. Poor man. He was resurrecting a fantasy world. *What's he going to do when they find out I'm just Jerrica?*

"Let's go to dinner. I reserved a private table. Do you think you can handle it?"

Khaki pants hugged his fit form well, and an olive green button down shirt revealed golden skin plus a snatch of chest hair. Not a tall man, yet not short, he carried himself with a confidence that drew one's eye.

His short wavy hair curled around his ears and his dark eyes sparkled from the memories she'd evoked. Beth had pointed out his attractiveness, and she had to admit he looked like he'd stepped out of a Hollywood magazine.

Hmmm. She had to agree with her former comparison. Not Frankenstein's monster. Gregory Peck-ish. His left eyebrow elevated and the corner of his mouth curved up. The room's temperature skyrocketed.

"I think I'll be fine," she whispered and brushed past him.

Brock took the stairs, enjoying her grasp on his sleeve as they came through the door of the restaurant. He slowed to give her time to assess the room. But her attention seemed superglued to the patterned carpet. Her hand fluttered up to press against her midsection. Best find a chair.

A few couples swayed on the small square dance floor. Some kind of festive occasion. Given the cake, he'd guess birthday? Anniversary? Anyway, the piano player in the corner kept the music on old tunes. Jerrica's flared eyes showed apprehension, but not panic.

The waitress appeared, and Brock ordered steak while Jerrica breathed out a request for chicken. Jerrica couldn't take her eyes from the couples on the dance floor even once the food arrived. Perhaps it kept her from dwelling on the current arrangement.

Brock ordered an after-dinner coffee and a hot tea for Jerrica. So many things he wished he could discuss. He couldn't resist one nagging at the back of his mind. "Care to dance later? I'm sure we could just mingle in the crowd."

She narrowed her eyes. "I don't dance."

He sat back in his chair. "Jenna didn't dance either."

Jerrica held her cup aloft, shooting BB's of disapproval in her stare.

"As a matter of fact," he continued, "that was our first unofficial date."

The waitress delivered the dessert menu, and Jerrica busied herself behind the cardboard barrier. Nope. If she thought he was dropping off at the most interesting part, she was in for a surprise.

"Yes, we were both avoiding a rather stuffy, extravagant wedding celebration dance of a distant cousin of mine. Jenna really didn't know anyone, and we were already acquainted from church camp. So we struck up a conversation on the patio about our hatred of dancing."

Jerrica fidgeted in her seat, the curtain of her hair hiding her expression from him.

"I love your hair. Except when it conceals your face. You don't have to hide from me." He winked. "And you've been a bit stingy with the smiles."

She sipped from her water glass and gave him a cool blue glance. "You were a bit unexpected."

"And unwanted?"

A flash of fire swept her gaze, and she settled back in her seat and crossed her arms over her stomach. "Yes, that, too."

He folded up the menu. At least he could be thankful for her honesty, even if it did pain him. Best to move on to desserts. "I think I'll get the cheesecake. You?"

❧ ⋯⋯ ❧

She squinted at him. Cheesecake? Jenna's favorite dessert, perhaps? But he merely motioned to the passing waiter. She cleared her throat. "Yes. That's fine."

Jerrica's strained muscles eased when they were left alone once more.

He took a drink from his water glass. "So I have a question for you. Would you have been happy to stay at the Rankins the rest of your life never knowing who you really were?"

Oh, good. More about this messy situation. She shrugged. "No, probably not. I don't know, maybe. They *are* very good people."

"I'm not disputing that," he murmured.

"It's not just the agoraphobia. At least that's what Beth calls it. It's everything. Even at night I have nightmares. There's really no rest."

His face puckered. Stupid. Stupid, stupid. Why add more cream to the butter churn?

"What nightmares? Nobody's mentioned that."

She released a pent up breath and shrugged. "Lots of different ones. But one in particular."

"What's it about?"

Ugh. Sharing that? That was worse than having visitors in her workshop. Confound her mouth for letting it slip out. "It's nothing."

He leaned forward, all handsomeness and somber. "Tonight it's just me and you. Wouldn't it be best if I knew what might happen?"

She scrutinized the planes of his face and then cut her gaze to her hands in her lap. Phobic wasn't foolish, and she knew he had a very valid point. He appeared concerned, perhaps he even cared. But then, he thought she was Jenna.

Her fingers sought the table cloth corner, and she pulled the skin on the corner of her lip with her teeth. What if she awoke in the middle of the night thrashing in her bed? She shivered, hoping that would not be her surprise show for the night. Her fingers traveled to the napkin in her lap. She at least owed him a heads up. Just in case.

"I always dream the same thing. That's what makes it so...scary." She sucked in a deep, even breath forcing herself to relax. A losing battle. "I'm in a cemetery. At night. The wind is blowing and there's lightening all around. It's very dark. *Very* dark."

A lump swelled in her throat. "A woman in a long red dress has a baby in her arms. She's standing beside an open grave, holding the baby over the hole. I beg for the baby over and over."

She flashed a glance at the dancers now gathered around a large table with a cake, somehow hoping a happy occasion would lessen the horror of her dream. "This big hat shields the woman's face, so I can't see her. The baby is crying and I'm screaming. Just as I reach for her, the woman throws the baby into the grave. Then the wind whips off her hat, and she's nothing but a skeleton."

Sweat turned her skin to ice. She forced a twitchy smile to her face, but the faithful goose flesh covered her arms. "Beth usually shakes me awake."

"She's been a great comfort, hasn't she?"

Jerrica nodded. "I don't know what I would've done without her."

Silence stretched between them and she lifted her eyes.

He gave a gentle smile. "Thanks for telling me."

She let a soft groan escape. "You've been forewarned. Beth doesn't get much sleep on the nights I dream."

His eyes twinkled. "Well, if we're up late, maybe I can entertain us with sock puppets."

Despite the pall of the nightmare, her mouth quirked. "That could prove to be interesting."

The waiter arrived with the dessert, and Brock winked, brandishing a forkful of cheesecake. "May all our fears be chased away with cheese."

She tried to suppress the grin that rose, but failed. Instead she raised her fork, filled with the fluffy, baked treat. "Agreed. Bring on the cheese."

If only that charm would work. They locked for a moment. Her breath hung on a cliff edge. She forced her gaze to her plate with a wisp of a sigh. At least spending this short time with him would not be agonizing. Yet the truth was bound to come out in time. Her gaze lifted to his tranquil face. He'd hung all his hope on her.

What a tragedy to break his heart.

After dinner Jerrica called Aunt Ellen and Uncle John from Brock's cell phone. Tears rushed to her eyes at the sound of their voices, making a steady trail down her face. After talking with them and Beth for some time, she ended the call and handed the phone to Brock.

She prepared for bed in her own room, battling the nuances of a completely strange place. It smelled funny. Not a bad funny necessarily. Just a different funny. The mattress was hard, the pillows lumpy. The light shadowed in odd angles. She missed her pink room where she knew every sound and shaft of light.

Maybe it hadn't been such a good idea to call home, for a cascade of homesickness tugged at her. She slipped on her pajamas and got into bed, wiping tears away. How silly she was. Was she a child? Her eyes flicked down. *Blue* pajamas. Ick. Too much already.

She tossed the blanket aside and strode to her suitcase. Her hands searched for one of the books Brock claimed he'd written. When she pulled it to light, she realized she'd read this particular volume at least three times. With a shrug she settled back under the covers.

She examined the cover, striving to fasten her mind on something else. *Timekeeper's Prelude,* book one of the Frozen Pendulum series. She stared at the grandfather clock on the front cover. It didn't look familiar at all. Her eyes went to the author's name, Langston Roe. Was it possible he'd written it?

She heard a faint knock on the connecting door.

"I'm going to bed now," came his muffled voice. "Goodnight."

"Brock?"

The door opened, and he peeked around. "Yes?"

"What made you choose Roe?"

"It's my mother's maiden name."

"Oh."

"Goodnight." His head disappeared.

"Brock?"

He grinned when he reappeared. "Yes?"

"Don't lock that door." She fastened her eyes on the book in her hands, and her face heated.

He was silent for a moment. "All right, Jerrica. Goodnight."

Don't lock that door? That was embarrassing. Even more embarrassing? Experiencing the throes of that nightmare. Here. In a hotel. With Brock. No, thank you. Begging for a sock puppet show at midnight would be less mortifying.

She fixed her eyes on the novel in hand. Staying awake wouldn't be that difficult with all the weird noises and lights. Besides, since it'd been so long since she'd read this novel, it would grab her and take her through most of the night. With Brock as the author, it was more like research. She inhaled a long breath, checked to make sure she had a full water glass on her bedside table, and snuggled back against the pillows.

Several hours ticked by and, immersed waist deep in plot, Jerrica's eyelids fluttered closed. *Don't fall asleep.* Her fingers pinched the two halves of the book in her lap. Only half way through Langston Roe's novel. She blinked hard, weariness like sand against her corneas. The clock digits showed only one a.m.

How was she ever going to make it? Determinedly, she opened the book.

The next morning Jerrica appeared, bleary-eyed but triumphant. No panic attacks, no nightmares. No sleep. After a quick continental breakfast, they were back on the road. Jerrica could sense Brock's eagerness to be home. Exhaustion made it hard to notice anything else. She covered up in a velour throw and cozied her head against the shoulder strap of the seatbelt. The next thing she knew, the car's engine grew quiet.

"Jerrica, we're here."

She sat up in a fog of confusion and rubbed her eyes. Where was here? She opened her eyes to a large white Victorian house. She cleared her clogged throat. "You live here?"

The house rose at least three stories if not one more. A meandering front porch lined with columns and balusters wrapped around two round sitting areas, one on either side. The two rounded sections were topped with cone-shaped roofs. The wide stone stairs led up to a double door surrounded with huge windows on both sides.

"Yes. That's why I didn't make arrangements for you to stay elsewhere. I have so many rooms you can have your pick."

She looked around the well-manicured yard. The house appeared to be on the outskirts of town without being rural. Several other equally impressive houses from the same time period neighbored Brock's home. He literally lived in a historical landmark.

"It's...impressive," she said, groping for the right words.

"Actually, if the facts be known, it's expensive. The cost of keeping it up is outrageous."

"Then why do you stay?"

He shrugged. "Back when it came up on the market, my uncle said it was a steal. And it was until I spent as much on repairs as I did buying it. Besides, Jenna loved it."

He slipped the car back into gear and continued up the driveway to the four car garage. After opening the closest door with the remote, he drove in. Jerrica couldn't help but stare open mouthed at the enormous garage area as he went around the car and removed the suitcases. Together they carried the luggage to the side door.

They came into the kitchen which was large and white with dark woodwork ornately decorating the ceiling, baseboard, and over each doorway and window. A shining stainless industrial stove shone in the muted light, and a refrigerator lay hidden behind dark cabinet doors.

Through a century-old door, amber with age, they moved out into the foyer area that rose two stories high. The hand-polished dark stairs glowed as they arched grandly from the foyer up to a second story. The open stairway reminded her of the Rankins' home just a bit. Her eyes lit on the second door from the top of the stairs.

"What room is that?" she said as she pointed.

"Just one of the many bedrooms."

"Can I stay there?"

He studied her a moment and nodded. "Sure. My bedroom's here on the main floor. Actually, since Jenna's been gone, I've hardly been on any other floor."

He led the way up the stairs and swung the door open. He laid the suitcases down at the foot of the bed. The big antique four-poster, covered with a plain eyelet comforter, sat high above the original wood flooring with a plain white ruffle around the bottom. Jerrica's eyes took in the intricate woodwork. Sunlight filled the room creating a warm, welcoming aura.

In its day this house had been the ultimate. With the right kind of furniture, the right kind of decorating, this house could be a showplace. Just like this room.

Brock cleared his throat. "Well, make yourself at home. The bathroom is two doors down on the right."

Jerrica nodded her head. A strange thought blurted out. "It must be lonely to live here."

He put his hands in his pockets and rattled his change. Then he meandered to the door, his expression guarded. "If you need anything, my room is on the first floor. I'll be in the kitchen getting some lunch together."

No answer. Exit stage left. His quick exit answered for him. Pushing away the disturbing thought, she tidied her things. Suitcases in the closet. Done. No use getting overly comfortable.

She opened the door and wandered through the second floor with soft steps. No need to get too attached to the house either. She wouldn't be staying long. As soon as she convinced Brock she didn't belong here, she'd be on her way. She ignored the twinge of sadness as Brock's face invaded her thoughts.

She peeked into the other bedrooms. Every room empty. The echoes of her muted footsteps on the dark vintage wood floor sent a shiver through her. Several bedrooms and a couple more baths completed the floor. She came across the stairs that would have taken her to the next floor, but she decided to save it for another time. Time to work her way back to the kitchen.

Downstairs, she located it easily, and true to his word, Brock was buttering bread.

"I hope you like grilled cheese sandwiches," he said, then grinned. "Guess I'm staying in the cheese theme."

"Yes, I like them. Bring on more cheese." She yawned. "Brock, why are all the rooms on the second floor empty except for my room?"

His face grew pensive, and he searched her eyes for a second before going back to his preparations. "I called a friend of mine a couple of days ago, and he and a buddy moved a bed and dresser into that room. My sister came by and put sheets on and so forth."

"But how did you know I'd choose that room?"

A twitch started at his left eye. The glint in his eye hinted at something he didn't want to tell her. His dark gaze flicked to hers. "Sure you want to know?"

Chapter Eleven

O h, no. Dread mounted in her chest as she took in Brock's cagey expression. "I guess."

Brock laid the cheese between the bread and flipped them into the hot frying pan. "It was Jenna's favorite room. Something about the lighting. She intended to convert it into her own art studio."

A chill raced up her back. These similarities bordered on spooky. Brock seemed to know what she would do before she did, like a puppet master. And she was the puppet. The sock puppet. She tamped down the uneasiness that rose. "I see."

"I'm trying not to compare you to Jenna. I know you don't want that."

Uh, huh. Sure. She shot him an annoyed look. "Then I guess we had better get solid proof I'm Jerrica. Then we can get back to our lives."

❦ ⋯⋯ ❧

Brock winced when he heard her separate their lives so easily. He knew who she was. So did Uncle John and the entire family.

Only she remained in the dark. Maybe he should just tell her what they'd done. Nope. He'd better feel her out. It could be too much, too soon.

"Then I guess we should make an appointment with Dr. Cob."

"Excuse me?" She rested on the edge of the stool behind the counter.

"Your dentist. I mean, Jenna's dentist," he amended at her hard look. "He can take x-rays and compare them and give us the answer we need."

Jerrica shook her head. That wild look settled into her eyes again. She crossed her arms over her stomach. This wasn't starting well.

"No."

"Jerrica, they'll be able to compare—"

"I'm not going to any doctor." She jerked herself from the stool and backed toward the door.

"He's not a doctor, Jerrica," he hedged. "Didn't you hear me? He's a dentist."

"No!"

"It won't hurt."

She huffed in short gasps. "He'll put sharp things in my mouth. Sharp horrible things that swell and foam…"

Brock lowered his brows. "What are you talking about?"

"No." She was near screaming now. "He's not going to touch me."

"Calm down. We won't do it if it upsets you." Panic attack blooming at three paces. If he told her now, she'd flip. What was he thinking? She was flipping now.

Yet he needed something tangible to placate her. Something concrete that she could not dispute. "Wait, Jerrica. I've just thought of a way we can get a positive I.D. without going to Dr. Cob."

Her face paled and she narrowed her eyes. "What?"

"Your fingerprints. I have a hospital document with Jenna's fingerprints. I don't know why I didn't think of it before."

"What will they do?"

He moved closer and raised his hands like a horse trainer calming a colt. "They just put ink on your fingertips and stamp it on paper. Then they can compare the prints."

"Who does that?"

"The police."

"Oh." She licked her lips.

"Like your Uncle Robert." Brock reached for her hands and pulled them gently from her stomach. She blinked at him, and a surge of love pumped through him. Jerrica, so like a delicate, hand-fashioned glass figurine. Ready to shatter at any moment. "I want to do everything I can to make this easy for you."

"All right. Maybe."

Phew. "Good. So how about a drive after we eat?"

A drive. What a waste of time. There was no point getting to know the area since she'd soon return to Tennessee. Yet, she had to admit, this whole adventure had driven away some of her fears. When this fiasco was over, and she was back with the Rankins, she could at least look back and appreciate what she'd accomplished.

Brock drove all over town, from the park on the east end to the library on the west. He pointed out the church where they'd married on the north side and filled her in on the new businesses on the south side. Parts of town boasted the large Victorian homes, many of which had become apartment houses, funeral homes, and some grand showcases of the past. It was a pleasant, clean, small town, but Jerrica found it hard to take a real interest.

Finally Brock turned on a southbound road that meandered into the country at the edge of town. Jerrica caught her breath as her head swiveled from window to window. The bottom dropped from her stomach. Somehow, this appeared familiar.

"Wait." Jerrica could barely breathe. What was it about this country intersection? "Turn here."

He followed the direction she indicated.

"Where are we going?" The amusement on his face slid away when he met her confused eyes.

"I...don't know," she whispered.

Jerrica straightened in the seat and leaned forward. They rode in silence for several minutes while the car wound along the curvy road until they came to a T. She stared long and hard down the dirt path.

"Take this road."

After at least five miles, they arrived at a highway. Why was this so ingrained in her mind? She pointed a shaky finger. "Now right."

Brock followed her directions, his gut twisting as they rode some two miles down the highway. He knew a quicker way to arrive at this vicinity and wondered why she'd zigzagged through the country. A curve approached. What was Jerrica doing? Where was she taking him?

"Stop, wait."

"What?" He slowed and threw a glance into the rearview mirror.

"I missed a turn. Go back."

She missed a turn? A turn to...what? Brock spun the car around in a driveway and swung around to head in the opposite direction. She grew more agitated as they approached the next country road.

"Here, here. This is it. Turn right here."

The paved country road rose sharply up a hill. Just to the left, a cemetery came into view. A chain link fence encircled the large headstone-littered lot. Even though it was early summer, the grass had already begun to take over the cemetery, standing knee high. Rock patches interspersed the drive, and Brock pulled in next to the double metal gate large enough to admit a car.

"There." Her voice sounded strangled.

Brock turned into the grassy unkempt drive. A cemetery? He'd promised John he'd take care of her and now, she'd totally lost it. He'd pushed too hard, too strong. The Rankins would never forgive him.

"Jerrica, listen—" He slowed the car to park and turned to grasp her.

But Jerrica took advantage of the stop, flung the car door open, and bounded out. He exited the car in a rush, praying she wasn't heading blindly into the midst of the highway beyond the hill. The thought gave urgency to his legs, and he began to run. He called her name, but she continued to race through the monuments.

There was no hesitation in her gait as she hurried across the overgrown lot. She ran straight for the graves in the northwest corner. She fell to her knees and covered her face with her hands.

Her grief greeted him as he came abreast of her kneeling amongst the weeds. Relieved she hadn't leaped the fence into oncoming traffic, yet he ached at her brokenness.

Brock paused to catch his breath and read the name splayed across the tombstone as he approached. Marcene Price. The double headstone revealed another. Ken Price.

He knelt next to her, rubbing a hand across her back. "Who are these people?"

"My mother," she snuffled, "and my father."

Brock swaddled his arms around her while his cognition spun. Were these some kind of relatives? Never once had Jenna mentioned where her father had been buried. He blinked at the other name. How could her mother be here? She was very much alive. Maybe a first wife?

His gaze took in the dates. Their deaths were separated by a little more than a year. His wife would've only been fifteen at the time. How could she have led him here if she hadn't known of this spot?

"I don't understand," he murmured into her hair.

She shuddered in his arms. "I told you she was dead. Cancer. I just didn't know...Dad would be here too."

Brock cradled her until she'd revived some composure. A swirl of confusion fogged his brain. This couldn't be right. Jenna's mother was alive and kicking at the Auberry Center in Evansville. She attended their wedding.

Jerrica pulled from his embrace and went closer to her mother's headstone.

"They put the wrong name." Her fingers traced the letters. "Her name was Margaret."

She pivoted, a wild look in her eyes. "We have to get it changed. I don't know why they put Marcene. Why didn't I have them change it?"

She backed from the headstones and peered at them, grasping her head with her hands.

"Yes. I remember now. My father died in an auto accident when I was fifteen," she murmured. "My mother was diagnosed with cancer shortly after that."

"Jerrica, are you sure?"

She rose, anger hot as lava in her eyes. "What do you think I'm doing, making this up as I go along?"

"Sorry." He took a deep breath and ran a hand through his hair.

Enough shock for one day. If he could, he'd get her fingerprinted and prove her identity out front so there could be no denial. Then he would tell her about her mother. Her *real* mother. The amnesia had been enough to shoulder, but now it appeared he'd have to deal with false memory. A shaft of dread pierced his soul. Would she start having hallucinations like her mother?

His glance fell to the tombstones, and he shook his head in wonderment. Still, she knew the exact locations of these graves. How could she have known that?

Her lip curled with disdain and she pointed at him. "I'm sure about all the hours I spent at that hospital with my dying mother, all the treatments, shots, smells, pain."

A sarcastic bark of laughter burst from her. "I may have amnesia, but even my subconscious remembered that."

"Hey, listen—" He stepped closer, and she jumped back with a shake of her head.

"I don't know for sure if I'm Jenna or not. But I know at one time, I was here, that I lived somewhere near, and I had a family. That's more than I ever remembered in the Smokies for the last three years."

Brock bobbed his head once and rattled the change in his pocket. He didn't believe her. He probably thought she was crazy. She swiped the tears and crossed her arms tightly. There weren't too many things she'd been sure of in the last three years, but this one thing she knew was the honest-to-God truth. These were her parents.

She turned back to the headstones. The more she stared at them, the more familiar they seemed. Even the fence line revived her memory. And the sound of the passing cars from the highway. Yes, she'd once been here. How could she have forgotten?

"I want to get some flowers." She sniffed, unsure why his disbelief stung.

He nodded, standing like a cemetery statue. She turned, hiding from him and stomped to the car.

Jerrica's mind throbbed, striving to recover more memories linked to the graveyard, but none would step forward from the amnesia fuzz. All the way into town she sat with her arms crossed tightly, racking her mind for clues. But it'd gone blank. She sighed with frustration and smacked her forehead.

Brock purchased floral arrangements in town. They drove back and decorated the graves. Jerrica stood for a moment and admired the sunflower wreaths she'd picked out. They looked fresh and homey. A fresh wave of grief hit her, and she dabbed at her face with an overused tissue. She glanced at some of the other arrangements with faded plastic flowers and grimaced. Mom and Dad deserved more than a generic gaudy basket of plastic flowers that seemed so prevalent in cemeteries.

She covered her face with her hands. How would she know anything about gaudy memorial arrangements? This place had become a boiling eddy of confusion and clarity. Would she ever get it sorted out?

A twinge of guilt cut through her. Brock. He'd been so understanding, buying wreaths, and driving her back out here. And what had she done? Yelled at him. Just like Beth. She groaned. Another person to apologize to. How would she ever get through this with her sanity?

She should say more. His puzzlement glared obvious. Or was it something else? Perhaps he knew something, or thought he knew something. Like the room she'd chosen. And her favorite color. She clutched her stomach. What was next?

What surprises lurked around the corner?

Brock wiped a hand in a slow swipe down his face as if he could erase the muddle in his brain. Ensconced in his home office, his fists came down on his desk on either side of his laptop as he stared at the computer screen. Here he had all this information from Haywood McCoy, enough to write fifteen or sixteen separate articles, and he couldn't string two words together.

He stared at the man's bearded face in one of the many pictures he'd taken with his hands wrapped around a greenware bowl. Scraggly beard, eyes filled with suspicion. Or hate. Or both.

Crazy mountain man hadn't been too chatty, and neither had the young grungy boy. Delbert? But what they hadn't said, spoke volumes. He shut the laptop. Who cared? Certainly not him at the current moment. His mind simmered on the hot topic of the cemetery trip. And Jerrica.

He stood and paced. *I should just tell her. Tell her everything.* He paused at the window, the distant streetlights casting shadows across the manicured lawn. If she was demented, what harm would it do? Yet—she hadn't seemed confused or irrational. Grief-stricken, maybe. But not confused.

And she remembered the exact roads to guide them there. A short groan simmered in his throat. She remembered random roads and didn't know her own husband. Nothing seemed to make sense.

He padded from his office into the dark kitchen, not bothering to turn on the light. If it weren't so late, he'd shoot some hoops to occupy his mind. But Jerrica lay asleep upstairs, and a bouncing basketball wasn't exactly conducive to a good night's sleep.

He yanked the refrigerator door open and squinted at the limited selection. Being gone for several weeks had a tendency to cause food to spoil. He grabbed a water bottle and shut the door with a shrug. Food didn't really tempt him this late at night anyway.

He ripped the cap off and took a long swallow. Maybe he couldn't play basketball, but he could get outside and enjoy the night. He returned to his office and unplugged his laptop. Maybe the peaceful quiet of the night would encourage some inspiration for his articles.

Outside on the patio furniture, he opened the computer and let the screen light up. He stared at the monitor for a full minute before he lowered it to his lap. Why torture himself? No article would be written tonight.

The house blocked the weak light from the streetlights, so his gaze drew to the stars in the black sky, an expanse that pulled his thoughts to his Heavenly Father. He leaned back and propped his feet on a chair. He whispered his thoughts aloud to the only One who knew the score, who knew how it would end and help him endure the trials.

"I never dreamed I'd get my wife back, Lord. Yet she's not mine anymore. She's a stranger." He took a swig of water as thoughts pumped in his head, the quiet of the night like a balm to his soul. "I don't understand why You would bring her back and not allow us the relationship we had before."

He shut his eyes and thought of their wedding picture in the drawer of his desk. His mother, father, brother, sister-in-law, and his sister stood on one side while Jenna's mother stood with her on the other. How would this ever sort out? She most certainly didn't appear dead in that photo.

He set his water on the glass top of the wrought iron table and stuck his thumbs under his biceps. His head tilted back and he closed his eyes. How he wished he could peer into the future. Heck, if he could do that, he'd just turn back time and never lose her in the first place. He inhaled the fresh scent of the pines on the north side of his property, and his head bobbed forward.

Chapter Twelve

J errica sat on her bed, cross-legged on the white comforter, the only light filtering from the small lamp on her bedside table muted with a red scarf. She'd tried to sleep, but warm sensations of foggy previous events thwarted her every attempt. Even her most successful sleep inducement of counting actual sheep had failed. She snatched the white smooth rock from the bedside table and turned it in her hands. Katie's lucky rock.

She rubbed it hard until her hand warmed up. "I wish you were a genie lamp. I would wish to have my memory back."

But her mind didn't dwell on the piece of cold white quartz. Instead words formed and ricocheted through her brain like a security message on a website, blurred, warped, familiar. It resembled a chant or a rap. It started out very vague and grew stronger as she sat there. She mouthed the words as the remembrance tingled her brain.

"But such as..." she whispered, and paused. "And God is faithful..."

What was it? She thunked the rock on the bedside table and gripped her head, massaging her scalp against her skull. If only she could rub it into focus. A distant memory of teenagers chanting together. Fire. Darkness around.

"'Will provide the way of escape.'" The words flared and she grasped them. "'so that you will be able to endure it.'"

Jerrica caught her breath. It was a Bible verse. How did it start?

She stood and paced, biting her thumb nail. "'No temp-tation,'" she snapped her fingers to the beat, "'has o-vertaken you but such as is common to man. And God is faithful...'"

She paused as she lost the thread, and then repeated it again from the beginning, and this time she did not stop.

"'Who will not allow you, to be tempt-ed beyond what you are able. But with- the temp-tation, will provide the way to escape— also—and you will be able to en-dure it!'"

She leaped into the air with a happy cry and ran to the full length mirror in the corner by the window. Her hands grasped the wooden frame and she rattled it in glee. Then she leaned forward to stare into her pupils. Now where in that scrambled brain had this verse come from?

The chant ran over and over in her mind to the sounds of a group of teenaged voices. Perhaps church? Camp? A cookout of some sort? Hadn't Brock mentioned something about church camp?

But instead of pondering its source, she stared at herself, gripping the mirror, and thought of what the verse really meant. It clearly spoke of overcoming the temptation of sin. Perfect verse for teenagers. Or anyone, for that much.

Yet the part about enduring latched onto her. God would help her endure. He would never wish for her to live with debilitating fear. He wanted faith. And trust. She shivered and searched her limited memory.

It was true. Even though at times it seemed as if she couldn't bear the things she had to face, she'd pulled through. God had indeed kept His promise. A warm peace permeated her heart and caused her to give a small smile to her reflection. God helped her face her fears. That small memory nugget revived at the most opportune time.

It was late, and no doubt Brock was asleep, but she tiptoed from her room. The thick darkness made it difficult to navigate the unfamiliar house, but she had an immense desire to get some air. A yearning to view the dark sky with its glowing stars, gripped her. To experience the immense awesomeness of God in the quiet night never failed to comfort her through all the troubling times.

Tonight, she wanted to crow her gratefulness. Instead, she tiptoed downstairs and out the back to the patio. The French doors hung open. Stepping out, the warm breeze caressed her skin. The night embraced her.

In the dimness she could make out Brock in one of the white wrought iron chairs at the glass table with his feet propped up on another. He didn't move. She crept up and found his laptop computer still on, but Brock fast asleep.

She eased the computer from his lap and set it on the table and surveyed his shadowed form, arms crossed, head tilted back against the back of the chair as if he, too, had looked at the stars. Had he, like her, come to absorb the quietness of the night and feel God's solace and strength?

Poor guy. Even in the near dark, his face wore fatigue. Her hand reached forth to stroke his arm but she snatched it back. Her breath caught in her throat and moisture wet her eyes as she pressed her hands into her lap. A strange emotion twisted her middle.

Brock stirred in his sleep and his eyes came open. He blinked and then gave a sleepy grin. "Hey."

"I think you should go to bed," she whispered.

He moaned and stretched, throwing his feet to the ground. "Yeah, I guess. It was so beautiful out I couldn't resist sitting here."

"I know how you feel." She missed the wooded mountains. But the stillness and the stars were still here. She remembered Beth singing a song about God calling each star by name. What an amazing God. She took a deep breath as she searched the sky.

"What's in that brain of yours?" Brock asked quietly.

She glanced at him. He seemed totally awake now. "I was thinking of a song Beth used to sing."

"I know you miss them—"

"I do. But I was contemplating how God calls all the stars by name. Can you imagine knowing all the names of the stars? How incredibly amazing God is."

He was silent and Jerrica chanced a glance in his direction. He too, peered at the stars.

"You know, I just remembered something in my room a minute ago. Something I must have learned several years back, but I can't remember when."

After she had chanted the verse, Brock smiled.

"It's 1 Corinthians 10:13. I don't recognize that exact version, but that's where it comes from."

Jerrica nodded and played with the belt of her robe. "I thought it might be a Bible verse."

The silence pervaded a moment, and she dropped her eyes and stared at his handsome face, lit by the light of his computer. His eyes lowered and locked on hers.

"I owe you an apology," she whispered.

"What for?"

A nervous laugh bubbled up. "For being so ugly at the cemetery."

His lips twitched and he sat forward. "Jerrica, if there is one thing you'll never be accused of, it's being ugly."

Warmth cascaded through her, and she glued her eyes to the concrete at her feet. "You know what I mean."

He reached into her lap and pulled one of her hands into his. Her breathing slowed as he stroked her hand, and his sleep-thickened voice continued. "You know, this is a situation in unchartered territory for both of us. Most people never have to deal with what we've just dealt with the last several weeks. But at least I haven't had to reconstruct my entire life like you have. I think it's normal to be confused, even angry."

Her mouth parted and her eyes dropped to his hands as he rubbed her skin. Her heart stuttered in her chest. She blinked and raised her gaze to focus on his face.

"You're going to have tumbling emotions here and there. It only makes sense. If I didn't know what was going on half the time, I'd be practically crazy."

She leaned forward, her breaths mere huffs of air.

His hand came to caress her face. "The main thing to remember is not to be too hard on yourself. Got it?"

She blinked and pulled back, inhaling a deep breath. Oh, the man was like a magnet. She pressed her free hand to her chest.

"Jerrica?"

"Yes...um, okay."

He let her hand go and stood while she collected herself. A surge of unexplainable emotions pumped through her, and she shivered, missing the warm contact of his hands. He closed the computer and tucked it under his arm. She stood and rubbed the goose bumps on her upper arms. At least the hives had stayed at bay.

"May I escort you inside?" He chuckled and extended his other elbow towards her.

Jerrica swallowed and pressed her hand in the crook of his elbow. They walked into the dim interior and secured the doors. The street lights guided them with an ethereal light through the sheer curtains of the house, and he guided her to the bottom of the stairs where he paused.

"I'm sure each day will bring more clarity for you, Jerrica."

She licked her lips. "What if it doesn't?"

He inhaled. "Then, you build a new future."

She let go of his arm and sought the cool wooden bannister as she turned. He bade her goodnight but waited at the foot of the stairs until she reached the second floor. She dallied at the top, gazing at his vague form at the bottom. "Goodnight, Brock."

"Pleasant dreams." His form faded from view.

A new future? And would it be with or without Brock?

Long after they parted ways, she lay in the dark on her bed, tumbling that miraculous verse in her head. Fear tempted her at every turn. And if indeed she never remembered who she was, Brock was right. This aggressive, unwanted emotion impeded a new life. Yet anxiety clawed out, yearning to envelope her like a blackmailing cousin, familiar, yet repugnant. It was easier to give in to terror instead of reaching out and striving to overcome.

Building something fresh. Not a new concept. Since she had come to Indiana, she knew without a doubt that God was in control and with his help and guidance, she could lick her fears for good.

A continual pounding woke Jerrica from a sound sleep. The clock registered eight a.m. She groaned. It'd been late when she'd finally drifted off to sleep. She flipped over on the cushy bed and buried her head under the comforter. Why didn't Aunt Ellen get the door?

With lead feet she dragged herself out of bed and slipped on her silken blue robe. She opened her door and moved down the stairs as the pounding continued. When she finally made it to the bottom of the steps, she froze. Where was she? This wasn't her house. She pulled the wrap around herself tighter. Then like a grenade it hit her. Brock's house.

She backed up a few stairs, and her brain fumbled what to do. Finally she sat on a step. Who could it possibly be? Dare she answer it? Whoever stood there was being pretty insistent. Biting her bottom lip she collected her courage and walked toward the door.

With a twist, she unlocked the deadbolt and cracked the door open. There stood a pretty, young, dark haired woman.

"Jenna! It really is you." The woman clutched her hands beneath her chin, her mouth agape. "I'm sorry. My brother would kill me if he knew I was here. He's not home is he?"

Jerrica could feel her heart race. "I'm...not sure."

"I just couldn't stay away, and I was on my way to work. Well, I couldn't resist seeing you for myself. Brock said he'd call me, but you know how he is." The woman paused a moment and realized the awkwardness of her last statement. "I mean, well, never mind."

The man in mind came jogging up the sidewalk, dressed in running clothes and marked with sweat.

"Couldn't stay away and give us some peace, could you, Devi?" Brock bounded up the steps behind her.

The woman gave a start, grimaced, and wheeled around. "Oh, Brock, I'd probably still be waiting next year for you to call. Besides, when have I ever listened to you?"

"True," he drawled sarcastically. "It looks like formal introductions are in order. Jerrica, this is my little sister, nosy and obnoxious as she is, Devi. Devi, Jerrica."

"Jerrica?" Devi repeated with some puzzlement. "I thought—"

"We haven't received a positive I.D. yet," he cut in, a strange light in his eyes.

Devi raised her eyebrows. "I think it's pretty obvious who she is. But she ought to stay with me considering you're not sure."

"In that one bedroom apartment?" he asked. "Face it, Devi, I have enough room here to christen the place 'Langston Inn.'"

Devi shrugged. "I guess. Surely we could continue this conversation inside."

"No, Devi, dear," he said with a twist of humor lighting his lips. "It's now eight-thirty. You're going to be late for work."

Devi sniffed. "All right," she agreed reluctantly. "It was nice seeing you, Jenna...oops, I mean Jerrica."

"Yes," she murmured.

Brock slid through the door and closed it as soon as his sister was down the first flight of steps. "I apologize. I should have known she'd show up."

"It's okay. She seemed...nice."

He let out a stream of air. "Sure," he agreed as he ran his hand through his hair, "she is. But very scatterbrained."

He pushed aside the curtain, and Jerrica saw him wince and shake his head.

"What is it?"

"She almost pulled out into traffic without looking. She worries me." He stayed at the window for a couple of minutes.

She looked down and realized she was still in her robe.

He turned away from the window. Leave it to Devi to show up on the first morning back. Good thing she wasn't a cat. With her immense curiosity, her nine lives would have been spent before she reached first grade. He pulled a small towel from his pocket and wiped his sweaty brow and then flicked his gaze to Jerrica who still stood at the foot of the stairs.

His eyes ran over her form before he realized what he was doing. Her robe had opened, revealing a portion of body-hugging silk pajamas, and he straightened. Memories of touching her, holding her against him had kept him awake long after Jerrica had retired last night.

They'd never shared a bed, yet his hands remembered their passionate embraces and whispers of promises. His lips throbbed with the thought of her imploring lips on his. The longing of holding her near washed over him, and when his eyes returned to hers, a certain amount of reservation resided there, and she tugged the robe closed.

"I better change." She ran up the stairs.

So much for that. Better just shower and rummage a breakfast. His stomach growled to accentuate the point. He spun and headed for his bedroom.

Back at the kitchen in twenty minutes, he pulled the fridge door open. One egg left and stale bread. Sounded like French toast. With the sausage links from the freezer, he'd have a complete breakfast. He set to work and the popping grease seared away the fervent emotions that tugged at his thoughts. He was just flipping the toast from the frying pan as she entered the room.

"How did you learn to cook so many things?"

He shrugged. "I've been on my own for some time now. I guess it's a matter of survival."

Jerrica fetched the silverware from the dishwasher while he brought the plates to the counter. They settled on the stools and filled their plates. He said grace and they tore into the meal.

"Do you have any other family I should be aware of? You know, just in case they should drop in too?" She gave a small laugh.

He grinned. "My parents live in Indy as do my brother and his wife. Then there's my uncle, but he never stays in one place long enough to count. My grandparents left us kids with quite a nest egg which is nice in a way. But for Devi, it's mostly an excuse for escaping her responsibilities."

"I see."

He stood and rinsed his empty plate in the sink. His eyes fixed on her. She looked so fresh and invitingly soft. He tamped down his body's response. "I was thinking we'd head down to the police station today and get you fingerprinted. What do you think?"

"Oh." She sat a little taller in her seat, and her fork stilled in her plate. One emotion after another played across her face. "Today? Oh, today. To-day. I suppose it's the reasonable thing to do."

The helpless look she shot him churned his gut. He was more in love with her than he'd ever been in his life. She was Jenna Langston. But what would he do if she refused to be Mrs. Jenna Langston? How would he ever recover?

Chapter Thirteen

The police station smelled funky. Like burnt coffee. And sweat? Either way, not conducive to comfort. The place milled with uniformed and plain clothes, looking official, toting sheaves of papers. They sat in a quiet hall with several chairs and a few bored patrons. Not the stuff to stifle panic.

"I'm not sure I can do this," Jerrica whispered and squeezed her hands together.

She hugged her middle and leaned forward, letting her hair swing forward to close off her features. A one act play. Pull the curtain. Brock placed a gentle hand on her back and rubbed her stiff back. Why did she always allow his touch? She couldn't deny it brought a snatch of security.

Brock bent toward her. "It's a simple procedure. They'll take us back into the fingerprinting area, ink your fingers, and roll them across the documents. That's it."

They called Jerrica's name, which cut off any more conversation. Brock steadied her as she lurched forward. The uniformed policeman completed the process in record time and returned them to the waiting room. After about a forty-five minute wait, they were escorted into another office where a secretary sat behind a huge desk. She was the thinnest woman he'd ever laid eyes on, but her bony fingers flew across the keyboard as she took their personal information.

The secretary left for a few minutes and reappeared with several documents. She re-seated herself and rotated her stack of copies in front of Jerrica.

"I'll need your signature here by the two X's and your initials here," she explained. "Then here and here. Please read this so you understand what you are signing. I'll give you a few minutes."

She stood and left them alone. Jerrica's brows cinched together as she flash read the paper. Finally she handed it to Brock. "I can't really focus on what it's saying. Would you?"

Brock took it and skimmed the information. "It's okay to sign."

Her hand shook as she took a pen and scratched her name on the forms. The secretary entered as she finished the last one.

She glanced over the documents and then stapled them. "All right, folks. Results will arrive at your home in three to six weeks at the earliest."

Jerrica gasped, and Brock cleared his throat. "Is there no way we can get it sooner?"

"No, sir. I'm afraid not. They're back-logged in Indianapolis right now, so it could be even longer."

"But, ma'am, this is extremely important." Brock persisted.

The secretary glanced at him with little disguised irritation on her thin face. The narrowness of her face made her eyes even larger. "Hate to tell you, but the murderers and drug dealers come first here. You'll just have to wait in line."

Jerrica gripped the chair's hand rest with one hand and sealed her hand over her mouth. Eyes closed, Brock's impatient harrumph met her ears.

"Look, this is a matter of putting a woman's life back together. Don't you think that's of some importance? It's a simple matter of comparing two sets of prints."

"Sir, the live-birth document you presented is not an official government form. It must be verified." She gave a sniff as her eyes took in Jerrica's distress. "I wish I could help you."

Jerrica stood. "It's okay, Brock. Let's go."

He apologized to Jerrica in the car and she nodded. It wasn't his fault. When they arrived home, Brock sequestered himself in his office, muttering something about writing. She welcomed the chance to hermit out the next couple of hours in her bedroom. Every day a battle.

After a couple of hours of solitary, Jerrica opened her door. One could only mull the injustices of the world for so long.

She wandered to the bottom floor of the house, peeking in each room. Toward the back of the house, she came across a door slightly ajar. With a gentle hand, she pushed it open, and her breath stilled in her throat.

The walls were painted a chocolate brown, and a huge four poster bed rested against the far wall. Brock's bedroom. A different kind of anxiety made her cast a glance behind her before she stepped inside.

A matching dresser stood against the outside wall, and small nightstands flanked the bed. A picture rested on the far one and, after a slight hesitation, she gumshoed toward it. Brock and a woman in a blue dress. Of course. Blue. The woman that looked very much like herself. Too much.

Jerrica perched on the edge of the bed and cupped the frame in her hands. The couple beamed at the camera, the woman's head nestled against Brock's shoulder. The girl looked no older than a teen, and Brock looked younger without some of the care-lines that now creased the planes of his face.

My, he was drop-dead handsome. His coal black eyes sparkled against his tan face. Had she ever seen Brock smile like that? No. Always had a touch of sadness lingering around his eyes, a hollowness in his cheeks.

Her gaze shifted to the woman with chin length hair, blond highlights sprinkled throughout. Her bright blue eyes looked slightly off to the side, as if she had other things on her mind. Like something to hide? Jerrica shuddered and put the picture down. The likeness was freakishly unsettling.

The room darkened slightly, and her breath snagged when she whipped her head around. Brock stood sentry at the door. Jerrica jumped up and covered her mouth with her hand. "I'm sorry. I was just exploring when I found your room. This picture caught my eye."

He walked closer glancing at the frame before settling back at her.

"You shouldn't be in here." He didn't seem pleased. Or did he?

Her eyes widened. His proximity both unnerved and fascinated her. "Why not?"

His eyes raked her face and she wanted to squirm. His hand raised and caressed her upper arm, sending a quiver of extreme awareness down her spine. She drew in a deep breath, and licked her lips. His dark eyes dropped to her mouth. Then his arm froze and dropped to his side.

"I think you had better leave."

She choked over a lump in her throat, very conscious of the heat of his eyes. Part of her wanted to stay and explore the fire. Part of her wanted to run. "Brock...I—"

"Go, Jerrica," he growled.

Jerrica flew through the door.

Zap! Lightning ripped the black sky. The grave yawned below her. On a bank of freshly dug soil the woman in the red dress rose above her, dangling the infant over the hole. Laughter echoed. Jerrica clawed the muddy bank to get closer. The baby's wails filled the voids of thunder, and Jerrica's muscles cramped with exhaustion. The storm overhead lit the night sky with stark flashes, revealing the open grave.

The baby shrieks melded with the peals of thunder. *Rock a bye baby…*

Rain plastered Jerrica's hair into her eyes, and she lifted a muddy hand to swipe it away. Thunder resounded around her, quaking the ground. Jerrica screamed and cowered, raising a hand as a shield. When the reverberation subsided, the pink blanket fell away from the child into the dark hole.

"Give her to me." Her voice barely rose above the storm. The rushing wind spoke with low moans. *When the bow breaks, the cradle will fall.* The distorted lullaby crescendoed with a rising howl.

The next flash of light lit up the headstones surrounding her. Nothing but blackness beyond. The tombstones began rocking back and forth, as if walking, coming closer and closer.

A whimper tore loose from her throat. She had to snatch the baby and get out of here. Frantically she clutched at the muddy grass to pull herself closer.

"She's mine. Don't drop her." Jerrica inched toward the tall woman.

Rising to her knees, she struggled to stand. While the wind keened and the lightning flashed, the woman flung the child into the open grave.

The baby's frantic cries mingled with hers as it disappeared from view. Discordant tinkling bells played a slow warped version of "Brahms' Lullaby" that rivaled the storms intensity. The baby's shrieks repeated over and over in rhythm to the horrific overture.

Jerrica clutched her head. "No!"

She struggled to the edge of the hole, but there was nothing but darkness. Her eyes returned to the woman whose long red dress flowed around her. "How could you? Why couldn't you let me keep her?"

Jerrica struggled to a standing position, and the woman turned toward her. The wind whipped the woman's ghostly hair about her face. Suddenly the wind gusted with might and tore the hat from the woman's head. A bony white skull rested on the woman's shoulders, snakes of pale silver writhed on her head, and her macabre mouth opened in laughter.

Jerrica screamed.

A pair of hands grabbed her. In desperation she struggled and fought to escape. The baby was gone. *Gone.* How would she ever find her? Jerrica had to escape. She sprouted wings and pulled harder, struggling to become airborne.

Her wings flapped to launch herself into the air, but someone held her fast. That horrid woman's skull leered below. Fire flared around her. Her name echoed from the rim of the surrounding darkness, and she slowed and paused, gasping for breath.

Time decelerated as she came out of the fog of her nightmare and realized she still screamed. A shadowy face came into focus. A strange room. A man. Not the woman in red. Brock.

"She threw the child in the grave," Jerrica bawled, gasping for oxygen. "I couldn't reach her. I couldn't get to her. I tried so hard. So, so hard."

A thousand shards of agony pierced her, and she quaked from horror. Tears streamed down her face as she sobbed into his shoulder.

"It's all right. It's just a bad dream. It's not real, Jerrica. You're okay."

She panted and clutched his arm. "Her head was a skull. *A skull.* The infant fell into the grave. She took her away. The lightning—oh, please, help me, help me reach the baby."

She melted against him in a ball of helplessness.

༄ ⸱⸱⸱⸱⸱⸱ ༁

Brock wrapped her in his arms, trying to still her sniffles and shaking body. Her piercing scream had startled him awake. He stroked her hair from her face and rocked her gently as he prayed. His soul cluttered with sorrow from the torment she lived through.

Several minutes passed before she calmed enough for Brock to loosen his hold. She whimpered and clung to him. Her eyes shot wildly around the room as if expecting the object of her nightmare to pop out from the shadows.

"Jerrica. Listen. It's all going to get straightened out. You'll see," he crooned.

Fresh tears washed down her face. "No, she won't leave me alone. She always comes back."

Her face pressed against his neck, and he handed her a tissue from the night stand. Small spasmodic jerks shook her body with every breath.

"Do you want to go get some coffee downstairs?"

"No." Her grip on him tightened. "I just need to sit here a minute."

She hiccupped, and her breathing slowed. Several minutes elapsed before she pulled away and wrapped her arms around her drawn up legs.

Brock's skin chilled without her warm body pressed against him. "I can bring you something if you like."

Her wide eyes shot to him. "No. You can't leave. Please don't leave."

"All right. I'll stay as long as you need." He sat in silence on the side of the bed.

Ten minutes later, she eased herself under the comforter, grasping the edge with white knuckles. She lay still for several long moments. Her body began to relax and finally her eyes drifted shut.

"Well, I guess everything's under control," he murmured, watching her eyes flutter closed.

Her eyes snapped open, and she snatched his hand as he rose from the bed.

"Don't leave, Brock. Please," she pleaded. "I can't stay here alone. Not now."

He fixed his eyes on the hand she gripped before looking back at her face. "Let me pull up a chair and I'll stay right here."

"No, lie here, next to me. Please, Brock."

He pressed his molars together. The woman was pleading with him to get in her bed. He closed his eyes for a moment. When he opened them, she was gaping towards the closet door, her eyes enormous and full of fear. Doubts of her mental stability resurrected in his head.

"All right," Brock heard himself say through his teeth. He lay facing her, as she refused to surrender his hand.

Then she wedged closer and buried her head against his chest. "I'm sorry."

He heard her muffled voice and knew she was crying again. He felt her body draw up against him. Although he longed to be closer to her, he knew it was best that he was on top of the comforter instead of under. He contented himself with drawing his other arm over her body and gathering her against him. Such sweet torture to have her close, yet bleak to be so far away emotionally. It would be a long time before he slept.

Brock woke the next morning to fresh scented blond hair against his cheek. He blinked at the ceiling. Where... Jerrica's room. In *her bed*. And the same woman was now on top of the comforter snuggled into his chest.

He tightened his arms around the fragile woman. Her warm, pliable body burrowed closer. He groaned softly and lifted his head to kiss her forehead.

Longing reared up as he brushed a lock from her face. "Oh, Jenna. I've missed you."

He readjusted his body and cradled her head in the crook of his arm. He bent his head and brushed a soft kiss against her lips. As if he couldn't stand to stop at that point, he lowered his head again and allowed his lips to linger there. Her lips moved in response and a thrill shot through him. Then as suddenly as it had begun, he was thrust away.

᠀ ······ ᠀

"What are you doing?" Jerrica gasped.

He sighed and flopped back on the bed. "I would have thought that was obvious."

She brought her hand to her mouth. Her cheeks cooked like a caldron. How had he gotten in her bed? "What are you doing here?"

He sat up on one elbow. "You are the one that begged me to stay. Don't you remember?"

Recollections of the night before rushed to her brain, and her face burned fever-hot. "But that doesn't explain why you were kissing me. I'm not Jenna."

Had she ever been kissed like that? She was still trying to push aside the complete and overwhelming sense of pleasure of waking up with his lips on hers.

He rolled out of bed.

"So you have been so good to remind me since I found you," he said wearily. "I'm going to my bed. Alone."

She sat ramrod stiff in her bed. A sense of loss shivered over her skin as if a comforting blanket had been jerked from her body. She rubbed her hands down her arms to rid herself of those incessant goose bumps and inhaled fully to clear her thoughts. What was she thinking? She hardly knew him.

Her thoughts left the obvious pull of Brock and settled into a more uncomfortable, but familiar, loop. That horrible, haunting dream. How many times had she snuggled in bed only to awaken to the same nightmare? So many she'd lost count. This time it had been stronger than ever, more detailed. More real. She shuddered and shoved the comforter away. The room, now so filled with light, seemed an unlikely vehicle for such disturbing images. She pressed her hand to her heart and wandered to the window.

Looking out on the pure summer morning helped chase away the ghastly images lingering in Jerrica's brain. She turned toward the open bedroom door. She'd been so crass to Brock even though he'd comforted her. Why couldn't she have at least expressed some gratefulness? Because of that kiss. Nothing in her memory banks had stirred her like that. And there were certainly worse ways to wake up.

She looped the ends of her hair around her fingers. Then yanked. Here she was, right back where she started. With a grumble of irritation at herself, she snatched clean clothes from her suitcase. Hopefully a shower would rinse away all her loco thoughts.

Once she emerged clean from the bathroom, dried her hair, and dressed, she headed downstairs. She stood in the kitchen and pondered what she should do. Brock was nowhere to be found. At the direction of her thoughts, her mind filled with the tender kiss she'd received first thing in the morning.

She shoved away the thought. Yet perhaps she could show her appreciation for his comfort with a little breakfast. Appreciation for his calming presence that is, not the kiss. Although...She shook her head, chiding herself. *Idiot.*

She yanked the refrigerator door open to break the cycle of her thoughts. Brock had picked up several grocery items after they'd returned from the police office, so she selected some fresh eggs from the refrigerator and found a package of banana nut muffins in the pantry.

Humming to herself, she whipped the omelet around the bowl, adding chopped ham and cheddar cheese. Banana nut muffins browned in the oven as she slipped the second omelet

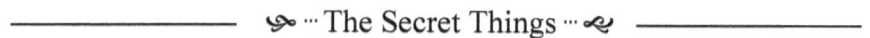

from the pan. After adding a cup of coffee to the tray, she steered herself in the direction of Brock's bedroom.

Chapter Fourteen

She gave a soft knock on the door. Reviving naught, she knocked again, a bit louder. At Brock's muffled "come in," she swung into the room with her breakfast tray.

He sat up, rubbing his eyes. "Breakfast in bed?"

She gave a small smile, noticing his voice was a few timbres deeper and still sleep scratchy.

"I...wanted to thank you for being there last night."

He cleared his throat. "I'm sorr—"

"No," she interrupted. "Please don't."

She drew her eyes from his. The rugged five o'clock shadow across his jaw only brought the morning kiss into sharp focus. She couldn't bear for him to apologize for kissing her. "I was just as much at fault. I hope you like ham and cheese omelets and banana nut muffins."

His mouth spread in a wide grin, showing his white teeth and the smile lines around his eyes. Crazy handsome. Crazy stinking handsome. *Focus on the coffee cup. Don't spill it.* Her hands sweat as she approached the bed and propped the tray over his lap.

"None for you?" One of his brows lifted. Part of that charming smile lingered around his mouth.

"I'm...finished." Big fat fib. Flashing a tepid smile, she hurried out the door to the kitchen to do just that.

Brock closed the door and carried the large box to his office. He knew what was in the container, and the usual thrill shot through him. It never ceased to amaze him when he held his newest release in his hands.

He fetched a box opener from his middle drawer and ripped through the packaging tape. The open flaps revealed the book cover with the grandfather clock's face, the Roman numerals distorted by the flying shards of glass. He pulled one out. *The Shattered Bevel* by Langston Roe, the second book in the Frozen Pendulum series.

He grabbed his phone. "Dial Treydon Rogers."

The line buzzed in his ear and was answered on the fourth ring.

"Yo, Brock. Got the new shipment, eh?"

"Yeah, it looks great."

Laughter sounded over the line. "You see they got the moon dial on there?"

"Sure did. That's exactly the one I wanted."

"Anything for you, buddy. We even added your old mug next to your bio this time. And how's the third book coming along?"

Brock cleared his throat and wandered to the window. Jerrica blocked his brain. "Uh...I'm kinda at a standstill."

"What? Well, no hurry. Your deadline is months off. I'm sure by the time next week rolls around you'll be feeding me a new plot twist."

Brock pulled the curtain slightly, letting his eyes feast on Jerrica, who'd stepped out of the house and meandered to the swing on the patio and sat down. Clad in snug jeans and a t-shirt, her form tugged his gear into neutral.

His agent's voice relegated to Charlie Brown's teacher squawks. Jerrica pulled out a small journal and pen. So graceful. Gorgeous. Her legs drew up underneath her as the tree's lacy shade danced over her. "What did you say about next week?"

A snort sounded in his ear. "The ICRS? Ring a bell?"

Brock sagged and released his hold on the curtain. How had this major event skipped his brain? His eyes flicked back to the beautiful woman lounging on the swing. Through the sheers she appeared like a dream sequence. He turned away. That was a snatch too close to reality.

Treydon, right. At this rate, he'd be jobless. Brock cleared his throat to salvage the conversation. "Oh, sure. The International Christian Retail Show. Yeah, about that..."

"No, no. You're slated to be at our table signing books and charming the ladies, remember? This is why we pushed up the book's release date. Are you recalling any of this?"

Brock settled in the office chair and flicked the calendar on his desk. "Listen, Trey. I've got some major setbacks here, and I—"

"I don't care if it's a mass burial of your whole family. Bring the caskets. There's no way you can skip this. Not this late. It won't reflect well."

Brock rolled his eyes. Trey the drama king. The man didn't possess one iota of sympathy in his stocky body. "This weekend. Got it."

"I thought you would. And don't forget the Aston Publishing House's gala on Saturday night."

"Sure thing, boss." He tried to keep sarcasm out of his voice, and he almost succeeded. Brock rang off and rapped his knuckles on the oak desktop. With or without Jerrica, he had to go.

He grabbed a copy of his new release, jotted a brief note on the inside cover, and headed to the patio. Ice the gala. And Trey.

He swung through the back door and devoured the sight of his lithe wife, perched in the swing. He pulled a wrought iron chair over and settled next to her. She gave a timid smile.

"Bored?" He lowered himself into the seat, breathing in the sweet air of a perfect summer day.

She gave a shake of her head as she met his eyes. "Not bored, exactly. Just...restless. I always worked in the workshop at home."

"There are some art supplies in the closet in the room next to yours. You're welcome to check it out."

"Okay, thanks."

"And downtown is the Hoosier Heritage this week on Main Street. They usually have a bunch of booths with crafts if you're interested. It's an annual event." He glanced at his watch. "Might be interesting to see some of the similar crafts you worked on."

Her eyes grew large. "Downtown?"

"Yep. We could catch a walking taco for lunch." He winked.

She shrugged and hunched her shoulders.

"You know, our wait would be over if you'd go see Dr. Cob."

Fear sparked in her eyes. "No."

Okay, time to change the subject. He leaned forward as he held up his book. "How about a new read?"

She gasped and snatched it from his hand. "I've never seen this one. Where did you get it?"

"Came in the mail this morning. You're the first to get an official copy."

Her mouth agape, she searched his face and then studied the book in her hand. "Wow, thanks."

"No problem. You know, you've done some amazing things this week."

Her head came up, and her brows descended as she tilted her head to the side. "What? I haven't done anything."

He linked his hands between his knees. "Yes, you have. I don't think you realize what you've accomplished in the last week.

You've gone from total paranoia to someone who is beginning to get a handle on those fears."

She eyed him and nodded slightly. "I suppose."

"You stayed in a hotel, ate in a strange restaurant, met my sister." At that he rolled his eyes heavenward. "I think you've come a long way. We ought to celebrate with a walking taco."

"Downtown? There would be so many people. So crowded."

Brock looked into her eyes. "Two weeks ago would you have guessed you could've stayed in a hotel?"

"No, but—"

"I'll be there." He kept his voice low. "I promise not to leave your side."

She clutched the book to her stomach. "Okay, I'll try."

He nodded. Excellent. He tucked the St. Louis trip away. Plenty of time to discuss that later.

"If another person calls me Jenna, I'll..." Tears welled in her eyes as they darted around the crowds. She ducked behind one of the many portable canvas tents that lined Main Street.

Please, Brock," she pleaded, her lip quivering, "take me home."

"Home?"

She scrunched her hands into fists. "Yes. I mean, your home."

Brock took a deep breath, peering so deeply into her eyes she was sure he discerned her innermost thoughts. The ones duct taped and wrapped with mental barbed wire. The droop in his features proclaimed disappointment. Oh, how she wished she had the fortitude to stay.

He laid a hand to the small of her back. "All right. Let's cut through here."

They slid between the downtown buildings and soon arrived at the car. With relief she slid into the passenger seat. She'd barely been able to choke down her taco before people recognized her with their gawking stares. Back from the dead.

That taco shoved at the back of her throat threatened to make a messy reappearance. This would be a perfect night to disappear into the woods. Anxiety's chicken claws clutched at her chest.

She kept her face turned toward the window as they drove. Once back, Brock pulled to a stop inside the garage, and she flung the door open, and raced inside, taking the stairs two at a time. The tears she'd been holding burst from her as she slammed the door shut.

Brock clenched his jaw at the bottom of the stairs. He wished he could magically erase her hurt and fear away. But he couldn't. That was one adventure that hadn't worked, and he should have known better. He'd forgotten she'd be recognized.

The rest of the evening was a bust. Brock strode through the kitchen with yet another cup of coffee in his hand. At least he'd gotten several articles written. He refilled his cup and wandered back to the bottom of the stairs and glared at the closed door at the top of the steps.

Something had to be done. He couldn't let her hide in her fear alone. With determination he set the cup down on the small hallway table and strode up the stairs. He knocked several times, but when silence ran a shaft of fear through him, he burst in. The room was empty.

Where had she gone? Terror gripped him that only compared with the horror he felt when he'd learned of the crash of Jenna's plane. *Dear God, had she left again?*

He searched the house, one room at a time, calling her name. This never would've happened if he hadn't pushed leaving the house this afternoon. He searched through the three floors, the attic, and finally ended in the basement. Every floor vacant.

His eyes darted to the small basement window where, beyond, lay only darkness. Jerrica must have taken one of her random jaunts. Only now she was in unfamiliar territory. He hurried up the stairs and searched the grounds for any sign of her but ended up back on the patio, alone.

He sat down on the padded chair and covered his face with his hands. It was too soon to call the police. All he could do was wait. Wait and pray.

"Oh, God. Where is she? I just found her, and now she's gone again. I won't be able to lose her a second time, Lord. Help me find her. She's new to the area and could easily lose her way. Keep her safe in your loving arms. Help her to recover her memory, and ease her sorrow, pain, and fear. Please bring her back, dear Lord in Heaven, please. I beg you with my whole soul, bring her back safely." He poured out his heart aloud, choking on unshed tears.

When he finished he looked up and ran his hand through his hair. There she stood before him.

"Jenna." He rushed to her and enfolded her in his arms, his right hand gently cupping her head against his chest.

"Thank you, Lord, thank you," he whispered against her hair.

~ ...... ~

She stood, whalebone stiff, before easing her arms up to hug him back. Had he really been that worried?

He let her go, brought his big hands up to cup both sides of her face, and peered into her eyes. Raw torment lay etched in their depths. This man had truly meant every word he'd prayed. An overwhelming sense of sorrow shrouded her for having caused his agony. He then clutched her back into his arms.

"I'm sorry," she murmured against his chest. "I didn't mean to frighten you."

"It was like losing you all over again." His voice hitched.

Later, alone in her room, Jerrica sat on her mussed bed, her arms wrapped around her knees, observing the moonlight streaming through the large ceiling to floor windows. Brock had been so distraught. Even now it gave her a shiver to think about the anguish in his eyes. She knew it was only a matter of time before Brock would learn the truth; that she indeed was not Jenna, his lost love.

She closed her eyes and tucked her chin to her knees. How would she leave him, all broken and full of renewed grief? Moisture squeezed through her lashes. In such a short time, he'd become...important to her. How could that be?

Again she imagined his arms around her, strong, yet so tender. The essence of being needed. Another tear started in the corner of her eye, followed by streams of others.

How she longed to remember what her life had been before her memory loss. Had there been anyone like Brock who loved her? She bowed her head, praying through her sorrow.

Lifting her head, she knew there was only one thing to do. No matter how painful, she must find out. She swallowed. A fierce longing rose up within her to be Jenna. To just acquiesce and embrace being this woman.

She grabbed the book he'd given her today and flipped to the back cover where his picture and bio were displayed. For the first time, a photo had been included. No smile lit his face. She sniffed as she flicked to the front of the book and noticed writing on the first page. Her breath caught in her throat as she read it.

Chapter Fifteen

"To a woman of ultimate mystery who holds my heart deep within a labyrinth of secret things.—Deuteronomy 29:29"

She reread the simple line, mouthing the words in a whisper. His heart? Why had it never occurred to her that this man loved Jenna, and therefore, shifted that love to her?

Her heart thudded and she took a shuddering breath. Hadn't she felt it in his embrace? Tears bit her eyes. What a mess. The poor man. No, it wasn't fair to Brock to steal his wife's identity. She would search for the truth. Brock would be heartbroken when he discovered his love was indeed dead, and she, just Jerrica.

The next morning, after a night of tossing, she awoke and dressed. It was late. She opened her door and crept down the stairs. As she went, she could hear the television in the midst of flipping from channel to channel. She treaded through the entryway to the left, where Brock reclined in his chair, remote in hand.

"Good morning."

She rolled her shoulders and gave a small stretch as she approached the couch. "Morning."

Sports. News. Cartoons. She'd never seen so many channels. Black and white movie. No—that was Audrey Hepburn. Shuttling down a long set of steps.

"Stop. Can you go back?"

He shot her a puzzled look but flicked the channels back.

"There. *Roman Holiday*! I love this film."

She settled on the couch, wrapping her legs beneath her. A small blanket with St. Louis Cardinals splayed across it lay next to her, and she cozied up underneath it. "Do you mind if we watch it?"

A grin played at his mouth. "Not at all. And please, feel free to use my blanket."

At his wink she felt heat invade her face. Was he teasing her? "Thanks. One must always have a blanket handy when watching old movies."

"Really?"

"Shhh." Gregory Peck had arrived, the little rascal. Ready to put his plan into action to get an exclusive interview. How alike this film was to her life. Brock a writer, she, someone who wanted to escape.

It felt comforting, somehow, to watch the familiar movie. Interesting to share it with someone new. Special.

As the credits rolled, she gave a blissful coo. Satisfying and uplifting as always. Happily-ever-after. What a cheery way to start the day.

The TV burst into black. Brock set the remote down. "So, I have to tell you something."

The brightness began to fade into gloom.

"Okay." She sat up and rubbed the blanket from her legs. Now what?

"You're not going to like it."

St. Louis? Jerrica's chin plummeted, her gaze fastened on Brock. Was he kidding? Her skin crawled at the thought. The craft fair all over again, only larger. Much larger. People everywhere, all in a hurry to get somewhere in that stifling city of tall buildings packaged in faceless windows and concrete.

He'd given her the option of going with him, staying behind alone, or with his sister. It would be too time consuming to take her to the Smokies, although Brock had offered. Besides, was she three?

She sighed. Some options. Staying in a hotel didn't seem as foreboding as it once had. But the nightmares always followed. Could she stay here with her horror reruns knowing Brock was not here to wake her, to comfort her?

She tried to think through the craft fair visit. Could there have been a way to escape the climactic anxiety? *Focus on what was normal, why you went there.* There'd been a boy with a homemade gun of sorts. A popgun, perhaps? And what about the crafts she had seen? Wreath, signs, handmade purses? Yes. Had there been more than one doll booth? She covered her face with her hands.

All she could remember were the faces as they came to stare at her. Leering faces tilted and gaping, examining her like a covey of medical residents gaping at ginormous, anomaly plastered on her cheek.

"Is that really you, Jenna?"

"We can't believe it, Jenna."

"Jenna, where have you been?"

"We all thought you were dead, Jenna."

Jenna, Jenna, *Jenna.*

Brock left the recliner and mumbled something about breakfast. She stood and hurried from the room. How could she go to a huge rumbling city? How she longed to talk to Beth and tell her how totally impossible the situation had become.

The quiet, unobtrusive farm hidden away from crowds and the rush had helped her block fear. Jerrica lay on her bed and closed her eyes. But she couldn't run from the fear. And she certainly couldn't hide from it. It only followed her. And she knew she couldn't go back until evidence proved who she was.

She picked up the phone and dialed the Rankins. At least hearing their voices might ease her tension and help her see reason. An hour and a half later she crept downstairs to a cleaned kitchen and a homemade breakfast sandwich in the fridge.

She sat at the counter, ingesting about the best sausage, egg, and cheese sandwich she'd ever had. Why hadn't Aunt Ellen ever thought to combine breakfast food in such a way?

Brock. What a gentleman he'd been. Kind. Encouraging. And so freaking understanding. The perfect silver screen hero. He deserved a little compromise. Yeah.

She rinsed her plate and deposited it into the dishwasher. Then she meandered back to the room where she'd spotted his computer. The door was closed. Jerking her head and fisting herself taller, she knocked.

At Brock's invitation, she turned the knob. He sat at his desk, laptop open before him. Working. Doing his magic, spinning words into living realms. Interrupting him couldn't be helped. She had to tell him of her decision before she changed her mind.

Brock rose to his feet and headed toward her. She held up her hand to stop him. Sensible thought would flee if he got too close.

"I've reached a decision. I can't stay here alone. I won't stay with your sister. I'll have to go to St. Louis with you even though as I stand here, I'm positive I'll die while I'm there. I can't get on an airplane. So if we can get there despite all my, 'can'ts,' then I'll go with you. I'm...really sorry."

He moved to touch her and she jerked back.

"No, please." She put a hand to her nauseous stomach. "I think I'm going to—"

Jerrica rushed from the room with one hand on her stomach and one over her mouth. Hello, breakfast sandwich.

Brock pulled the suitcase from the hall closet and rolled it down the hallway to his room. The elation of knowing Jerrica had agreed to accompany him soured in his stomach as he thought of her nauseated face as she'd lurched from his office earlier. He blew out a lungful of air and sank to the edge of his mattress. With his head clasped in his hands, he prayed. All her misery had to be leading to some memory recovery, didn't it?

His phone buzzed on the bedside table, and he clamped a hand on it.

"Hello, Bro."

Brock swiped his hand over his face. "Hey, Glenn."

"Mom and Tisha. Incoming in like an hour."

He jumped to his feet. "What?"

Laughter met his shock. "Sorry. Wish I could say I was lying. But I've been up to my neck on this house Dad's building. The storm washed out the bank we'd built up with a retaining wall—"

"Are you telling me Mom and your wife are on their way here? Now?"

"Thought I made that clear."

Brock pulled the phone from his ear and stretched his neck with irritation. This was the last thing he needed right now. The last thing Jerrica needed. Why had his mother called last night? Shoot. Why had he told her about the gala? He stepped to the window. "Why didn't you stop them? I told you how delicate this situation—"

"You tell me how and I'm all in."

No way to argue with that. "This couldn't be worse timing. We'll be on our way to St. Louis tomorrow."

"Have they ever had good timing? She gave you a week. Count yourself lucky. At least you are forewarned."

"Yeah." He ought to ask about the family. But right now he was just too downright aggravated. "Gotta go. Thanks, Bro."

"You got it. Enjoy."

Brock gritted his teeth and pitched the phone on the bed.

Jerrica pushed up from the bed and set a hand to her stomach. Most of the tumbling and clenching had eased. Hives still at bay. Voices floated up the stairwell, muffled through the heavy oak door. High voices. A woman? Devi? No, it seemed more than one. She swung her feet to the floor, padded to the door, and pressed her ear to the wood. Very muffled, but decipherable.

"Yes, Mother, but this is not a good time."

Mother? Another voice, also a woman's chirruped in.

"Oh, come now, Brock. We won't stay long. Your mom and I were worried for you."

"You know the situation. I asked you all to give us some time."

"And we did."

Silence stretched and Jerrica leaned closer.

"Either way, we're here to help Jenna, that poor dear. She needs the company of women."

Brock's voice grew softer and softer until their voices disappeared altogether. Jerrica groaned and dove back into bed. Would this never end? So many people were getting involved. Now she had to face his mother? Panic rushed through her, and she rose to pace the confines of her room.

She paused at the window and gripped the curtains. If only she could tug them down and wrap them about her and disappear from all the turmoil both inside and out. Her breathing slowed, and she turned her head to glare at the closet. She could hide in there. Perhaps there's a hidden door she could fall through. Like Alice.

Do something a sane person would do.

After inhaling deeply, she turned and strode to the pile of dirty clothes in the corner. She'd promised Brock she'd accompany him to St. Louis. That meant laundry. Yet a casual trip downstairs might put her face to face with the new demons downstairs. No. Demons probably wasn't the best analogy. Fiends? Monsters? Trolls? Drat. No, no, and double NO. She didn't even know them. How unfair.

Yet how unfair of them? Why had they just sprung from under their bridge to haunt them? Brock's voice clearly hadn't been welcoming. She hugged the clothes to her and raised her chin. Still, wasn't it better to meet them head on with the knowledge of who they were? Or kinda.

Hmmm. Obviously her lungs hadn't received that message. Why did fear have its clutches so deep in her psyche? A rush of trembling rattled through her, and she prayed the migraine would bypass her this time. God, oh, God. There's only two of them. *Could I possibly face them and triumph?*

The first step is always the hardest. One step. Then two. *Roll the window down, Jerrica.* Step, step.

Soon she stood at the door, fumbling to find the knob beneath the mound of clothing. At last the door clicked and swung open. The stairway gleamed at her. Distant mutters indicated a kitchen conversation in full swing. If memory served right, to get to the laundry room she'd have to cut through the kitchen. Of course.

She edged down the stairs, forcing the rushing air that escaped her lungs to slow. Hello, lungs, check your email. Brain says relax.

Sun streamed in the door, the sidelights, and the stained-glass transom at the top. God's glory, the sun. It gave her courage to creep the rest of the way down the steps. She paused at the bottom, facing the light, letting the rays warm her face.

"I don't care what you say, we're here to—Jenna!"

Jerrica swung toward the sound and the older woman rushing towards her, her arms spread wide for a hug. The fancy white pantsuit and coifed dark curls didn't seem to dampen her enthusiasm.

"Mother. Stop."

Indeed she did, a troubled look on her face. Her arms plunged to her sides. Brock came around her and spun to set up a stance in front of Jerrica.

"We don't know for sure if she's Jenna."

"Don't be daft, Son. Look at her." Another woman with a shoulder-length dark hair stood next to Mother dear, hands on hips, gaping at her.

A tremor made her arms clutch the clothes tighter to her chest. Jerrica moved her head ever so slightly to hide entirely behind Brock's big body.

"This is why I wanted you to wait." His deep voice held a thread of steel.

The large grandfather clock in the same hallway ticked away the seconds. Then a short half-hour bong. No one spoke. She glanced at the pendulum. How much time she'd wasted always being afraid. She closed her eyes momentarily before she broke the silence. "It's okay, Brock."

He pivoted, his face opened in incredulity. "What? No. You don't have to do this, Jerrica."

She fixed her eyes on his black ones, a soft light kindled there. "I can do it."

He searched her face for a moment and then nodded. "All right."

When he moved aside she faced the two women standing tandem. "Hello."

The older woman's mouth twitched and moisture made her eyes sparkle. "We're just so glad to see you, is all."

The younger woman covered her mouth with the back of her hand and wrapped her other arm around the older woman.

Brock cleared his throat. "This is my mother, Vivian, and my sister-in-law, Tisha."

Jerrica gave a small nod. The two women fought tears for a few moments before his mother spoke again. "We thought we'd never see you again. We thought—"

"Mother."

She nodded and accepted a tissue Tisha had wrangled from her purse. The woman gave a stiff smile. "Forgive us. You do look so much like Jenna."

Brock stepped a little closer. "So she's been told several times."

"Don't be fresh, Brock." His mother raised her chin and shot him a hard look with her dark eyes. "You have to give us a moment to collect ourselves. This is quite unexpected."

Brock gave a muffled growl beside Jerrica. "I'm pretty clear on how shocking it is."

Jerrica stepped forward a bit. "I'm sorry. You've caught me at a bad time. Let me run and get this load started. Then perhaps we can sit in the living room."

Brock stared at her as if she'd sprouted a unicorn twirl.

She attempted a smile. Partially successful. "I'll be right back."

With that she scurried through the hall, past the gaping twins, to the kitchen door and powered on to the laundry room. Once there she pressed the door closed and tried to still her thundering heart. This would not be easy.

She took her time loading the washing machine and adding the soap. With exaggerated slowness, she shut the lid. Nothing to do but head back into the living room.

She silently padded through the kitchen and into the hallway when the doorbell rang. The tenseness in her body increased and she froze. Brock appeared from the left and strode to the door.

"Hi, I heard Mom was here. And Tisha." Devi shot through the door then came to a standstill when she caught site of Jerrica. Her mouth dropped into the stunned smile. "You're keeping all this company to yourself, aren't you?"

Brock sidled up to Devi and motioned into the room. "Go, little sister. I need a minute."

After giving a mock salute, her face a childish pucker, she marched out of sight. The squeals of the greeting echoed to Jerrica down the long hall.

Brock parked one hand in his pocket and rubbed his neck with the other. He stepped a few paces closer. "Sure am sorry about this. I had no clue they were coming until they were well on their way."

Jerrica gave a small shrug. She eyed the huge walnut clock, snipping off time with each sway of the pendulum.

He hated seeing her give that uncommunicative shrug. Like she'd moved back into herself. Where she'd been when he first met her. It ate at him, and he longed to thunder into the living room and command the ladies to leave. "You don't have to go out there."

She nodded, and he wondered briefly what that meant. He stepped closer, and she raised her aquamarine eyes to his. With the muted sunlight, they glowed with intenseness and...fear? Yes, always fear. A sharp prong of anger made him tighten his lips. Why did his mother have to corner her like this? "I'll ask them to leave."

He spun and felt a hand catch his elbow. "It's okay, Brock. I think I can do it."

Conversation ceased the moment he walked in with Jerrica. His mother gestured to the empty place beside her on the huge sectional sofa. Jerrica drifted closer but settled on the large square ottoman.

"So, how are you?" His mother crossed her hands on her knees and fixed her eyes on Jerrica. The other two women followed suit. Brock shook his head while the women centered her in their crosshairs like psychotic snipers.

"Fine." Her face paled.

Brock stepped forward. Time to stop this attack.

His mother glanced at him and flicked her wrist. "Get us some coffee, Brock. We girls need some time."

He settled into the recliner in the center of the room between the warring parties. If his mother thought he was leaving Jerrica to be gobbled by wolves, she could think again. "Coffee can wait."

"Oh, pooh with you." She turned her gaze back on Jerrica. "Well, you look good, although you've let the highlights grow out of your hair. I always thought that brightened your face."

"Cinnamon highlights would be divine." Devi popped in, nodding enthusiastically. "I personally prefer to darken my hair."

Brock rolled his eyes. "This is what you came to talk about? Dying hair?"

His mother adjusted herself to get a full view of her son. "You're downright rude today."

He could scarcely stem the grunt that came from his throat. "Rude is coming when you've not been invited."

Her penciled-in eyebrows rose. "If we waited for an invitation, there's no telling how long that would be."

Tisha joined the conversation. "So you're going to St. Louis?"

"Yes, tomorrow. Early. Very Early." Brock answered when Jerrica hesitated.

Devi parked a hand on her hip. "And you've got clothes? She needs a dress. And a manicure. That's a must. And of course, a new do."

"I brought my jewelry samples. I could simply cover you in our newest pieces." Tisha brought forth her hand, displaying a sparkling bauble on her finger and jangling the numerous heavy bracelets on her wrists. "This is the latest from the catalog. I'd be glad to lend you any piece. This necklace pairs up with the entire ensemble. Isn't it gorgeous? And so versatile. If I had my manikin, I could show you all the possibilities."

Brock stared at the heavy chain at his sister-in-law's neck. Somehow he couldn't imagine Jerrica wearing any heavy jewelry. But she gave a stiff smile and slight nod. He narrowed his eyes at them.

Devi jumped up. "I have a brilliant idea. We could go shopping. Like now. You could be completely outfitted in a matter of hours. I know a great walk-in salon. We could all get our nails done, and they might even fit you in for a cut and a color."

Jerrica also rose, but the familiar shadow of panic filtered across her face. He shoved himself out of the chair. "I think maybe that would be a little too much help, right now, ladies. If you'll excuse us."

But his words were a little late as Jerrica fled for the hallway and then sped up the stairs. Yep. Just what he figured. He turned to find the women standing a few steps behind him, eyes filled with odd curiosity. This time he did grunt. "Did I not ask for a little time?"

Devi crossed her arms tight and glared at him. "Fine. But we're going to help whether you want us to or not. Come on, ladies. We have a gala to shop for."

The other two chimed in with agreement and shot daggers at Brock and worked their way toward the door.

"Fine, super." Brock held the door open as they sauntered down the front steps, discussing the wisdom of heels versus flats. They piled in his mother's car, and he waved. And knowing they couldn't hear him, he smiled and added, "Good riddance."

Chapter Sixteen

Jerrica cast her gaze around her bed at the ten formals that lay there in a rainbow of colors and styles. What in the world? Small, hot explosions started at the base of her neck. Oh, not now. Not with three of Brock's family below anticipating a fashion show. She rotated her head and rubbed the base of her neck. So this is what a chipmunk felt like when trapped in its burrow.

She ran her eyes over the selections. Is this what Jenna did? Flaunt about in finery? All righty. She'd pick a dress. And quickly. But no runway. Not a chance. She fingered the bright yellow creation in front of her. The plunging neckline made heat flow to her face. Not in a jillion years would she wear that. She hung it on the back of the door.

It proved easy to reject two others merely on color. Fuchsia, uh, no. Mud-colored teal. Not a chance. She chucked the red satin as well. Too flashy.

Without much more thought, she culled the white one too. Too much like a wedding. That left two black, a purple, a beige lacy dress, and an aquamarine clear as the sky in June. She approached the latter and ran a hand over the sheer material. It generously covered all the important areas and even sported capped sleeves instead of the thin spaghetti straps.

With a sigh she slipped it on and turned toward the mirror. It clung to her curves and made her feel quite exposed. Still the small scar on her shoulder was completely concealed. She quickly shrugged out of it, trying to drum up some thankfulness. The women downstairs had gone to a lot of trouble on her behalf. Unfortunately, she knew the next step was jewelry. Somehow she would side step the salon and the manicure.

A knock sounded on the door, and she quickly bunched the rejects in her hand.

"It's me." Brock's low voice drifted through the door.

With a smidgen of relief, she opened the door a crack.

"How 'bout I take the dresses you don't want, and alert the wardrobe entourage downstairs of your selection?"

She turned pained eyes up to his. "They said something about jewelry."

"Humph. Well, give me the one you've selected also, and I'll let them titter and flitter about it by themselves. You should rest."

Feeling like a complete chicken-hearted, lily-livered troll, she agreed and passed the dresses to him.

With his mom set up in his room, Brock crashed on the couch recliner. And even though Tisha and Devi had snuggled up on a couple of air mattresses in an extra room upstairs, thankfully he couldn't hear their college-dorm gossip. Good grief, how old were they? He just hoped Jerrica couldn't hear it either.

His wife had never returned down the stairs. And although his excuses sounded thin, even to his own ears, he could care less. He'd told them they needed some time to themselves. No matter.

They would leave on time in the morning and let his family mosey on out at their ease.

On the dining room table through the doorway the white stack of boxes caught his attention. At least Jerrica had plenty of wardrobe choices. Women like that sort of thing. He fixed his eyes on the tray ceiling and drifted off to sleep.

By six o'clock the next morning, he collected the suitcases, carried them to the garage, and hefted them into the trunk. Jerrica's luggage felt practically empty as he tossed it inside. He collected the boxes from the dining room and met up with Jerrica, fully dressed with purse, sneaking down the stairs.

"Did you take enough clothes?" He asked, keeping his voice low.

She shrugged. "I hope so. I guess I should have brought more from home."

He patted the pile of boxes. "Well, I know for a fact, my family bought a few extra things."

Her mouth opened, and she shot him a sideways glance. "What are you talking about?"

"Come here." He led her into the kitchen and propped the boxes on the counter.

She pulled the top off the first box. Inside were several pairs of pajamas in pastel shades, trimmed in lace, soft and delicate. She blushed.

"All courtesy of my invading family members, I might add at this point. Although this addition to your wardrobe was their idea, I did suggest a few colors."

The next box contained a pair of capris, several jean shorts, and a couple of short spandex skirts. "They're...nice."

Brock snorted. "You don't like them."

"It's not that." She fingered the seam of the shorts.

He frowned. "So what's up?"

She chewed her pinky nail. "I don't wear shorts."

"Jerrica," he said with exaggerated patience, "it's a hundred degrees in the shade. I really think shorts would be more practical."

"I know."

He fitted the tops over the boxes before motioning with his hands for her to elaborate. "And—"

She rubbed her hand along her right thigh. "I have a scar and it's...I just can't wear shorts."

Brock turned and stacked the two boxes together and pulled out the last large one at the bottom. "Fine. Let's get to the last box."

He worked to keep the irritation from his voice. Jerrica shrank from him, and a blast of remorse coursed through him.

Jerrica's wishy-washy, wimpy mood this morning didn't help battle off the verge of tears, and she closed her eyes. Why did everything have to be such a fight? Why couldn't she just be like everyone else and wear the stupid shorts and flitter about in happiness? Everyone had gone to so much trouble.

She opened her eyes and the next box was open before her. Nestled in the tissue paper, the gorgeous tea-length, aquamarine dress shone. Atop the satin material lay designer jewelry, a bangle bracelet and rings, glistening in the light.

"It's all beautiful. Really." She gave a small laugh as she caressed the silky fabric. "I never did ask why I needed all this. Are we going to the prom?"

"Sort of." Seriousness lit his dark eyes.

The implication hit her like a scorned woman's slap. The smile left her face. "There's a party in St. Louis, isn't there?"

"Yes," he replied as he helped put the stunning dress inside the white box. "The owner of the Aston Publishing House, Colonel Robert Preston Aston himself, has an open house on Saturday night during the retail show."

She gave a slight tremulous smile. "What luck."

He balanced the boxes in one hand and put his other hand into his pocket for the keys. "Yeah, well, I knew you'd be thrilled. I tried to tell them you probably wouldn't go."

She pulled in a quivering breath. Why didn't she think about this yesterday? Formal dresses, duh. Her stomach twisted in knots. The visitors and their demands had occupied her mind so much she'd forgotten to contemplate the reasoning for such frippery.

Her eyes traveled over the boxes Brock picked up and carried to the garage. She'd have to remember to thank his mom, sister-in-law, and sister. Even though the thought of attending a formal party nearly sent her bolting to Nicaragua. Jerrica tried to clear her throat before bile blocked the passage completely. They stepped out into the garage, and he pulled the door shut.

A *huge* formal party. A sickening wave hit her stomach, and she pressed a hand against her middle. She hesitated. "Shouldn't we...say goodbye?"

He stopped at the passenger door and opened it for her. "Nope. Told them we'd jet on out before they moved in the morning. So we're off."

She walked on pirate peg-legs until she came even with him. Off to St. Louis. For the next week. Her belly lurched again as she felt the blood drain from her face. A huge bustling city. And a gala. A hooping, stinking, freaking gala. Internal organs did the wave. Nausea rose up her throat. "House open?"

The acid contents battering at her esophagus wiped away her need for an answer, and she sealed a hand over her mouth, bolting up the steps. The door burst open at her fumbling fingers, so she flew to the bathroom to retch in the open porcelain ring. Trembling, she cleaned up and tried to slow the spasms in her abdomen.

Once she returned to the back door, she pulled her stiff face into some semblance of a smile. "You know me too well already."

"You okay?"

She nodded stiffly. As okay as she could get.

The city proved to be absolutely the most suffocating place she could ever remember visiting. The highway turned into this monstrosity of a road with six lanes with concrete overpasses going every direction at once, overstuffed with cars and loud trucks Jake braking through traffic. Formidable semis exploded past them at unbelievable speeds.

Then the enormous black river. The Mississippi? Jerrica could care less. It was all she could do just to slouch in the seat with her hands over her ears. She heard a mumbling and realized Brock spoke.

"What?" She clenched her trembling limbs.

"I said, the car company would be disappointed to see you covering your ears. It's supposed to have a serene silence in the noisiest of places."

"Well, they obviously have some work to do," she grumbled through gritted teeth as another semi swooshed by, making the car feel as if they had been pushed a foot off the road.

"Look, Jerrica." He pointed off to the left. "You're going to miss the arch."

She pushed his hand back toward the steering wheel. "Keep both hands on that thing."

"I'll drive with no hands if you don't look."

"Fine." She peered out the window through the haze. A huge silver arch caught the sun and gleamed in the distance. She gasped. "That is the most terrifying thing I've ever seen."

Brock threw back his head with a hearty laugh. "Only you would call one of the most noteworthy structures in America, horrible. Do you know you can go to the top and look out?"

She widened her eyes. "Are you trying to kill me?"

He gave that grin that wrested her breath away. "And you have to ride these little tiny capsules to the top."

She shivered. "You are infuriating, Brock Langston."

A hint of that smile pulled at the corners of his mouth. "It's hard to believe you are the same little hillbilly that traipses through the mountains populated with bears. Who spelunks through dark, unexplored caves."

"It's different." How? She couldn't explain. His attractive profile soon blocked the mammoth structure. "Have you been to the top of that thing?"

"Oh, yes, ma'am. I had to hunker down in those little seats. I think only about six people can fit in the capsule."

Sweat formed in a line across her upper lip. "You're a horrid man. To think I was beginning to believe you had some shred of decency. All you can do is...is scare me, and—"

"Excuse me? Could I interrupt this little tirade? We're here."

She caught her breath and glanced around. They were parked in front of a sizable hotel, windows decorating the entire front façade. A concierge with a sharp white shirt and tie approached the car. Jerrica continued to suck in her surroundings while Brock made arrangements. A small park lay on the other side of the road, and beyond, that arch. Frightening. Brock opened her door to help her from the car.

He smiled. "You've got to admit, my ploy worked. You grew so angry, you didn't even seem bothered by the traffic."

"What a dirty little trick."

He grinned, and a quiver shimmied in her stomach. Not from nausea this time. From nerves? She wasn't sure.

"Care to check in?"

Jerrica gulped. "What floor?"

"The twenty-third."

Forty-six flights of stairs. The man surely despised her. "I only suspected earlier. Now I'm convinced. You're trying to murder me."

How would she climb that many stairs every time they left and returned? She clung to his elbow as they followed the bellboy with a cart of their luggage. Inside the wall of windows, the ceiling soared several floors.

Everything around them shone, from the black marble tile to the glittering chandeliers. Easy cheesy diners partook of lunch in the raised restaurant to the right. Lucky devils. Spending the lunch hour in urban gab, ha, ha, ha. Imaginary conversations filled Jerrica's brain.

I've a massage at two, yoga at three, and Isabelle has her ballet recital this evening. When's the next rooftop party? I love the view of the river from your place. And I just adore your husband's veggie burgers. Titter, titter. Spas and pedicures.

They continued to follow their guide up a slight ramp, just down from Starbucks and the gift shop. The bellboy stopped in front of the six elevators. Jerrica stuttered to a stop, yet people rushed on, clutching attaches and wearing business dark.

The elevator door slid open and in went their guide and luggage. He blinked at them in question, holding up an arm to stop the door. Brock stood with one foot in the empty elevator and one foot in the hallway, suits sidestepping him.

He smiled and motioned her in. "Come on, Jerrica. You can do it. Remember, it's the twenty-third floor. We couldn't possibly take all the stairs."

Twenty-third. "'The Lord is my shepherd, I shall not want....'" *Brock maketh me enter petrifying elevators.*

"But..." So this was the demise of the heroine. Tragically slain on black marble at the foot of an elevator, chalk outline of her dead body, blood dripping from her open mouth. Trampled by dress shoes. She rubbed her hands up and down her upper arms and bounced with reluctance.

A couple came up beside her with hesitant glances.

"Here, you go ahead," Brock motioned the couple to take the elevator. "We'll be right up."

The couple smiled and thanked him. The doors shut out the bellboy's puzzled face.

Brock walked to Jerrica who covered her face with her hands.

"I'm sorry, I'm sorry, I'm sorry!" she mumbled shaking her head.

She could do this. He was absolutely positive. Brock reached up and rubbed her upper arms to dispel the goose bumps. "Listen. Just stay against me and don't look around. You won't even know we're in an elevator."

It surely didn't help that the elevator was glass on one side. They'd have a perfect view of the Mississippi. But he wouldn't be stupid and point that out. He pressed the elevator button again.

"Here's what we'll do." He wrapped his left arm around her shoulders and dropped his head to speak lowly into her ear. "Just keep your face against me and hide your eyes. It'll be over before you can count to thirty."

"What if it stops? What if it falls? What if the doors won't open?" Her voice crept toward hysterical.

"Yes, the papers are filled with such tragedies." His laughter rumbled from his chest, and she smacked his arm. The elevator dinged and he dragged her with him.

"Just a little farther," he coaxed as she tensed. Her grip tightened on his shirt as she whimpered, pressing her face against his chest, drawing the gazes of several around.

But at last they were in, and he began counting. "One, Mississippi, two, Mississippi, three Mississippi..." He prayed they reached their floor before he got to thirty. He flicked his eyes up and watched the numbers change on the panel. Nineteen, twenty...Jerrica shuddered. The elevator dinged. They'd arrived. He pushed her to the hallway. "Thirty Mississippi. We're here."

She kept her head burrowed against him and mumbled, "On the twenty-third floor?"

"Yes," he grinned, enjoying her closeness. Reluctantly he eased her away and forced her hands from her face. "We're safe."

"Uh-huh."

"You made it. You conquered the elevator and now stand upon floor twenty-three." He raised his hands in mock victory.

Her tongue swiped her top lip, face pale as lilies. "Yay, me."

He put his arm around her waist and urged her to walk. It didn't take long to locate their two bedroom suite and a relieved bellboy. Brock slid the patient man a large tip and shut the door.

Jerrica blinked several times as if waking and looked around. She'd ridden the elevator. A slice of thankfulness and accomplishment slowed her soft pants. "'He makes me to lie down in green pastures; He leads me beside quiet waters, He restores my soul.'"

Her eyes traveled the main area. Lovely room. She glanced at Brock who was busy turning on lights. Still, she was a little miffed by his earlier traffic trick. Her stomach steadied. Why did the cave seem safe and an elevator so terrifying? Wow. As if she'd make sense now.

She glanced at the bathroom near the door, wandered through the living area, and peeked into the two bedrooms, before stepping into the one that was to be hers. She wandered to the window to let in the sun.

Holy Comoly. The river and arch greeted her, asparkle with the rays of the sun. Her gaze transfixed on the drop to the ground. Hello, Sergeant Saliva-Stealer.

She couldn't pull her eyes away. Like bystanders at a fatal wreck.

Several gaming boats were tethered near the concrete bank. She raised her eyes. The silver arch reflected back at her and mocked her fear. Surely Brock could've reserved a room closer to the main floor. Had that too been another trick? Dizziness enveloped her. She put her hands over her face and sank to the floor with a groan.

Chapter Seventeen

J errica closed her eyes and willed her stomach to calm.
Look at the carpet. Nice and clean. *And on the twenty-third floor.*

She slid her hand into her pocket to retrieve a tissue and felt Katie's smooth stone. *Katie—think about her instead of being so high.* She pictured little Katie singing her heart out at the front of the church, her little hands clasped over her head. A tune danced through her mind, "Jesus is the rock of my Salvation, his banner over me is love."

Katie. Her dirty little angel. An overwhelming urge to pray for her weighed on her heart. When she finished, a peace descended, and her own fear dissipated. She stood. Time. To. Get. Normal.

Dinner arrived as she stepped into the main room, and Brock had the TV blaring the St. Louis game, the organ leading the charge call.

The announcer called out, "It's a swing and a miss for strike two."

He glanced toward her as the bellboy laid the meal on the small table. "You mind if I watch the game?"

Jerrica shook her head, hiding a smile at his reluctance to pull his eyes from the screen. "No. It's fine."

Room service. Her companion's peace treaty for making her do the elevator. Oh, and the twenty-third floor. Extravagance accepted.

Brock tipped the man as he left and returned to pull out her chair before seating himself across from her. He flicked on the mute and blessed the food.

Jerrica picked up the fork to dive into the enchiladas. "So who are you for?"

A pause before he answered, eyes fixated on the batter. "St. Louis, of course." A short groan. "Oh, man. Why'd they play him today? His average is below two hundred."

"Sorry, but I'm a Cubbie fan." Her fork stopped midway, and her mouth hung open. Brock turned to look at her. She glared at him. "You knew that didn't you?"

He nodded. "You just now realized that, huh?"

She put down the fork. "Why does this seem to happen when I'm eating? It's positively nauseating. I love Mexican food. And don't tell me you already knew that!"

"All right. I won't." A glint lit his eye.

She stared at him a moment, narrowing her eyes. "Now what?"

He rose from his chair, went into his bedroom, and returned with two t-shirts. "I didn't give you everything the ladies picked out for you to wear. I saved this one for the game on Thursday. I was hoping we could go."

With a sick realization, she picked up the t-shirt he threw her. The Chicago Cubs' logo sprawled across the front of the jersey. He held his up to his chest where it proclaimed the St. Louis Cardinals.

Too. Many. Coincidences. She whirled and stumbled blindly for her room.

She held tight to the metal guard rail at the entrance to Busch Stadium. People surged around her to hand tickets to the takers. Why, why had she agreed to this again?

"Oh, I shouldn't be here." She shielded her eyes from the melee around her.

Brock blocked her on three sides to protect her from the crush of people. "Jerrica, make a decision. We can't stand here much longer."

"I know you went to a lot of trouble to get these tickets, and these...shirts, but I just can't push myself through that gate. The concrete—" She motioned above her head.

"People have been coming here for years and lived to tell about it. It's a fairly new stadium so I'm sure it's up to code. It's completely safe. Much like the cave."

"So you say."

He pulled her within his embrace and murmured in her ear as she trembled.

"Jerrica, I'd never place your life in danger, you must know that."

Tears stung her eyes and she sniffed. "I know."

"Can you just trust me?"

"It's not that."

"It is. Trust and pray. Close your eyes and I'll take you in."

Her eyes darted about. What were these people thinking as they herded past her? Thousands of pounds of man-made concrete hovered above their heads. And the sheer volume of people. They were nuts. And Beth called *her* fears irrational.

"Okay." She choked.

Brock held her against him, and she squeezed her eyes shut, praying so hard her lips moved with each word. She could sense him weaving her in and out of hundreds of other humans, but she dared not open her eyes. Food smells berated her nose. Hot dogs, nachos, popcorn. She concentrated on the olfactory buffet and ignored the people's voices rising to a low collective roar. Before she knew it, he eased her into a seat.

"Let up on the death grip. We've made it." Brock whispered into her ear.

Slowly she opened her eyes. They sat fairly close to the field in the first tier. But as her eyes trailed up to the balconies, her heart fell to her feet.

"Oh, oh, how can they sit up there? Samson could bring this place down with a shove." She covered her face with her hands. "Oh, I'm going to be sick."

"What? No, Jerrica, not here, please not here." Without missing a beat, he grabbed a tub of popcorn from a nearby vendor, dumped the popcorn, and handed it to her. But she managed to squelch the urge.

"Sorry." She blinked at him then turned her gaze to the irritated popcorn man.

After clearing things up with the vendor and the tub tucked close to her seat, Jerrica's nerves settled. She kept her eyes forward and ignored the balconies behind her. "Oh, my. Now I need the restroom."

Brock guided her to the ladies' room and waited near the entrance. It took all her courage to enter the concrete guillotine with a steady stream, no pun intended, of other lady visitors. She refreshed herself and returned. "I'm really sorry, Brock."

"Jerrica, constant puking isn't healthy." He dug in his pocket and handed her a mint.

"I didn't, you know. But I probably still need this." She raised the mint in her hand and forced a smile. "Thanks for being so patient."

"Well, I'm not sure about the halitosis, but I'm not taking any chances," he grinned.

He led her back to her seat as she kept her eyes glued to the concrete walk in front of her. Once seated Jerrica studied the people around her. Funny how they appeared as interesting as the game. Some were fixated with their phones, and she wondered why they bothered to come. She even managed to giggle at a few vendors' antics as they tried to drum up customers. The inning ended with the Cardinals ahead, and Brock swung towards her.

"Kiss me."

"What?"

"We're on the kiss cam. Hurry."

His face blocked out the sun, and his lips met hers. The laughing crowd surrounding them faded as his mouth moved against hers. And then it was over, and she gasped in surprise.

He grinned. "Sorry. Can't let the kiss cam down. Or our fans."

He gestured around them, and she slunk into her seat. All eyes seemed fixed on them. "Thanks for being a good sport."

A noise escaped her that she'd hoped sounded like a laugh. The joke was on him. She wasn't surprised by the suddenness. She was stunned at the emotions churning through her and the disappointment of the lack of further samples.

Sweat gathered on her lip and she dabbed at it. It had to be the heat making her feel so odd. So off balance. Or the concrete. Suspended. She licked her sunburnt lips. Yes, that was it. Her presence in this stadium had knocked her equilibrium off center. Once she was back at the hotel, her need for Brock's security would dry up like a dog's water bowl in the Sahara.

Brock gripped the steering wheel and glanced at Jerrica, her head lolled against his shoulder. The game had run late with extra innings, and she was wiped. His lips quirked. She'd been a soldier to take on overcoming the fear of the game.

Pride swelled his chest. She'd always been a trooper, jumping in when others hesitated. And getting caught on the kiss cam, well, it couldn't have worked out any better. He only wished the cam had frozen on them. She'd been dazed at first, but her lips had responded to his.

He gave a sigh of relief. Each day she seemed to overcome yet another fear. Maybe she'd recover from this trauma in time. However, he didn't relish discussing her mother again. He knew he had to tell her the truth, but he just couldn't bring that up now.

Brock glanced at the top of her head as she nestled against him, her hands limp in her lap. Things were going too smoothly right now to spoil it.

He pulled to the front of the hotel, handed his keys to the waiting attendant, and roused Jerrica. She was so sleepy, she put up little fight riding the elevator. He guided her with stumbling steps into the suite and to the door of her room. She mumbled something and disappeared. He turned and made his way to his room.

After a shower, he prepared for bed, thankful for the soft feel of the pajama pants against his skin after a long day. His hand lowered for his t-shirt when a knock sounded at the door. What was she doing up? Uneasiness volleyed through his gut as he strode to the door. But the hesitant smile on her sleepy face reassured him, and he ran his eyes down the length of her robe, belt snugged at her waist.

"Sorry, I know it's late. I sorted through my stuff and didn't know if you were still up or not."

"Yeah, me too. What's up?"

She cleared her throat. "Thank you for...everything. I mean, you know. It's been so difficult and all. I just appreciate all your understanding and willingness to put up with my antics. You were incredibly patient. A lot of guys wouldn't want to mess with a crazy woman."

Her soft open expression sent a ricocheting desire to reach out and pull her to him. Just the thought of her lying next to him in bed made his hands come up, but he diverted them into his still-wet hair. "You're not crazy, Jenna."

Something odd crossed her face. "Well, anyway, thanks."

He stepped forward as she turned. "About tomorrow—"

She snapped her fingers. "Oh, yeah. I'm going to stay in. I think I need some...time. I'll call Uncle John and Aunt Ellen. I haven't talked to them in several days. And I'll read and I've got my journal. You know, it's probably best with the crowds, and you being busy with the book thing."

He nodded. Her eyes skimmed down his chest, and she stumbled. He grabbed her as she gasped. "Hey, you feeling all right?"

She pulled from him. "Yes, I'm fine. Just sleepy."

He scratched his head as she hurried to her room. With a shrug he returned to his bedroom and shut the door with hesitation. He'd called her Jenna. Perhaps why she'd rushed away. At least she hadn't corrected him.

With a groan he sank to the side of the bed and planted his head in his hands. He'd only been with her a few weeks, and the love roaring through his body unsettled him with its ferocity. What if she chose not to stay? His thoughts fell to intense prayer.

Jerrica clutched the robe to her chest and leaned against the closed door as her heart thundered. Hadn't she told herself when he opened the door bare-chested to keep her eyes above his chin? And she'd been incredibly successful until the very end.

His chest had unnerved her enough, but the birthmark to the left of his navel had almost laid her on the floor. Hot lava bled into her head, and she gripped her skull as she staggered to the bed.

"It looks like brown paint spilling out of your bellybutton." She'd laughed, and her junior high friends giggled next to her.

He'd grinned. "Get in the pool and quit bothering the lifeguard."

She'd stuck out her tongue at him and cannonballed into the water.

Jerrica panted. Oh, dear heaven, she'd known him as a young girl. Cold reality sluiced through her feeble confidence. Who was she? Her brain churned in warp drive, and she collapsed, burying her head into her pillows.

Jerrica woke late Friday morning and, after a peek into the main room, she realized she had the place to herself. Refusing to analyze last night's discovery, she returned to her room and laid out her outfit choices on the bed.

The white shorts with the tie-dyed t-shirt lured her. Devi had probably picked that out. Her fingers rubbed the burn scar that ran down her right leg. She had no business putting it on. Yet, she was here. Alone. Who'd know?

After a shower she slipped on the clothing which was slightly loose, but she shrugged her shoulders. At the mirror the warped skin on her leg screamed at her, and she swiped at it. Brock must bring out her daring nature because she thrust her chin out and decided to wear the outfit anyway.

With her favorite throw, she parked herself on the couch in the main room near the phone with her books. Aunt Ellen's voice cheered her as she answered.

"In St. Louis? Oh, my, Jerrica. I would've never thought."

Jerrica lowered her head and smiled. "I even went to a baseball game last night."

Silence pervaded the line for a couple of beats. "Glory, hallelujah. That's wonderful."

Her eyes rested on the burn on her leg, and she glanced away. "He's at the retail show now. I was hungry for some news."

"Well, I'm afraid we had a close call here."

Jerrica froze. "Uncle John?"

Aunt Ellen's voice dropped. "No, Katie."

Chapter Eighteen

Jerrica's breath snagged. "What happened?"

Aunt Ellen's tsk-tsk echoed across the miles. "Almost hit by a car. Right around lunchtime on Wednesday."

Just about the time they'd arrived at the hotel. Oh, how that child had laid on her heart. "Is she all right?"

"Not a scratch on her. No one can explain it. She was in town with her father, and she ran plum out in the middle of a parking lot. She fell, and the truck went right over the top of her. Right smack dab over her. Can you believe it? How she knew to lie still, I have no idea."

She snugged the blanket up to warm the shiver that raced through her. "You know, I had the strangest inclination to pray right around that same time."

"Well, it's a good thing you did. Without the Lord's help, she wouldn't be with us."

Katie had been so close to death. How she wished she could be there to hug away the child's terror. As Aunt Ellen continued to chat about the area news, Jerrica's mind wandered. Time was so precious. Every minute. Why did she let so much of it be swallowed in fear? *God help me not to waste my days. Help me.*

"Honey, I just want to share one last thing with you before we hang up."

"Okay." Jerrica tucked away her thoughts for later.

"Make sure you look up Ecclesiastes 4:9."

Jerrica laughed. "You're not going to tell me what it is, are you?"

Her aunt's chuckle said it all. "Nope, darling girl, I'm not. Always take time each day to spend with the Lord."

"Yes, Aunt Ellen." She grinned, reciting like a school child. "I love you and tell everyone I miss them"

"Will, do. Love ya, dumpling."

She lost no time looking up her aunt's verse. "'Two are better than one because they have good return for their labor.'"

Indeed the things she'd accomplished with Brock's aid.

It was after dark when the door clicked open. Jerrica, deep into one of Brock's novels, jumped and choked in surprise. She flicked her eyes to the cover she held as Brock strode closer.

"Problem?" he asked.

"No, you just startled me."

He dropped into the chair opposite her. "Sorry. My novel giving you the jitters?"

She widened her eyes. "I would ask you what's going to happen, but I don't want to ruin it."

He smiled, tiredness etched in his face. "You eat?"

She glanced at the clock. It was already nine-thirty. "Yes. I had something sent up. I hope you don't mind."

"No, that's fine. We had sandwiches around six." He reclined in the chair. "Did you know everyone is writing a thriller these days?"

"Oh?"

He chuckled. "Yeah, almost everyone who bought a book had to tell me they were either writing a novel or were going to. You up for some swimming downstairs?"

Horror of horrors. Jerrica could just picture herself, burn marks and all, in a bathing suit. The ladies had tucked a little two piece number under her nighties. Oh. My. Stars. That was most definitely out of the question. She could just see everyone gawking at her burn scars and Brock right there along with them.

"We could take a drive," she mumbled, doubting. "Or just watch TV. I recorded the game for you."

"I already heard the score. Maybe we can just turn in early. I begged off for part of the day tomorrow. Let's do something."

She shrugged. "Okay."

The next morning Jerrica yanked her suitcase open. Brock mentioned visiting the zoo, and she only had one pair of jeans left that were fairly clean.

"Jerrica?" His voice filtered through her door.

"What?" A sound of irritation crept into her voice.

"Why don't you wear one of those short outfits?"

"I wore one yesterday."

His muffled voice continued, "But you didn't step foot outside."

"I can't, Brock, you know I can't." She heard him sigh behind the door.

"Jerrica, I don't know anything anymore." His voice grew fainter as he left her door.

A moment later she heard his door close. A tremor snaked through her. She was getting so tired of not being able to do things, normal things that other people did without a thought. Hadn't she prayed about not wasting time? Precious minutes?

A boldness made her snatch up the short outfit. With a shot of defiance she left the room without her robe and marched through the living area to the bathroom. Just as she neared her destination, he came out of his room and shot her a glance, which turned into a long double take of her in her satin nightie. Her face flamed.

Her breath stuck in her throat. "I..."

There were no words.

Brock crossed his arms and leaned against the wall as he continued to stare at her. That signature eyebrow shot up, and a grin appeared on his face.

"I..." she tried again. *Buy Rosetta Stone now*. English version.

"You should wear that more often." His voice appeared thick.

She lunged into the bathroom and slammed the door.

Forty-five minutes later she sat on the side of the tub contemplating the bathroom's doorknob. Her hair was pulled back into a simple barrette, and she had on the soft blue shirt and jean shorts. Her feet were fastened into the new white sandals Beth had picked out before she had left. There was no reason to stay in that room any longer. None whatsoever.

Again her hand went to the scar that ran almost to her knee on the outside of her right leg. Most of the scarring had been on her torso, across her back and wrapping around her abdomen with a small area creeping up over her right shoulder. A capped-sleeved shirt easily hid it, but the shorts exposed her thigh. She lurched at a knock at the door.

"I hate to rush you, but I need to run a razor over this face of mine."

How had they scored a suite with one bathroom?

"Are you still in there?" He gave a bark of laughter at his joke.

"Jerrica?" He knocked louder, his voice rising.

"Let me in." The door shuddered, the doorknob twitched. "Jerrica, are you all right?"

More thumping against the door. She reached and turned the lock in the door. He burst into the room, his eyes flashing with fear that melted into anger. He grabbed her shoulders and gave her a small shake.

"Don't ever do that to me again."

Breath left her. "I'm sorry."

She rushed from the bathroom to her bedroom and slammed the door shut. The tears came as she hit the bed. He just didn't understand. Grabbing a pillow she smothered her head in it.

The door opened behind her. She froze, squelching the hiccups. It seemed a long time before she felt his finger trace the scar on her right thigh that she'd exposed in her flight from his anger. She couldn't move or breathe.

"It must have been very painful." His low voice caught her attention. He pulled the pillow from her face and lowered himself to the bed.

"I can't wear these shorts," she whispered through her tears, turning her face from him.

Gently he turned her to him and rubbed his thumbs beneath her eyes.

"No, I think you can't wear this eye makeup." He chuckled before growing serious. "I didn't mean to scare you, but I thought something might have happened."

"You think I'm a nutcase."

"I don't. I think you're beautiful."

She wiped her face, blackened with mascara. "Oh, yeah, just beautiful with mascara running down my face and a scar covering my leg."

He swept his hand across the scar and she trembled.

"Brock?"

"Shhh," he murmured as his face came closer, and his lips covered hers. The long sweet kiss sent a dizzying sensation rippling through Jerrica, and she rolled over onto her back. Brock brought himself up and over her, his arms wrapping around her. She lifted her arms to wrap around his neck, one hand finding the curling hair at his nape, still damp, as the kiss deepened.

He broke away, stood, and shuffled to the door. His gaze bore into hers as he took a deep breath. She propped herself on her bed, her stare probing his thoughts. His eyes raked her body and came to rest on her scar.

"I can't do this. I want you to be sure."

Strange how cold she felt without him. She stood and approached. "It's because of the scar, isn't it?"

His gaze swept her, desire still in his eyes. "You know that has nothing to do with it. I think we should slow this down."

She covered the scar with her hand, lowered her head, and turned to her suitcase. "I need to change."

"Please don't. You're beautiful and that scar changes nothing."

"But you—"

He took a deep breath and ran his hand through his hair. "What I'm doing now has nothing to do with your scar."

Feeling brazen, she turned and walked toward him. She leaned forward, just short of touching him and whispered, "What does it have to do with, then?"

A pulse pounded in his neck. Her bravado waned as his masculine scent drifted to her nose, and the cords in his neck tightened. He spun and left the room.

Instead of shaving, Brock spent the time waiting for her in his bedroom, praying. Praying for patience, praying for understanding, praying for control. Eventually she appeared at his door, still dressed in her shorts. He rose, and they made their way to the front of the hotel in silence. Once in the car, Jerrica fiddled with the satellite radio, scanning stations before settling on classical music.

"Mozart," she murmured as the next song started.

He shrugged. "I don't know. Maybe."

She turned her head to him, her face tense. "No, I know it is."

He raised his head a bit and nodded, not quite comprehending her tone.

She turned back to the window. Her expression was decidedly sullen. Perhaps she blamed him for the scene at the hotel, now that her brain functioned. He sighed to cover a muted growl.

Didn't she know that if he'd stayed in her room any longer, she'd truly be his wife in every way? And she would've despised him. She wasn't in the same place as he. He loved her beyond any obstacle.

She, however, still groped for who she was. Despite obvious clues. All this chemistry between them surely just brought more confusion for her. From the corner of his eye he saw her hand creep to her throat as they went under an overpass. What a paradox she was.

They arrived, parked, and entered. The sunny weather made it the perfect day to stroll through the place. The temperature rose, but under the shade trees the breeze cooled their skin. They walked in silence for a moment as Jerrica glanced at the crowds. Brock took her hand and gave a reassuring squeeze.

She turned to him, and he cocked a smile. "So I'm forgiven?"

Her brows shot up. "For what?"

"For kissing you at the hotel." He shot her a wicked glance. "Or for stopping."

Her mouth fell open. "Brock Levi Langston, I—"

She halted in the middle of the zoo road and snatched her hand from his. He stepped back from her, watching the emotions flit across her face. While she battled the new memory, he eased her to a nearby bench. Once seated, she avoided his gaze

"Don't say it." She held up her hand.

He slid his arm around her trembling shoulders. She obviously needed a moment to compose herself after his middle name had tumbled from her mouth. He raised a brow, yet couldn't resist. "I suppose this would be a bad time to ask about going to the gala tonight?"

Her eyes searched his, her face the color of ivory. "*Is* your middle name, Levi?"

He nodded.

"It's not looking good for my position of not being Jenna." She choked.

He rubbed her shoulder. "You act like it would be the worst thing ever."

She stared at her hands. "No, it wouldn't. But it makes me feel so off balance."

"I know."

"I don't really know what to say, what to think. I..." She slouched against the back of the bench.

He leaned back and gripped her upper arm. She didn't resist when he snugged her against his body. "Let's not dwell on it for now. Just something to ponder."

"I suppose." She sat up, but didn't pull away. "Since I have no idea where to go from here, I'll just change the subject. Let's just discuss this party thing. Part of me wants to go."

"Which part?"

"The part that isn't afraid."

"I guess I'm not familiar with that part." He chuckled.

She pulled from him and scowled. "Brock, it's not a joke. Everything is just a mess."

He reached over and took her hand in his. "I know, but sometimes, if I get you worked up enough, the part that isn't afraid shows up. And I really want to see you in that dress."

She refused to look at him. "You'll have to start now to aggravate me enough to attend that fancy shindig."

"That can be arranged." He laughed again.

❧ ⋯⋯ ❧

The afternoon passed quickly, and Jerrica counted it yet another victory as she'd only paused behind buildings "to get normal" twice. The seals charmed her as the zoo workers threw fish to them. It didn't even matter to Jerrica that it became crowded. Watching those shiny black animals dive in and swim acrobatically to be the first to snack had been captivating.

The "animal show" planned for the evening, however, was much less appealing. Once back at the hotel, she viewed herself in the full-length mirror. The long aquamarine dress brought out her eyes stunningly. Her freshly washed and dried hair fell in volumes of gold around her face. Not a salon cut and color, but passable.

Again her gaze fell on her reflection. No. She couldn't possibly go. Just trying on the charming dress. For just a moment. Or two.

She pressed her hand to her churning stomach. Still, she was pleased with her appearance. Part of her wanted to let Brock see her. Appreciate her. What a confidence booster it would be to watch appreciation jump in his eyes.

The gauzy sparkle of the material caught the light, and she clenched and unclenched her hands. It wasn't that she didn't want to attend. It was just that same old enemy. *Fear.* Realizing she shouldn't let it steal her time was so totally different than not allowing it to do so. She sank to the floor beside her bed. *Oh, Lord, show me a way.*

As she prayed, her face pressed into the mattress. The bed gave way beside her, and she peeked through her hands. Brock had settled to his knees next to her. He brought up his left arm and laid it across her shoulders. His other hand covered her praying hands. How wonderfully assuring to feel his warm strength. His support.

The verse Aunt Ellen had shared on the phone burned through her brain as she prayed. Two were indeed better.

And suddenly she knew the answer. It knelt next to her. She raised her head. "I'm going, Brock."

The party percolated in full swing by the time they drove up. The home boasted a wrought iron and brick fence with a guard house, complete with a uniformed security officer demanding invitations. The house itself took up a city block and the lawn and gardens yet another. The stone mansion was immaculate, lit majestically as they drew near. The landscaping spared no cost with a huge fountain and blooming bushes artfully trimmed.

The home boasted several floors with stone gargoyles hunched in sentry on the rooftop. A fairytale mansion. Or a wicked witch's castle. All in the perspective. Hers leaned toward the latter. Shocker.

Dear Dr. Frankenstein. Please seal your basement laboratory with the large padlock. Scratch that. Nine tons of sand will work better.

Inside resembled a palace filled with chandeliers and polished stone floors. Ornate pieces of art filled the corners and the stairway landing. One huge abstract sculpture took up the center of the foyer, a gargantuan iron column of flames. Colored spotlights gave the rusted flames a life as they eased on and off, drawing one's eye up the structure.

Water cascaded down a stone wall near the stairs that led to the balcony, and windows covered the far wall that rose up two stories. People dressed to the hilt in silk and satin floated about the entire floor and even filtered up the steps, drinks in hand. Surely she'd laid eyes on the world's entire population in the last two days.

Servers in black uniforms circulated with hors d'oeuvre platters. Beyond, French doors opened to an intricately designed garden that boasted tables and benches throughout to offer privacy for its occupants. A band to the left played classical tunes, and folks waltzed on the white shining dance floor. The crystal hanging overhead sparkled dizzily and appeared to be falling as Jerrica dared to glance up.

Brock, dressed in a full black, double-breasted tuxedo, easily fell into the group of well-dressed men around the dance floor. Yet, with his tanned face and dark eyes, he was drop dead handsome and drew more than his share of feminine glances. If everyone could have just dropped off Wile E. Coyote's cliff at that point, Jerrica could have easily allowed herself to enjoy the finery.

Brock steered her to a table near the right side next to the wall, picked up nametags, and settled both of them in a couple of chairs. Five others were already seated.

"Jerrica, this is Matt Peruski, associate editor, and his wife, Sofie. And this is the editor-in-chief, Treydon Rogers and his escort—"

"Natalie, Natalie Ospry." The Marilyn Monroe look-alike positively purred as she introduced herself. She stood and held her hand to Brock and lowered her torso in an already too low-cut dress. Focus point. Grand Tetons eye level.

Jerrica gritted her teeth and held back a snort as an unfamiliar emotion swelled inside her. She may be an amnesiac, but she recognized jealousy. Her gaze settled back on the woman's feline features, positively purring at Brock.

Wasn't she a peach? Perhaps there *would* be enough anger to see her through this challenging evening.

Chapter Nineteen

"Nice to meet you," the blond purred, her eyes glued to Brock's.

Jerrica forced her arms not to lock across her abdomen in her normal withdrawal reaction.

"You as well." Brock cleared his throat and leaned toward Jerrica. Nati-cat had no option but to seat herself. He motioned to the final man in the remaining seat. "And this is Randall Sipes. Randy hangs around up there at Aston's, but I don't think he really has a job, so to speak."

The man with thick black glasses glanced at Jerrica who peeked at him.

"Don't believe that con artist. He's just a writer, a rag writer I might add. He makes his living on lies. What I do is art. I'm the cover illustrator for Astons."

"Yes, Treydon's lauded your absolutely fascinating work, Randall," Natalie inserted, giving Brock another once over. Her full red lips curved into a Cheshire smile. "But I must say, I've always wondered what goes around in a writer's head? Give us a peek..."

"Brock," he supplied.

"Brock. Ummm. Nice strong name. Where do you get those ideas?"

Jerrica's ire rose another dozen fractions. Perhaps Treydon felt the tension too, as he leaned forward and draped his arm around the beauty's shoulders.

"So you've read my novels?" Brock inserted.

Natalie smiled and tossed her mane of iridescent blond hair. "Not exactly. But Treydon has told me so much it seems as if I have."

Brock's editor put up his hand conspiratorially and joked, "The closest she gets to literature is *Cosmopolitan*."

"Treydon," she admonished, pursing her ruby lips in a playful pout.

"So, Jerrica, how did you and Brock meet?" Randy interjected.

"Yes, tell us. Regale us with your tale of romance." Natalie pressed a glass of burgundy wine to her artificially full lips. Too full. *Rubber-baby's-buggy-bumpers.* But in the woman's eyes shone a direct challenge.

Regale you? Anger simmered vomit. Jerrica's imaginary response went into overdrive.

Perhaps you won't mind terribly if I barfed on your sequined, scarlet dress?

Or perhaps I could start out with that and then say, actually Brock might be my husband, but we don't know for sure because we're waiting for the Federal fingerprint match?

More? I'm a Smoky Mountain hillbilly, or at least that's the latest default setting for now. I adore prancing about the mountains and sequestering myself in workshops and even caves. You'll find it interesting that I'm fearful of practically everything—

including this whole weird over-the-top celebration thing, crowds and cities.

On a side note, just to be frank, your dress is too revealing—thanks, but no thanks for the close-up—and your interest in my date is beyond polite. Now, if you would excuse me, could I now flee from you and your arrogant attitude and condescending companions? That'd be great.

Instead, Brock answered for her. "We've known each other for years."

He slipped his hand down and eased her hand from clenching at her stomach. She took an unsteady breath to calm herself, and comfort flowed from his grip.

"Let's dance, darling," Treydon suggested to Natalie whose eyes were still firmly fastened on Brock.

"We just did, dear. Now Brock, perhaps you'd allow me to warm you up on the dance floor?"

Jerrica's innards burned.

Brock answered without a hitch. "I don't dance, Natalie."

"Pooh. What a shame." Out came the lips.

Off dashed Jerrica's droll musings. NYT Headline on Macy's Thanksgiving Day Parade Disaster: Overfilled Dumbo Balloon Collides the Time Warner Building. Dumbo's lips were obliterated. City crews still cleaning up lipstick.

Jerrica stabbed herself with her thumbnail to keep from going buggy. Brock rubbed his hand softly over hers.

"Very well, Treydon. Let's show them how."

Natalie rose, and Jerrica couldn't help but feel drawn to her movements. What a stunning woman, tall and reed thin in a red, sparkling dress. Skin tight and screaming, look at me! Her hair tumbled to her waist, skin glowing with an artificial tan that only heightened her beauty. Like an A-list movie, everyone at the tables around them gaped at her sauntering away. Brock whispered into her ear.

"Poor Treydon."

She turned to him. "What do you mean? She's probably the most gorgeous woman in this room. Maybe the world."

"Exactly, just like his first three wives. They're all fluff and no stuff."

"I guess appearances can be deceiving," she whispered.

Matt stood up across the table and helped his wife from her chair. "We'll leave you two with your sweet nothings while we dance. Excuse us." Matt smiled at his wife as they walked away.

Randy smiled and rose as well. "Off to the bar."

Left to themselves, Brock reached over and brushed his hand against her right shoulder blade. "Appearances mean very little."

She caught her breath when his dark eyes blazed into hers. "Physical scars bother you a lot, but it's only the outside. It's not what matters."

"Is it showing?" She grappled with her dress sleeve.

"You see? Sometimes you fear appearances. You fear people, concrete, a bit of scar showing. It doesn't matter." His breath brushed the skin beneath her ear.

Tingles of awareness rippled down her neck, yet fear nosed in. "Please, Brock. Is there any way we can leave?"

"No. Come with me."

He pulled her from the chair and steered her through the crowd. She dropped her eyes and followed him through the open French doors and into the garden until they left the other couples behind. The voices behind them grew fainter as he steered her between the garden statuaries and landscape. He finally stopped beside an arch flanked by a copse of pink budding Rose of Sharon bushes that filled the air with their sweet incense.

He drew her closer and she didn't resist. "Jenna, I'm sorry, Jerrica—blast. I know I've demanded a lot from you. I don't know of a more challenging point in my life."

She laughed softly. "Me either."

He chuckled with her, gathering her in his arms. For a moment he just gazed at her. Like a precious piece of art. It was both discerning and delightful. The intoxicating scent of the garden and his cologne mesmerized her. The evening insects serenaded them, and the sounds of the party drifted down to the private grove.

He leaned forward and kissed her so, so tenderly. Then he pressed his temple to hers and cradled her. She leaned forward and laid her head against his neck and soaked up the warm security of his arms. Jerrica wondered if he could hear the hammering of her heart. Their sighs laced the atmosphere of the garden surrounding them, melding them with landscape.

After several minutes, Brock pulled away and took her hand. "Better?"

Better? The earth now sang. Fear, jealousy, sarcasm now replaced with elation, wonder, and serenity. She nodded, not able to actually speak. Brock guided her back to the house while she strove to hang on to the powerful sensations. They alleviated her anxiety enough that she felt equipped to weather the party finale.

Jerrica managed to stay long enough to partake of the meal. Finally, Brock rose to leave, but Colonel Aston himself showed up, Treydon Rogers in tow, insisting on being introduced to Brock's date. They got away as quickly as possible, and the ride back to the hotel was a quiet one.

Once they arrived at their suite, Jerrica headed straight to her separate room. The atmosphere was too sparked with temptation to chance being alone with him any longer.

Yet, as she settled into her bed, her thoughts resurrected the stroll in the garden, the moonlight bathing them in iridescent light. Brock's hand in hers, his gentle kiss. It reminded her of...something. But she couldn't get a firm grasp on the foggy cloud of recall in the distance. A blessing in disguise.

Was she being dense? So many memories had come to light. Lately, Brock's stories of his marriage with Jenna didn't seem like his life with another. It seemed like life with her.

She exhaled a long breath of frustration. It couldn't be. Her treacherous mind revived the time spent in the garden with Brock once more, her heart tumbling at the memory of him pulling her close. She pressed her head against her cool pillow.

How rapidly she attached to this man who had come into her life so abruptly. She willed away any more thoughts and closed her eyes.

On Sunday Brock brought church to the living room of their hotel via the Wi-Fi. She knew it didn't take the place of going to worship, but she appreciated his gesture of understanding. He set up his laptop on the coffee table, and they seated themselves on the couch, Bibles in hand.

The speaker from a large local church delivered a moving message of how faith replaced fear. And even though she hadn't actually attended, it seemed as if the sermon had been tailor-made for her. She wrote down the verses he gave, intending to look them up later and commit them to memory.

After they worshipped, they spent the rest of the day resting and reading. Jerrica took the opportunity to ponder the verses of faith. The opposite of fear, so the speaker had said. The day balmed her in a restful, refreshing way.

For the next several days, Brock left her alone at the hotel and rejoined the show that had brought him here in the first place. He came stumbling in, near bedtime, but always wanted to chat. It became something she looked forward to.

Thursday dawned and she packed her things. Once loaded, they drove out of the city and stopped to eat at a fast food place. Then back on the road. The nervous tension vacated her body as they exited the busy area.

Still, a fruitful trip. She'd accomplished many things and hadn't kept Brock from doing the same. It was a quiet ride home, and she dozed through most of it. Brock carried her suitcase to her room as the evening shadows grew long. He handed her an unfamiliar box.

"What's this?"

"A little something I picked up in the city."

She set it on her bed and took the top off. Inside were professional watercolors, acrylics, and oils. A large round palate and a set of thirty professional brushes nestled next to the paints. She lifted her head, lips in an O.

"Oh, and this." He brought out a large bag containing several canvasses stretched over wooden frames and several art pads of different sizes.

"I thought since I'd be getting back to work tomorrow, closing myself in my study, you might enjoy a little painting." He dusted his hands as she turned her eyes on him.

"You've bought me so much already. I don't know what to say."

He set her suitcase by the dresser. "Nothing to say. Well, I'm off to check e-mails and read the paper."

"Brock." At the door he paused. Her chest swelled with gratitude and...some kind of deep warmth. "Thank you. Thanks for everything."

Every day since he'd left his wife's suitcase upstairs more than a week ago, Jerrica's precious face stayed imprinted in his brain. Brock stood up once more. His office chair seemed most uncomfortable today. Ergonomic lie. He was supposed to be writing, but all he could do was pace.

Pace to the window where he could watch Jerrica nestled on the patio swing, art pad on her lap. The lacework of sun through the trees highlighted her hair and made her seem almost dreamlike. He shook his head. What a pathetic sap. Next thing he knew he'd be writing romance.

About all he'd finished this week was standing at the window, barely getting five pages written. Almost afraid to take his eyes from her in case she dematerialized into electrons.

His gaze dropped, and he was pleased to see her in a pair of shorts. She looked so relaxed. He cringed when he thought of what he had to do. The trip to the city had brought them closer. Much closer.

Yet the subject of her mother couldn't stay hidden. Perhaps he would mention it after a few days, when she had some time to adjust. Who was he fooling? He was avoiding telling her, knowing it would destroy the delicate thread of trust they'd forged in St. Louis.

He didn't relish revealing her mother lived in a mental institution in Evansville. For the last three years he'd paid the woman's bills. Tried to visit her. He cinched his jaw. Next week. Maybe by some miracle the fingerprint match would arrive in the meantime. Then he could be openly honest about her mother. A mother she seemed so certain was dead.

Brock forked his hand through his hair and glanced at the clock. Too early for lunch, which disappointed him. He craved being close to her, if only over a bowl of soup. She'd mentioned her aunt and uncle on the way home, and he formulated a plan to visit soon if she wanted to go. The way his writing was going, he could easily turn it into a four-day trip. Maybe this weekend.

He stood for several more minutes, gazing. Loving her from a distance. Finally he decided to tell her about the plans to go to Tennessee this weekend. It'd give him a reason to sit beside her in the swing and talk.

Jerrica flung the window of her Smoky Mountain bedroom open, yanked up the screen, and leaned out to fill her lungs. The dark was filled with sweet moist air. Brock's suggestion of coming back to Tennessee was a balm to her spirit. Just absorbing the nuances of her home eased her tension.

A boom in the distance reminded her where Aunt Ellen, Uncle John, and Beth would be. Enjoying the fireworks while she embraced the silence of the house. Except for Brock. Poor man. He must be terribly disappointed in missing the festivities of the Fourth.

She pulled back in and shut the window. If memory served correctly, Mavey put on a nice show for such a small town. And she could see it from Beth's room. She threaded her way out the doorway, walked down the shadowed hallway, and entered the bedroom. Sure enough, the room lightened with the explosion of color in the distance. Their location on the mountain elevated them just enough to catch the show above the trees, yet keep the noise to a minimum.

After opening the window, she eased her body to the slightly pitched porch roof. With a smile tugging at her cheeks, she crossed her legs and leaned back against the house. She'd spent the Fourth on this porch roof last year, too. How strange she was. Afraid of St. Louis, the ballpark, the zoo, yet calmly perch on a roof or meander through a dark cave. It made no sense. No sense at all.

God, show me how to eliminate these ridiculous fears.

A window opened to her left. Brock stuck out his head, his line of vision taking in the spectacular fireworks. Jerrica studied his faint profile with the next burst of light. They'd been through so much already. That same warm sensation filled her insides.

Did he regret being married to a person who didn't even know him? He'd taken on all the challenges with such bravado, she couldn't help but admire him. A smile lit the side of her cheek. Still, the little boy in him couldn't seem to resist the charm of a little gunpowder and fire.

"Nice show, huh?"

His head swung in her direction, and he gave a chuckle. "I never know where I'm going to find you."

"Sorta keeps you on your toes, right?" Was she flirting?

He disappeared for a moment and then his leg shot through the opening followed by his entire body. With care he scooted over the coarse shingles to bump knees with her.

Brock chuckled. "Hey."

She smiled, the moon emitting just enough light to illuminate his face. "You didn't have to stay in just because I couldn't go in town. I apologize for being such a circus freak. Again."

His brows drew together. "You're not a freak. You're you."

"But you're missing the whole festival."

A slow smile stretched across his face. "I'm right where I want to be."

She scanned back at the new display in the sky. "Can I tell you something?"

"Anything."

Was he serious? That man really put himself out there. "When you first came, I thought you were Frankenstein's Monster."

He stiffened, but his face remained in shadow. "O—kay."

"Sorry. Will it make you feel any better that I amended the notion and decided you were more like Gregory Peck?"

A grunt. "On a writing assignment in Rome? Does that make you the princess?"

"No. I'm merely the lowly Peasant of Fear. Or Circus Freak. I answer to both."

A snort of laughter met her ears. "I might agree to the first, but not the second."

A particularly intricate explosion burst into the air below them. Brock pointed. "Now that's some serious gunpowder."

Serious. Yes. "I have something else to confess."

"Oh, boy. You thought I was Jack the Ripper? The Unabomber?"

A small snicker escaped her. "No. Nothing like that. This one is about me."

His hand slid into hers. "You've come a long way. St. Louis proved that."

"Uh-huh. But, what if the big one's still out there?"

Again a boom. "The big one?"

"That big yet-to-be-discovered unknown. One that makes my brain melt down. One I can't handle. Do you think that is possible? Not being able to handle what comes along?"

He cleared his throat before answering. "A few years back I memorized 2 Corinthians 4:8-9. 'We are afflicted in every way, but not crushed; perplexed, but not despairing; persecuted, but not forsaken; struck down, but not destroyed.' I think God's enduring hope is contained in those verses. The Lord also promises to be by our side always."

He memorized verses. Just like she did. She sniffed and fixed her gaze on the blue rocket that exploded into a myriad of colors. A distant muffled boom followed. How many times had she felt completely crushed, in the grip of fear? "Did you memorize that verse when you heard about Jenna?"

He grew very still. "I did."

Tears came to the back of her eyes to think of his grief and pain to experience such a deep loss. It would be very easy to boohoo big time right now. "I'm sorry you had to go through that."

"I'm sorry you have to go through this." His voice was hushed. "I know you still can't fully believe it, but I know you're my wife."

Her lips tightened, yet tears rushed to her eyes as another explosion lit the air. The evidence piled higher each day.

Brock's eyes took in her face. "Don't be angry."

She lowered her head. "I'm not. I'm...confused. So totally confused. Much of what I thought was honest-to-God true, isn't. I've had so many memory recalls since meeting you, it's frightening. It's just so hard to believe I would forget everything. It makes me wonder if I'm crazy."

He caressed her hand in his. "You're not crazy. You've pulled back to protect yourself. It's a natural response."

Despite the seriousness of the conversation, or maybe because of it, she giggled. "I think you've bumped up into Beth's spot. My new unofficial shrink."

A low rumble emitted from his chest. He adjusted his legs, laying one out flat and pulling one knee up, never letting go of her hand. "Nothing a little sock puppet show can't cure."

A fit of laughter grabbed hold of her.

His hands jiggled hers. "I like hearing you laugh. You were so carefree as a teenager."

She stared at his profile. Even though he spoke to her as Jenna, she didn't bother to correct him, but fell into his recollection. "Was I?"

"Yeah. A buddy and I financed our college tuition by lifeguarding-slash-maintenancing our way through church camp. You were one I always remembered from year to year."

The memory of the birthmark near his belly button bubbled in her brain. She kept her voice carefree. "Oh. Why?"

He shrugged. "Well, you were adorable. Of course, I say this from a standpoint that you were just a teen and I, a college student. So I entertained no romantic illusions at that point."

A snort burst out. "I would hope not."

"Not that it didn't stop you from sharpening your flirting skills on me. You and your little gal pals. Your freshman year, if I remember correctly, you were so skinny, and you could flip off that diving board without fear."

"Me?"

"Oh, yeah. If you weren't flipping off the diving board, you were flipping across campus."

"I...don't remember any of that."

He shrugged against the house as yet another display of light spiraled in the distance. "One particular year you did backflips from the sanctuary to the dining hall. Quite a feat. Drew quite a crowd."

Jerrica remained silent and nibbled her lip. Had she been so outgoing? Would she ever be free of the binds that kept her memory prisoner?

"You had all the little boys drooling after you, fighting for a seat by you at the chow hall. Pretty entertaining."

"Great."

"Then your senior year came. Whoa, something had happened to you."

Jerrica's brows puckered. "What do you mean?"

He laughed. "Oh, it happens to most girls."

"What?"

"You grew into yourself." His gaze locked onto hers.

Her mouth dropped open. "I don't know what you mean."

He cleared his throat with an artificial cough and continued. "Let's just say it wasn't just the high school boys that were drooling."

She couldn't resist tilting her head a bit coquettishly. "Like you?"

He rested his head against the white siding of the house. "You better believe it. But I went back to college to finish. Then, lo and behold, we linked up at my cousin's wedding."

The crickets chirruped around them, and the scent of honeysuckle floated to the roof. He leaned forward while a burst of light shimmied behind him. Yet the light and the hot moist air couldn't explain the heat that wavered between them. She couldn't look away.

"You were yet to turn eighteen, and I still couldn't stay away."

"You robbed the cradle."

"Not exactly."

An ache fluttered in her chest as his hand tightened on hers.

"Your mother gave her blessing, and we hardly parted after that."

She pulled away from him and yanked her hand free. "My mother would never do that."

A blast of air sounded from the man next to her. "She would and she did. Had the wedding arranged in a matter of months."

Why did he have to ruin the moment? After flipping over to her knees, she crawled to her window, and then poked her head back. "Just when I think I'm understanding some of this mess, you tell me something so outrageous, I know you're lying."

She slid inside Beth's window and slammed the sash shut. Her fists collided with her hip bones. Well, that would leave a bruise. A gruff huff escaped her lips, whether from anger or the chemistry of being so near him. Both physically and emotionally. She pressed a hand to her chest. A dark shadow appeared at the door.

"It's true, Jenna."

Jenna. She shouldered around him and strode down the hallway. "Stop it, Brock. My mother is dead."

He grunted behind her but didn't follow. Once she reached her room, just to add a pointed exclamation mark, she slammed the door.

Brock stood in the hallway, eyeing the closed door in the near darkness. Just when he thought he was making some progress, she shoved him away. Literally. He pushed his hands deep in his pockets. Mentioning her mother had turned the tone of the conversation fast. Why he'd chosen that moment, he'd never know. He could be kissing her at this very moment.

He spun, sending a hand through his hair. No fixing it now. At least the air was cleared. Jerrica was in for some surprises soon. He hoped she recharged here in the mountains, for she had to face the big unknown. Had to face her mother. She would have to lean on God's promises, on His words.

He returned to the guest room and pushed the door shut. "'Early to bed, early to rise.'"

Must be the mountain air that set him to quoting. Uncle John would be proud. No sense in hashing around the scene, though he'd been close to stealing another kiss. If she'd allowed it. If only he'd kept his mouth shut and leaned towards her instead.

The room lit up for several seconds, and Brock wondered if Mavey was putting on its fireworks finale. Then everything went dark with only the moonlight for company. He scrubbed his fingers through the stubble on his chin. What did the future hold? Would they celebrate the Fourth of July as a couple next year? Or would she be here, while he gallivanted from one hotel to another, pitching books and squelching her memory?

He dropped to his knees and leaned against the quilt-covered bed. No time like the present to entreat the One who kept it all in the palm of His hand.

Chapter Twenty

A unt Ellen had breakfast on the table by the time Brock reached the kitchen the next morning. Uncle John sat in his usual Captain's chair, sipping java. Beth cleaned and sorted eggs. It was as if he and Jenna had never left. Yet his wife was notably absent.

"Good morning." Aunt Ellen greeted as she flipped one last egg frying in a greasy pan.

"Morning."

Beth turned a sunny smile on him. "Sleep well?"

"I suppose."

"You sure missed a great fireworks show last night." Beth carried the egg cartons and deposited them at the bottom of the refrigerator.

He lowered himself into the usual spot at the table. "Actually, Jerrica and I got to see some of it."

The room stilled and three gazes locked onto him.

"What?"

"Jerrica and fireworks don't mix." Beth shuddered her head like a shiver.

He shrugged. "She's done a lot of things she didn't used to do."

Beth sat in the chair opposite. "Interesting."

Aunt Ellen placed the plate of eggs on the table to join the bacon, sausage, and gravy. "Better go urge her down, Beth. She must be sleeping in."

Brock leaned back in his chair, enjoying the smell of the country breakfast. Coming here was like stepping back into his grandparents' kitchen. Aunt Ellen turned and pulled huge browned biscuits from the oven. Beth reappeared at the door. Her face said it all.

Brock rose. "She's not there, is she?"

Beth shook her head, regret evident in her eyes.

Aunt Ellen pulled the oven mitts from her hands. "I'm sure she's around somewhere. Let's just all sit and eat."

"I need to find her." Brock pushed out of his chair and moved to the back door. "I apologize for leaving breakfast."

The older woman waved a hand at him. "Go on with ya now. We understand and we'll keep a couple extra plates warm."

Brock pushed open the screen door and pulled the storm door shut behind him. His stomach rumbled in disappointment, leaving the food behind. Yet a thread of dread snaked through him. She'd been doing so well. He hoped she was just off tending her crafts in the barn, and that last night's conversation hadn't sent her into the mountains.

But a quick check at the workshop revealed an empty barn. His gaze traveled to the lower section below where he'd exited the cave several weeks back. He grabbed a flashlight from the barn and set off.

The weeds had grown quite a bit since his last visit. Uncle John hadn't mown down this slope, and after wading through waist high weeds, he had to pull away a swathe of Virginia Creeper vines to reveal the low opening to the cave. With a deep breath of reluctance, he shouldered his way in.

He clicked on the beam, thankful for strong batteries and made his way forward, hunkered over. As the ceiling rose to full height, he stood and inhaled a lungful of dank air. He couldn't resist running the beam over the ceiling, reading the names burnt there and remembering his conversation with Jenna, the cut on her knee, her beautiful legs. He pushed away the wisp of indulgence and entered the corridor that would lead him through to the main cavern.

The going was slow, with the rocks below him slick with moisture, while the ceiling waited to take a chunk out of his head. He reached the row of columns where the path narrowed when echoes reached his ears. Jenna? He flicked his light off for a moment, hoping to catch sight of any beams ahead. The sound of two faint voices bouncing off the cave's walls made him resist flipping back on the only light in the pitch blackness.

He closed his eyes and tried to lock the mumbling echoes into words, but failed. They grew distant, and he raised his head and opened his eyes. To his left came the slightest flicker of light. Seemed strange considering the exit loomed in front of him and shortly angled right.

He peered through the complete dark trying to find it again, but failed. Forcing himself not to move, he allowed time to tick by until he was satisfied the owners of those voices had moved on.

He flicked his flashlight on. Could Jenna be down the new pathway? Only one way to find out. He pivoted on the balls of his feet and headed left, squeezed between formations and down an unfamiliar route. His beam searched the passageway as he picked along.

The path rose and the dirt appeared drier. To the left and right of him were raised shelves of cave floor, with the ceiling only about three feet higher. Soda straws and columns decorated the shelves. He flicked the beam down. It almost appeared as if this trail had been hand dug.

Through the shelf on his left he could see the same path continue around a hairpin bend. He sidestepped more rock formations and continued. A shaft of light could be seen now some distance ahead. *Sunlight.* It grew stronger and stronger as he approached. He flicked his flashlight off as he reached the turn to the right that would obviously guide him out of the cave. With some stealth, he peeked around the corner and peered up. The path rose sharply. With a set of stairs. *Stairs?*

Two figures moved past the cave entrance, and he ducked back. He froze. The light brightened on the dirt floor again so he chanced a second look. Ceramic pots filled two broad benches at the base of the steps and lined the edges of the stairs all the way to the top. Large crocks, small ones, and every size in between.

Men's voices drifted down to him from the entrance, one gruff one and one youthful. Safe to say Jenna wasn't at the top of the stairs. And from the looks of the evidence, this cave had somehow transported him to the other side of the mountain straight into Haywood McCoy's lair. Memories of bullets buzzing by his head sent him ducking back behind the wall. Best to retrace to the main path.

There was no way he was going to come face to face with that man unarmed. Haywood was a hundred rungs or higher on the crazy ladder. Besides, he'd come to find his wife.

He stepped out to take the dugout path when a phone rang above him. His muscles ceased his motion to an abrupt stop.

"I tell you, we're covered. How you calling me in the middle of the day anyway?" Haywood's voice trickled down the artificial stairwell. His heavy steps shuffled and his voice got clearer. Brock hurried around the U and ducked. If Haywood took the path, he was done.

"Git, Delbert, I mean it."

Silence lengthened. Then a curse. "I know. Now you're using all my battery with your jibberish. I done told ya everything. They ain't left yet."

Again the cavern grew silent and Brock waited.

"Marcy—" He swore a long streak. "I'm done with ya."

The snap of a flip phone closing echoed through the chamber, and heavy footsteps grew louder. Brock rose but stayed hunkered as he crept back to the main trail. As he scrambled back to the original entrance, Brock pondered the name he'd overheard and the fact the nasty recluse even possessed a phone.

He pulled his mind to his search. What did it matter that some old kook used the cave to store his wares? And used a cell phone. In a cabin devoid of electricity.

He worked his way back to where Jenna had first brought him into the cave, ever keeping an ear for sounds of trailing hippies. But he made it to the low entrance without incident and dropped to his knees to crawl out. The last several feet grew claustrophobic, and he was very glad to step out into the early sunshine.

Birds chirped in the canopy of trees overhead. The lay of the mountain had sprouted a thick crop of undergrowth, vines devouring bushes and trees, turning the plants into mounds. Brock searched his immediate area for poison ivy. Finding none, he brought up his eyes and scanned the options. Jenna had insisted walking straight ahead would lead him back to the house. But there was no indication through the underbrush and thick trees that this might be true.

He glanced left and right. The church lay to the left, so he set off right, swiping away tall brush and leaping over deteriorating tree trunks scattered here and there. It probably wasn't a great idea to set out alone without a real sense of where he was going, but he was determined to find his wife.

⁘ ······ ⁘

Jerrica pushed the drawer closed one last time and set the small box back on the shelf. She turned the set of wedding rings in her hands before sliding the set onto her left ring finger. A perfect fit. She exhaled in a rush. The only thing left to do was to confront Brock. Surely he'd recognize the rings if he'd bought them.

Would he be dishonest about it, like he had last night? She gritted her teeth. How dare he insinuate that her mother was alive. What more proof did the man need than the graves? She shrugged and settled on the low bunk she'd slept on what seemed like eons ago. Aunt Ellen would have breakfast up soon. She'd stayed too long.

Her eyes studied the sturdy log structure around her. So many times this place had been a sanctuary. Now, she blew more air from her lungs, if she were honest, it made her feel alone. Her brow grew tight with consternation. How she'd begged the Creator for Brock to drive off and leave.

At the present moment, the thought of him departing without her seemed almost unbearable. She'd grown to trust him, and the thought of him lying to her just didn't...sit well.

Maybe he was misinformed, or—something. She knew with everything in her being that her mother had passed, knew it to the depths of her soul. Yet believing Brock deceived her didn't make sense. She pulled the wedding band and engagement ring from her hand and stuffed it into a tight pocket in her jeans.

Maybe he'd lied about their whole relationship. Yet she hadn't remembered anything until Brock had entered her life.

She closed her eyes and clenched her hands. Even with all the strange things she recalled, still, it proved difficult to conceive that she could be Jenna. Distant footsteps opened her eyes. No four-beat pattern. Besides, the sun was up. The deer and her offspring would've already found a spot to rest for the duration of the day.

No, the footfalls grew louder, and the foundation of the cabin picked up the low, hesitant thumps across the soil like a speaker.

Uncle John? No, he wouldn't be coming from the northeast. She rose and drew to the door. As quietly as she could, she turned the handle and eased the door open.

Brock stood some twenty feet in front of the cabin. His face creased in welcome, and Jerrica couldn't stop the tendril of pleasure that trailed through her. She returned a small smile.

"Hey."

Her cheek dented. His simple greeting glided to her like a bashful flirt. "Hi."

His eyes scanned the area and lit on the cabin. "This your home away from home?"

She nodded.

"Not a bad little shack."

With a deep breath, she turned to assess the structure, sticking her hands into her pockets. Her fingers collided with the ring set. She bit her lip and kept her gaze on the cabin. "Uncle John does some work on it occasionally. Probably just for me."

The corner of his mouth deepened. "Probably."

"I'm late for breakfast, aren't I?"

"Yep."

She drew in a deep breath. Her weekend back home seemed to be disappearing into avoiding the ones she so longed to see. "Sorry."

He crossed his arms and shrugged. "Just glad I found you. Your aunt said she'd keep our plates warm."

She caught her breath. "You haven't eaten either? I'm always causing some kind of stir. I thought I could slip down here for a quick visit, and, I don't know, it didn't go quite that quick."

"Nothing to worry over."

His deep eyes bore into hers. She licked her lips. It was obvious why Jenna had chosen him. Even at this distance, she could feel the attraction pulse. Her stomach tightened. Probably hunger. Or anxiety.

He moved closer and her muscles tensed. She laid a hand to her middle.

"Listen, about last night."

She waved her hand in dismissal. "Forget it. Consider it the rantings of a nutty woman."

Beside her now, he reached out and took her hand. In clear daylight it was easy to see the tenderness in his gaze. Had that been present last night in the near dark?

"Stop insulting yourself. You're not nutty, weird, or anything else. You're searching, and we all understand that."

He squeezed her hand, and a breathlessness seized her lungs.

"Come on. Let's get back."

They strode through the tall undergrowth with their hands linked. And for once, Jerrica reveled in not being alone.

By late evening, Uncle John and Beth had left to check out a few of the cabin rentals, and Aunt Ellen had settled on the porch for a little reading. Brock had disappeared into his room, so Jerrica took the opportunity to head to the workshop. If she could finish a tubful of elf shelf-sitters, Uncle John would be ahead for the holiday rush.

With a contented sigh, she stopped at the goat enclosure and slathered affection on the hyper animals before heading off to the barn. To her left, Katie came bolting through the trees, threw down the huge bicycle she was riding, and jumped off. She swiped a hank of long bangs out of her eyes and gave a hundred-watt smile.

"You're back, you're back." She dove into a catapult hug. "I couldn't believe it when my brother told my mom. I hurried right over 'cause I know you need help with those sitting-down elves."

Jerrica laughed. "Oh, Katie, you are a blast of energy. How did your brother know I was here?"

Katie shot off to open the workshop door and turn on the lights. "I don't know. Wow. Those elves have real jingle bells."

She flounced over to the buckets of gold and silver bells and thrust her hands into them. Several of them overflowed and jangled to the concrete floor.

Jerrica parked her hands on her hips. "Remember, child. You're cleaning up what you wreck."

"Huh? Oh, sure." She rattled handfuls of the bells till it sounded like a dozen Santas arriving on Christmas night.

"Cool. A ginormous bell." She rushed over to a wreath Jerrica had started, utilizing bells the size of her fist.

"Yeah, easy there. I finished that yesterday. Think it'll sell?"

The imp nodded. "Definitely. Who wouldn't want a ginormous bell, circley-mabob on their front door for Christmas?"

A snort burst from Jerrica. "Exactly. And just for future reference, the circley-mabob is called a wreath."

She perched herself on the stool and started mounting heads on the velvet bodies that Aunt Ellen had painstakingly sewn. Katie leaped about the room for a few more moments, laying her grungy hands on nearly every project in the room. "So tell me about this accident you were almost involved in."

The child became immobile and threw out her hands. "Scariest day of my life."

"So I hear."

"That monster truck went zooooom, right over me. I thought I'd be squished for sure."

Moisture came to Jerrica's eyes. "I'm so glad that God protected you."

Katie shrugged and propped herself at the counter. 'Yeah."

"Wait. If you're going to help, go wash your hands. You know my rules."

Katie grinned and saluted. "Yes, ma'am. Oh, that's how we sang the 'Lord's Army' song at Vacation Bible School."

She jumped down and twirled. "Listen, I can make up my own song to the same tune. We did that at school. Here goes: I may never make an elf, good enough to sit on a shelf, clean enough to please yourself—that's you, 'cause nothing else rhymes—I may never get the head on right, but I can still sing silly songs."

The child parked herself next to Jerrica, still humming the tune. "You make up one."

Jerrica pulled the wooden head from the girl's hand. "Go wash."

"Okie-dokie, artichokie." She bolted for the sink. "Do your song while I wash."

With a steady hand, Jerrica held the wooden head until the hot glue held and then set it aside, crossing his stuffed legs. "You mean to the same tune?"

"Yep."

"Hmmm. Let's see. I may never remember ever-y-thing, get a contract to sing, never wear a diamond ring, I may never be as brave as a king, but I'm very glad to see you. How's that?"

"Meh, needs work."

A laugh burst from Jerrica. "I really did miss you, Katie."

"I know. I'm adorable." She grinned and crossed her eyes. "Oooh, baby, I'm camping in the back yard tonight. You gotta come check out our tent."

Jerrica's brow rose while the hyper child juggled a wooden sphere. With quick hands, Jerrica grabbed it before it bounced to the concrete. "Be careful. Who's tent?"

"Me-N-Booger."

"Ewww. Not sure I want to."

"No, he's a kid. My youngest brother. He's eleven. That's just what we call him 'cause he eats his."

Jerrica shot her a glare.

Katie shrugged. "I know TMI, right?! And G-R-O-S-S. I've tried to tell him how disgusting it is, but he's still pickin' and eatin.'"

"Seriously, let's change the subject. Quick."

Katie giggled. "Wait till dark, though, 'cause we're gonna have a fire and we've got marshmallows. I'll keep Booger out of 'em."

Jerrica cringed. "Good to know."

They worked side by side for a few moments. Jerrica arranged the fifth one in a row, legs all crossed.

Katie paused and tilted her head at the little homemade creatures. "You know. People really like those elf thingeys, but they're just plain creepy."

Jerrica laughed and leaned over to hug her little neighbor. Life was never boring when she was about. "I thought you said clowns were creepy."

Her eyes grew big. "They are. At least the elves don't have all that stuff on their faces. But they still just sit there and watch you. And that's just freaky."

Katie bounced off the stool and ran toward the door. "Welp, gotta go. I'll see ya tonight."

The smile on Jerrica's face didn't waver once for the next twenty minutes. Even when Katie slammed the door.

Chapter Twenty–One

After dinner Jerrica made excuses about finishing a few more elves and slipped out while Uncle John had Brock fast in his quoting clutches. She gave a small grin at his face, reflecting a shred of helplessness. She grabbed the mosquito repellent from the pantry. Katie's mother wouldn't remember to spray the kids down, and poor Katie and—dare she think it—Booger, would be covered in insect bites. Even if they only stayed out for a few hours.

Once out the door, she took off down the slope towards Katie's house and soon hit the dirt road. Uppermost in her mind. Avoid the Booger marshmallow. A snort threatened to escape, and she clapped a hand over her mouth. Seemed a sacrilege to giggle in the peaceful darkness.

The dirt on the road met her olfactory system, and a secret smile stretched across her face. It smelled like home. She'd miss that.

But Jenna had grown fond of the huge home she and Brock occupied. Or rather his "ginormous house?" Oh, yes. Katie would be sure to express it that way. Too bad she couldn't sneak the tot home with her.

The path to Katie's took some twenty minutes, but guided by a cloud-shrouded fingernail moon made it most pleasant. Still she was winded when she turned into the yard. Avoiding the run-down house, she set out directly for the back yard where a little fire illuminated a ragged comforter stretched across the clothesline. Katie gave a squeal and bounded toward her.

"I knew you'd come." She yanked her toward the door of her abode. "See, we got a sheet for the floor and sleeping bags."

A lanky boy sat inside with vacant eyes, mouth hanging open. His face appeared as dirty as Katie's.

"And who's this?"

Katie grumbled. "You know. Booger."

Jerrica suppressed a smile. "I'm sure he has a name."

"Naw. We all forgot it if he did."

The grimy boy grabbed a marshmallow from the bag and stuffed it into his mouth. "You're a poop head."

Katie set her hands on her hips and slung her chin at him. "Am not."

"Am too."

"Not."

"Am."

Jerrica bobbed her head back and forth to clear it, not sure what was worse. The use of English or the fact that Booger had now contaminated all the marshmallows. "Anyway. Are you two sure you're going to be able to stay out here all night? By yourselves?"

"Sure." Katie exclaimed, throwing her hand out. "We do this all the time. Besides, we got Thunderdog. He's a watchdog. He'll protect us."

Katie wrapped her arm around the huge German shepherd, shaggy-dog mix that had threaded his way through the far open end of the tent and let out a huge dog smile, his pink tongue dripping with saliva. "You should stay with us."

"Although it sounds fun with you, Booger, and now, Thunderdog," she pulled away a little to get a breath of air free of dirty-dog smell, "I'll have to say no. I need to visit with my family. I have to leave on Monday."

"Oh, man. You just got here." Her face brightened. "At least you can have a marshmallow."

Jerrica laughed and backed out of the doggy-scented tent. "No, I've had plenty to eat tonight, but I'll watch you cook one."

Katie's countenance fell for a moment before she recovered a bit. "Oh, all right. Gimmie the stick, Booger."

She wrenched the stripped willow from the unsuspecting hand of her brother and darted from the listing tent. "Here. Watch me."

Jerrica stuck her hands deep in her pocket, her smile dimmed by the ring she found there. But she shook it off and listened to the excited chatter of the child beside her. When the marshmallow caught fire, she waved the stick until it went out, and then gingerly popped it into her mouth.

"See? I cooked it by myself," she mumbled around the white mush in her mouth.

"Awesome."

"Sure you don't want one? They're de-lish-ee-o-so!"

Her laughter came low as she thought about the extra disgusting ingredient. "I'm going to pass. Come by and see me tomorrow if you can, okay? If you come with me to church, we could do some elves afterwards."

"Naw, better not. Ma ain't happy tonight."

Jerrica nodded, "Well, here. When you are done cooking and away from the fire, put on some of this bug spray. Make sure, ahem, Booger gets some too. But stay away from the fire. Got it?"

"Sure."

"Okay. Just keep the whole can. I better go." She gave a parting smile and waved at Booger before she crept to the edge of the yard. Behind her Katie tossed marshmallows to Thunderdog, laughing when he bobbed his head at the heat of the offering.

As she approached the house, she could hear a one-sided conversation, and from the sound of the voice and the smell of a cigarette, Jerrica knew it had to be Katie's mother, Marla Hawk, on the open front porch. She stepped out to veer through the woods and wished she had her flashlight. It would be tricky going with the moon's meager light.

"I told you. J is still here with her rich husband." Her hiss smacked with a northern, nasal accent. "What I want to know is, where's the money? We've been waiting a long time. Raising a kid ain't cheap."

Jerrica froze. What in the world? Who was J? Definitely sounded shady. None of her business. Though, she did worry about Katie. She angled to the tree line, wondering if she could navigate the woods without setting up a racket.

"Delbert keeps me informed 'bout their comings and goings. Besides, she doesn't remember a thing. Can't even go into town for the Freedom Festival, so what do you think she's gonna do? Run for president?"

Again Jerrica grew still. Perhaps she wasn't crazy after all. How many people in the Mavey area had amnesia? And hadn't Katie said something about her oldest brother knowing she was back? What would Mrs. Hawk care about her activities? She reversed her direction and approached the side of the house.

"I know, Marcy. Do you think I'm an idgit born four hours ago? We've done our part, been doing it for three years. Now you do yours. Get us the money." A chair screeched across the porch concrete. "When we agreed to leave Chicago, you promised we'd be swimming in it. I ain't doing any swimming down here with the yocals." A long pause. "That ain't good enough." A door opened. "Well, I know for a fact that Langst—"

The bang of the front door snapped the word in half, leaving Jerrica with her mouth hanging open. Langston? Brock's last name? She buried the ring set deep in her pocket and hurried through the yard to the road, anxious to get out of sight of Katie's mother.

Brock finally found a pause to excuse himself from the quotation marathon and made his way toward the back door. Jerrica had taken off again. This could get tiresome. He carefully let the door slide shut to avoid notifying the entire house of his departure. Where had she gone this time?

In the dim illumination of the moon, he could make out a figure advancing toward him down the slope of the hill some distance down the dirt road. He set his teeth and loped toward the dim form, hoping to high heaven it was Jerrica. As he drew closer, he recognized her, and his heart thumped to a slower pace. "Hey."

She paused in the road. "You following me?"

He shrugged. "Just concerned."

Jerrica fell in step beside him. "I just went to see Katie, that's all. So I'm not likely to be torn asunder by bears tonight."

Irritation snapped at him, and he pulled her to a stop. "Whoa, whoa, now. Let's set the record straight. There actually are bears in those hills and hollers and a lot of other dangerous animals that could indeed tear you apart."

She stuck her hands in her back pockets and lowered her head. Was she mad? Contrite? It was hard to read in the dark. "It only makes sense to be careful. That's all I'm saying."

Her head nodded before she looked up. "I know. I'm just so used to taking off. I don't mean to scare anyone."

She grasped his elbow and pulled him to a walk. "I am a little chilly, though."

A start of surprise arrowed through him. He disengaged his arm and wrapped it around her shoulders. "You wouldn't think it'd be so chilly in July."

"I know, right?"

When she didn't pull away from him, he soaked up the intimacy of the moment. He rubbed her upper arm, feeling the goose bumps across her skin. "Everything okay with Katie?"

"Uh-huh. I...suppose."

They walked in silence for a distance, and Brock inhaled the moist greenery at the edge of the road and raised his eyes to the last shadow of the mountains in the distance. The cicadas serenaded them, and the moon moved out from behind the cloud, brightening everything.

Brock paused their linked parade and turned her towards him in the middle of the road. He cupped her face and eased it up. He perused the beautiful planes of her face, and she stilled.

"I know this is all very hard to believe, but I care what happens to you."

"Even if I'm not Jenna?"

His breathing mixed with hers and proved intoxicating to his senses. "Yes."

It was true. He knew who she was, but this new her had grabbed his heart like the previous Jenna never had. And he knew in his heart that he loved her even more fiercely than he had before.

She brought her hands up to his forearms. "Brock, I—"

He lowered his head. If only he could taste her lips, just for a fraction of a second, it would make facing her fury worth it. When she didn't stop him, he touched his lips to hers and reveled in their softness, their fullness.

He trailed a string of kisses along her jaw and then returned to her mouth. He tugged her closer, and Jerrica's soft sigh spurred him on to deepen the kiss. Her hands ran through his hair, her lips eagerly seeking his.

What?

Then she yanked from him. "I think I know my way home from here."

She pivoted and began to run up the road. Brock let her go. His senses still reeled from her response. She not only let him kiss her, she'd kissed back. Fervently. He sucked in a deep breath, elated yet dejected. Hope buoyed in his gut. Once the double identity was put to rest for her, maybe they could salvage their marriage.

Uncle John and Aunt Ellen chatted companionably in the front seat of the van while Brock chimed in occasionally. Jerrica kept her eyes fixed on the darkening landscape as it passed, as the trees whizzed by. She pondered last night's moonlight make-out session. Like two teenagers in the backseat of his parent's Volvo.

There was no other way to describe it. She'd liked it. Waaaay too much. And now. Plum scared witless of her own emotions. She couldn't even trust herself.

She face-palmed her forehead. The eavesdropped conversation. Why hadn't she shared the strange one-sided conversation Mrs. Hawk had conducted on her porch?

Well, A, the kiss had thrown everything off. B, the kiss had thrown off everything. Yep. Pretty much covered it. *No matter how you sliced it.*

Brock. Wow. Uh. No. *No.*

Her heart thumped at the memory. Not from fear this time. *Think about the conversation, stupid, not your runaway passion.* Okay. Weird convo. Mrs. Hawk said J. and Langst—something. Had Katie's mother really been talking about her? Should she share the information with Brock?

Maybe it all meant nothing. She didn't need one more piece of evidence to prove she was as half-cracked as a dropped egg. Brock already had a front seat on her bizarre life. *The Bizarro Show of Jerrica Rankin*. Sock puppets not included.

His low chuckle drew her eyes. Uncle John and his stories. So back to the Mrs. Hawk saga. What did she know, really? No full names were actually used. Except Marcy. Whoever that was.

Looking into his deep dark eyes, doubting her as she spouted such drivel would just be the limit. Especially now. With this...heat between them. It had to stop. Immediately. How she'd lost her head out there, she had no clue. Maybe the moonlight. Maybe his gentleness. Maybe just his maleness. *Gorgeous Gregory Peck, she swooning in the moonlight.* She gulped to herself. Choose all of the above. Bottom line. He wasn't hers to want. Besides, didn't she have enough issues anyway?

Definitely. So keep the alone times limited. Yes. That would work. And no mentioning the Mrs. Hawk thingy. Craziness was already maxed out. With a sigh that drew Brock's gaze, she pushed both enigmas to the back of her brain.

Once home, Uncle John unlocked the front door. Only Beth was missing, who'd gone to a friend's house after the long evening service. The bluegrass quartet had outdone themselves singing both oldies and contemporary selections. Even her uncle's foot had tapped to the lively music. Good. Safe subjects all.

Brock seemed to enjoy it as well, though she wondered if it was really his style. Her aunt, as always, was more carried away with the meal afterwards. My, that woman could organize a fine church supper. A few weeks ago, spending a service seated next to Brock had been an inconceivable concept. Quite willy-nilly she was.

"Oh." Aunt Ellen jerked her hands to her cheeks in dismay. "In all the singing and food preparation, I've forgotten my purse. And my Bible. How could I have done that?"

Uncle John chuckled. "'Forgetfulness is a form of freedom.'"

"Go on with ya." Ellen swatted his arm while balancing an empty baking dish in her hand. "We've got to go back to the church."

Uncle John meandered towards his recliner. "'Twill wait till morning, my dear."

Jerrica's aunt took a hard stance in the middle of the room, eyebrows drawn. "John, I won't leave my pocketbook in the church house."

Brock cleared his throat behind her. "We'll go back and get it."

Surprise lifted Jerrica's brows.

Aunt Ellen's face wreathed in a smile. "Will you? Oh, bless your heart, you sweetie pie. I so appreciate this. John, give them the keys to the church house."

Jerrica pinched her bottom lip. Sure. Make a pledge to not be alone with him, and now this. Her sudden refusal to accompany him would peak Brock's curiosity. No sense in bringing any unwanted attention being a spaz.

After all, tomorrow she would have no option. They would drive home together. Alone. Then they would share that huge house. Again, alone. Fine. She would have to think of it as being no different than staying with the Rankins. He shot a crooked grin at her, and her traitorous heart thunked beneath her chin.

Well, so much for that thought.

His brows rose and a question lurked in his eyes. "You coming with me?"

Sure. Mella yella humming a cappella. Like her intimate exhibition of her wanton passion for Brock had never happened. Perfect. It worked right into her plan. She nodded and walked to the door. "We'll be right back Aunt Ellen."

The beginning of a smile lit Brock's face, and Jerrica looked away at the jump of delight in her belly. She tightened her lips. Why become so enamored with him with so much up in the air? She let out a shaky breath, not sure she could control her body's reaction to the lure of his personality. And, of course, his striking good looks didn't deter either.

They settled into his car, and Jerrica snapped the seatbelt before settling back in the seat.

"Thanks for coming along, Jerrica. It'll make it easier to navigate the roads."

She shrugged, glad for the concealing darkness. "No problem. She's my aunt after all. I guess I could go myself and not put you out."

His soft laughter echoed through the car. A pleasant sound. Yet just another characteristic she could list of things she enjoyed about him. She clenched her hands. What if she wasn't Jenna? A tiny spark of yearning made her catch her breath. He'd be free. Free to pursue someone new. Like her?

"Wouldn't be very gentlemanly for me to let you fetch your aunt's purse by yourself." They rode for a few minutes in the car blanketed in companionable silence before he spoke again. "You know that cave down below the workshop?"

Her brows wrinkled at the change in subject. "Yes?"

"I went in there and searched for you yesterday. Before I found you at the cabin."

"You did?"

"Yeah. Did you know someone else uses that cave?"

Jerrica stiffened. Her eyes fastened on his dim profile. "What do you mean?"

"I heard voices, and I followed them."

Truthfully, she'd heard faint echoes through the cave before, but she'd never had the interest to locate the origins of the noises. "What did you find?"

He adjusted his hands on the steering wheel. "I believe Haywood McCoy uses that cave. He certainly stores his pots in there. Maybe more. You know this neck of the woods better than I. Is it possible he uses it as a shortcut as well?"

"It's possible. There may be some clay in there, too. Who knows? I know he uses local materials. What did he say to you?"

Brock shook his head. "Didn't talk to him. The last meeting I had with him started out with bullets flying around my head. I wasn't about to pop out and pump his hand in welcome."

Jerrica gave a small chuckle. "No, I suppose not. One of Katie's older brothers works for him sometimes."

"Yeah, someone else was there. Sounded young. It might have been him."

Her thoughts went back to the conversation she'd overheard from Katie's mother, and a shiver when through her. Could the brother have been spying on her in the cave? Revulsion rippled through her. Brock's speed pulled her from her thoughts.

"You'll have to slow down or you'll miss the turn."

He obliged, and soon they were parking in the dark gravel lot. The woods whispered secrets around them as they exited the car, and Jerrica eyed the cemetery to the right of the church. Her repetitive dream popped in her head, and she shoved it away with a clench of her teeth.

A lone light illuminated the small white church's entrance. Insects buzzed about, slamming their bodies against the bulb's glass cover. Brock inserted the key and held the door open for her. She stepped into the small pitch-black vestibule hugging herself and then turned to flick on the light. Despite the fact this was her church, it seemed a little spooky at night.

"I bet she left it in the basement." Jerrica threaded her way down the hallway, turning on lights as she went.

"Did you see that light inside this room? Someone must have forgotten to turn it off."

She stopped and looked back at him where he motioned to a door.

"That's the pastor's study. I'm not sure we have a key for that."

Brock reached up and tried the door, and it yielded to his touch. "Huh. They must have forgotten to lock it, too."

The shadowed room only showed a glowing computer screen. Jerrica approached and flicked the off button. "That's strange. I wonder why the monitor is on?"

He shrugged. "Who knows? Mine comes on by itself at times."

They pulled the door closed and headed down the stairwell. The small open area, filled with tables, flooded with light when Jerrica flipped the switch. "I'm sure her stuff will be in the kitchen. I'll just run and grab it."

Chapter Twenty–Two

Brock jangled the change in his pockets as he waited in the outer room. Simple block construction painted white, with portable tables, made the room receptive to any kind of small function. Brown shutters closed off the kitchen bar. His eyes continued around the room. A podium stood in the corner and a little bookcase as well. They must use this area as a Sunday School room.

A small flash of light caught his eye. He moved toward the bookcase in the far corner.

"Got it. She'd put them in a lower far cabinet in the kitchen, like she always does." She stuttered to a stop. "What's up?"

"Come here." He motioned her over, and she approached, skirting the long tables.

"What?"

"Did your aunt leave her phone, too? If she did, it's all charged up." Brock picked up the small flip phone.

Jerrica's brows creased. "That's not my aunt's."

Brock turned it over in his hands before flipping it open. A generic skin glowed in his hand, revealing only the phone's brand. He pushed a button, but a password had locked it up tight. "Strange. I hope someone remembers where they left it. You can't get in to find out who it belongs to."

"It doesn't look familiar. And it's ancient. Someone definitely needs an upgrade." Jerrica gave a small laugh. "Just leave it. We can tell my aunt and uncle. You ready?"

Brock replaced the phone as an uneasy sensation flared in his chest. Flip phones seemed to be quite popular around these parts.

Brock organized the last of the suitcases into the trunk, hoping the lid would latch. The entire back seat and the trunk were now filled with Jerrica's possessions and a plethora of painting projects for Uncle John. Perhaps this was a good sign. She at least trusted him to bring most of her life along. She slipped into the car, and Beth walked Brock to the driver's seat.

Beth lowered her voice. "I've never seen her so relaxed. Almost happy."

He squelched the hope that rose. Beth had no idea what lay ahead. The reluctance Jerrica had shown the first time she'd left this house now fixed itself in him. If only they could stay and continue to let their relationship bud between them in the comfort of the Smokies. Unfortunately reality nosed in, and he had no choice.

Jerrica's brow puckered as she fastened her seatbelt. Had she overheard Beth correctly? Happy? Yes, she supposed she was somewhat, odd as it seemed. Brock got in, and she waved at her family collected on the porch. One last regret was she hadn't been able to see more of Katie, but she supposed the next time they returned she'd see her again. Jerrica couldn't help but compare this exit to the one a few weeks back.

Jerrica pushed the buttons on the radio and found a country station. She grinned cheekily when she smiled at his surprised expression. Much to her surprise she sang every word.

"I guess you've left the classical music behind and become a regular Carrie Underwood, huh?" he grinned.

The song ended, and she turned the station down a bit.

"Well, I can't say I sing well, but I am loud." She let a laugh tumble out. "Yeah, my mom loved country music. She always had it..."

She stopped in mid-sentence, and fixed her misted eyes on his. Covering her mouth with her hand, she swiveled her head toward the window and stared at the passing landscape. She missed her so much.

"You remember something else?"

"She liked Randy Travis." She sniffed. "I wish she were alive so I could talk to her just one more time."

A heaviness settled in her stomach. She wished she could remember more about her.

Brock turned the volume down a bit. "Maybe she isn't dead."

Not that again. She turned to glare at him, and a stab of pain knifed her chest. "Are we going to do this again?"

He tapped the steering wheel with the heel of his hand a couple of times. How he wished he could turn back time and let her belt out a couple more songs. Why hadn't he kept his mouth closed? Hadn't he learned anything from their rooftop rendezvous? "It's not that."

"Brock, I showed you her grave. How much more proof do you need?"

He sat up a little taller in his seat. Fine. He'd fried himself good already, he just as well spill it. The moment was already spoiled. "I'm just saying, be open to the possibility that she may be alive."

Jerrica blinked at him. "There's something you're not telling me, isn't there? I knew there was something the day we went to the graves."

He could feel her stern perusal. Brock firmed his resolve. "Here's the facts, Jerrica. Your mother is in Auberry Center in Evansville. It's a psychiatric hospital"

She spoke through gritted teeth. "She is not."

He kept his voice soft and low. "Then I'm paying to house someone else's mother named Margaret Price."

"Margaret Price?" Her voice had a strange squeak.

He turned to look at her then. "Yes, Jerrica."

Something like a meteor catapulted in Jerrica's abdomen. She pushed her back against the seat and pressed her head against the rest. There was no way she was mistaken. Absolutely no possible way. Not this time.

Tears bit her eyes, and she tightened her face to hold back the frustration. The silence hung between them. He had to know her mother was dead. He'd driven her there. How could he insist that her mother was in a psychiatric center? She closed her eyes in resignation.

Who was this lady Brock supported in the hospital? And how could Jenna's mother be named Margaret Price as well? A headache started at the base of her neck. There were just too many similarities between Jenna and her. Only one way to find out who this stranger was. Confront her.

"I want to go see her tomorrow," she said quietly.

Jerrica stared at the tray ceiling above her head then moved her eyes to each corbel in the four corners. Once more she rose and paced her dark room. Her mind had spun through the entire mess several times. It was exhausting, yet it was impossible to sleep. She glanced at the clock. Two-seventeen. She crossed her arms over herself and stepped to the bedside table. Inside the small drawer, her wedding ring greeted her with a gleam, and the wallet-sized picture of Brock and Jenna smiled up at her.

She settled on the side of the bed and took up the picture and studied it. She'd found it in a box in the closet amongst other photos. Beneath it she stared at another. Several young girls stood arm in arm in their one piece bathing suits in front of a lake. The girl in the middle, dressed in a blue suit, looked suspiciously like herself.

She threw both pictures back in the drawer and shut it with a decisive snap. As if she needed more thoughts racing around her head tonight. She stacked her pillows so she could sit up. There was a plethora of things she could be doing besides wasting time. Painting, crafting, reading. But her body was exhausted. If only she could shut down.

Sometime near dawn, she must have nodded off but woke with a start. Thankful for what little rest she'd received, she wandered downstairs to the couch, propped herself up on a pillow, and covered herself with a light throw. Yawn after yawn and finally she drifted off.

A snap of the mailbox lid woke her a second time. She sat up, stretched, and then tightened the belt on her robe. Had the mail arrived already?

Sleepily she rubbed her eyes and stood up. Might as well fetch it while she waited for Brock to show his face this morning. She cast her eyes to the large grandfather clock in the hallway as she padded to the door. Six fifty-eight. The postman was a real go-getter.

She eased the door open and walked out on the huge porch. In spite of her restless night, it was a beautiful dewy morning. The westerly porch still shrouded in shade greeted her with coolness. The mimosa trees sent bursts of pink near the sidewalk, and the red knockout roses transmitted a welcome sweet scent for a new day. She tried to focus on these lovely things rather than ruminate about the woman in the hospital.

The mailbox hung to the right of the front door so she ambled over, still groggy from lack of sleep. She reached in and pulled out several envelopes.

The stoop beckoned, and she settled on the front step to enjoy the cool morning breeze. Ahhh. Four steps down from Heaven.

After stretching her neck and shoulders, she looked at the pile in her lap. She flicked through each one. The last one had a return address of the Indiana State Police. Uneasiness began to churn in her stomach. The fingerprint match? Jerrica trembled as she pulled the envelope from the stack.

Fully awake now, she licked her lips nervously as she tore the envelope open with trembling hands. A simple white sheet of paper fell to her lap on top of the stack of mail. Quickly she scanned the print.

A perfect match. Both sets belonged to Jenna Loralynn Price Langston. Her legs grew limp, and she barely acknowledged the pile of letters streaming from her lap down the steps.

She didn't remember retrieving the letters, but somehow she arrived back inside to dump the other mail on the kitchen counter. Her head throbbed and a rainbow aura filled the right side of her vision.

She clutched the letter to her chest and mounted the stairs, keeping a steadying hand on the banister, fearing her legs would double beneath her. In her room she collapsed on her bed and let the tears stream down her face. She was Jenna. She was Jenna Langston. Hadn't she already known? So many clues, coincidences.

She was Brock's wife.

"Jerrica?" Brock's gravelly voice echoed up the stairwell.

She swallowed, shoved the letter into the envelope, and stuffed it beneath her pillow. At the door she pressed her face in the open crack, mustering a normal voice. "Yes?"

"We need to talk a minute. Can you come down?"

"No." A stab of dread shot through her. Her brain scrambled for an excuse. "I'm not dressed."

A few moments of silence. "You said you wanted to go to Auberry today. Are you still wanting to?"

Trembling forced her to sit right down, knees against the door. Now goose bumps. Soon hives would arrive towing the Sergeant. Fake mother and matching fingerprints. Two lethal bullets.

She should tell Brock. No, it would have to wait. Rainbow pulsations continued across her line of sight, and she blinked, trying to dispel them. Could she handle another revelation?

Was this the big unknown?

Her parents' tombstones flared into her mind. She'd been so wrong about everything, would she be wrong about this as well? Yet as surely as she sat there, she *knew* she was right. She *had* to see this woman.

"Jerrica?"

A shiver ran through her bloodstream as she heard that name drift upstairs. She wasn't Jerrica. Never had been. "Yes. Please make the appointment for later today."

Brock swung the black car around a sharp corner as they neared the grounds of the Auberry Center. On the north side of town with a long driveway flanked by shaded grounds, the landscape boasted peaceful, grassy meadows with inviting benches and huge stately shade trees. The massive building was fairly new and state of the art. A brick wall ensconced the entire area with a coded entry. He glanced in the rearview mirror as the huge gate swung closed behind them. They were now locked in.

The front façade was covered with mirrored windows decked with flowers cascading about the entrance. Several people accompanied by white-coated attendants strolled along the many walks. One patient began wrestling with an aide while another white-coated worker rushed to help.

Jenna turned her head. Brock probably wondered if he should reserve a room for her. She'd denied being Jenna, but she'd been wrong. Yet she clung to the one thing she did know. Her mother was dead. She sank lower in the vehicle and pressed her fingertips to her head.

"You all right?" Brock asked.

"I'm fine." She let her eyes drift to her husband.

Her husband.

He exhaled. "I know you think this is all a waste of time, but I've been footing the bill for this woman because I thought she was my mother-in-law." He paused to clear his throat as he parked. Turning to her he continued. "Jerrica, I just want to know who she is. If anyone should know her, it should be you."

Jenna, she mentally corrected, her lips tightening. "Uh-huh. I should. Me. Jerrica."

After an odd look from Brock, she emerged from the car and went into the building. Her shoes made a clicking sound as she walked down the foyer. She stemmed a desire to shush her own soles. A garden area appeared through the wall of glass to their left, and she longed to run to it. The need to hide spiraled within her. *Help me, God.*

It was a relief when they reached the carpeted area to dull the continuous clicks that mocked her. Brock spoke quietly to the receptionist and then steered her to the stairway on the left.

"For once I wish something could be on the first floor," he joked quietly to lighten the mood. "Dr. Oxby's office is on the third floor."

Jenna couldn't appreciate his attempt at humor. She wanted to insist they take the elevator. The third floor would be gravy next to the twenty-third. Yet her lungs had to be made of iron, for she could barely breathe. What surprise awaited her here? An unknown so big she couldn't manage it? Enough had happened today already.

They came out of the stairwell, and she allowed Brock to lead her through the winding corridors until they came to a door marked simply with "Dr. Oxby."

In a waiting room, Jenna collapsed in a chair near the door. This is a *doctor's* office. The words thundered through her head. She gripped the seat of her chair. Brock went to the receptionist's window. Thankfully, the room was empty. Brock sat beside her, and the silence seemed stifling. She worked to control the panic that rose. Fluttering. Heel, fear. Heel. Victorious.

Another door opened, and a nurse appeared dressed in scrubs. Hot pink. Scrubs by any other color is still scrubs. Medicinal clothing. "Dr. Oxby is ready for you."

Jenna gave a gargled choke. Short-lived victory. Brock rose.

"Could you give us a moment?" He held up his hand and knelt in front of her. "We don't have to do this today."

Jenna's eyes clung to his like paint on a barn door. Her hands came up, and she clutched his shoulders. "Please help me do this."

With a nod, he prayed. "God, we need help. Please hear our prayer."

He took her hands and she stood.

The nurse waited at the doorway with a serene smile. "Anything I can get you?"

Valium. Xanax. Probably not talking about that.

"No, we're fine." Brock answered as he wrapped his arm around her waist and edged her toward the door.

Jenna took a shuddering breath. He was right. They were fine. After swallowing a lump in her aching throat, she stepped through the doorway. Just another room.

The nurse led them back a long hall, opened a door, and indicated they should enter. A white-coated man sat behind the desk entering information into a laptop computer, but turned with a smile and stood when they came in.

"Ah, Brock," the tall, balding man stood and greeted. "Good to see you."

The man walked around his desk and shook hands with Brock. Jenna blinked hard and looked to the multi-colored carpet. Did it only seem like the room had squeezed smaller? Even the huge low-e window taking up the entire far wall didn't seem to lessen the strange warping.

"Dr. Oxby, how are you?" Brock returned.

"Fine, fine. So this is Jerrica?" He smiled and held out his hand.

Jenna, she was Jenna. A scream stood gated at the back of her throat, and Jenna crossed her arms in front of her to tamp down the urge to release it. That sterile white coat sneered at her.

She glanced at the doctor and flopped out a hand to him. Her old friend, panic, began to swell inside her, growing ever larger. The doctor acknowledged her with a nod and smiled, but his tiger brown eyes pierced her soul. She fastened her gaze to the deceptively cheerful carpet.

"Well, let's sit down and have a talk before you go see Margaret."

Jenna flinched as he indicated several upholstered chairs to his right, and she sank into the farthest one from the doctor.

"Well, Margaret has had a good day today until she found out she was having visitors and then..." He shook his head. "Your mother suffers from grand delusions."

"She's not my mother."

The doctor shifted in his chair. "Jerrica, it's possible you believe she isn't your mother but the fact is she—"

"She's not my mother!" She glared at Dr. Oxby. The white coat jeered. "And none of your placating statements will make that fact less true."

Brock covered her trembling, clamped hands. "Jerrica, we need to know what's going on."

She looked at him. "My mother is buried at Oak Hill Cemetery off Highway sixty-five in plot number fifteen, next to my father. I took you there. You saw it."

Brock nodded his head. "I know."

"And I'm not having some grand delusion like this...person who thinks she's my mother."

Dr. Oxby leaned back in his chair and steepled his hand against his mouth as his probing eyes took her in. "That may be so. But for the last three years this woman has been calling for Jenna, her daughter, to come and remove her from this facility. Somehow, whether you want to admit it or not, she may have some connection to you. And the only way we can find out for sure is for you to recognize her."

Jenna chomped her lip and concentrated on the threads of the upholstery on the arm of the chair. She *was* Jenna. So who was this woman?

"I'm not sure I can go in there." The thundering in her head beat to the drum of her heart. Sweat broke across her upper lip.

The doctor nodded. "I understand. You've had quite a bit of stress already. That's why she's in the observation room. So you can see her without coming into contact with her."

Jenna took a deep, shaky breath. "I can look at her and she won't know?"

"That's correct."

She knew what they waited for, but wasn't sure she could drum up the courage. Sergeant had been promoted to Sergeant Major as her lips grew so dry, it parched her windpipe with a squeezing ache. Like a direct throat-punch.

Brock stood and reached his hand for her. Closing her eyes she took her husband's hand and rose from the chair. He led her slowly through the door, following Dr. Oxby out a back exit to another set of rooms. Finally they stepped inside a long and narrow room with a large one way observation window on the left. Dr. Oxby indicated a couple of chairs along the wall.

"You can sit here until you're ready. She's the only one in that room."

Jenna glanced at the seats but didn't take one. She looked toward the window. Suddenly the phrase that Beth always told her popped in her mind. *The first step is always the hardest.* And here was her window. How ironic.

Brock supported her as she stepped forward. She gripped Brock's hands as she eased her gaze up, steeling herself for "the big unknown."

The woman sat at a small table drinking coffee. A big-boned woman, wearing red cotton sweat pants and a red t-shirt which hung on her, lounged there. But when Jenna's eyes took in the woman's face, she blanched.

"Oh." She gasped and twirled from the window. Everything tilted, and her legs came out from beneath her. Brock's arms encircled her and assisted her to the chairs along the wall. She covered her face with her hands.

"No, no." Her head exploded with pain, and she fisted her hair in her hands. "She's dead. It can't be her."

Somewhere in another world, Brock's arms gathered her, and his voice whispered soothingly. All she could see was the woman's face over and over.

"It's not her. It can't be her," Jenna choked.

"It's okay. We'll go. We'll get out of here."

"No," she sucked in a spasm of air. "I can't. I have to see. I have to know. I can't leave yet."

She tried to collect herself as Brock stood and talked quietly to Dr. Oxby. She knew her mother was dead. *She was dead.* Yet this person looked exactly like her. An old, weathered version. A pathetic, haggard faxed copy. A headache slammed into her forehead, and bursts of white hot needles sewed through her brain.

She closed her eyes and took a deep quivering breath to calm herself. Brock offered a tissue and a water bottle. She took the first and pushed away the second. Anything going down the gullet was sure to reappear. Brock squatted in front of her. It was several minutes before she settled enough to look again.

Brock searched her eyes. "You don't have to do this. Let's head home."

"No, please. I have to look at her again."

Chapter Twenty–Three

Clearing his throat, Brock stood and moved the other chair in front of the window. Jenna stood and melted into it. His hands massaged her tight shoulders. She bowed her head. *Help me, Lord. I need your strength and your wisdom right now. You said you'd never leave me, never allow me to be beaten down without the ability to face it. Please prove it to be true. Help me. Help me see. Help me remember.*

When she looked up, she battled against the frightening similarities between this woman and her mother. The woman smoked a cigarette and tilted her head back to exhale through the corner of her mouth. Dark circles bagged under her eyes, and her skin looked like thick, wrinkled, brown leather. The choppy, dark hair stood out as if electrocuted from her scalp.

A realization washed over Jenna like cool, mountain water. It wasn't her. The woman picked up the coffee cup, took a delicate sip, and crossed her legs. Almost entranced, Jenna's eyes followed her as she gathered the napkin near the saucer and dabbed her upper lip.

Jenna longed for the woman to look in her direction and then, as if she'd spoken the desire aloud, the woman cast an insolent glance toward the window. Jenna scrutinized her. Warm memories washed over Jenna of her mother sitting with her legs crossed, sipping coffee as if it was too hot, and then wiping her lip.

"Ladies always use their napkins," Jenna whispered aloud, remembering her mother's words.

A thousand years ago, or perhaps only a decade or so, a young Jenna grinned at her mother and imitated her. She'd righted the huge sunhat on her head and looked over at the enormous brown-patched bear that sat among the other stuffed animals she'd invited to her tea party.

"Did you hear that, Patches? Ladies always use their napkins." Small Jenna giggled, patting the toy on the head.

The here and now nosed in. The woman in front of her put the cup down and drew another long drag on her cigarette. Jenna peered closer and pressed her hands against the window.

"My mother never smoked." Relief coursed through her. She glanced at Brock for just a moment. "It isn't her. I thought it was for a moment, but now I'm positive it isn't. That person could never be my mother."

Brock lowered himself next to her. "Who is she?"

"I don't...know." Her eyes misted with tears. A tug pulled at her brain. "She resembles my mother. Her movements are similar. But I can't remember."

She covered her mouth with her fingers as she continued to peer at the woman. A foggy mist warmed her mind but refused to reveal any secrets. "I must know her, mustn't I? She's so like Mother."

Dr. Oxby came forward and mumbled a few words to Brock that she couldn't hear before he left the room.

"It's time to go," Brock said gently.

"I want to—"

"Not today. Let's go home."

Jenna fixed her eyes on the passing scenery during the two hour trip home. Brock didn't offer any consolation or try humor to lighten the mood. He allowed her to stew in her own tub of oxymorons. Now that the tension had eased, exhaustion hung on her like a wet coat.

Back at the house, they parted and went to their respective rooms. She paced the afternoon away, her mind a roil. At last she settled on her soft comforter, exhausted, and fell asleep.

When she woke, it was past bedtime, so Jenna rose and dressed for bed in her favorite nightie, the powder blue gown Brock had admired. The silky satin hugged her curves, long enough to cover the marks on her leg. Her emotions throbbed raw. How did one process the puzzling information she'd discovered today? Or the last several months?

She examined the scar in the mirror that showed through the split in the side. She was Brock's wife. And she longed for his comfort. Tears appeared and trickled down her cheeks as she rubbed the tender, mottled skin. Yet she was damaged goods now. Brock had married a whole person, and now he would be stuck with an amnesiac with both physical and mental scars.

Appearances mattered little, Brock said. Natalie had been all fluff and no stuff. Did he really mean that? Why did it seem her mind seldom had many thoughts independent of him? Fuzzy memories of his face close to hers grew clearer. Nuances of his body pressed to hers haunted like a specter. He seemed to be the one and only person who knew how to comfort and help her.

She studied herself in the full-length mirror. And she *was* Jenna Langston. Brock's wife. That picture was her and she'd loved him. A suffocating feeling lit her lungs. Perhaps this emotion wasn't just in past tense. She'd seldom let anyone touch her, but with him, it was different.

With a deep breath, she approached the small drawer in the side table and slid it out. Her wedding rings glistened from a small velvet box. She reached out, and with trembling hands, slipped them on her third finger. The diamond shot a gleam of approval.

Yes, her mind still stirred with uncertainties. And it was true, she couldn't get a fix on this woman at the Auberry Center, and it frightened the jeebers out of her. But she knew who *she* was now. Jenna Langston, Brock's wife.

She hugged herself, feeling very forlorn, craving Brock's calming presence. The ring felt unfamiliar on her hand. Her head came up. Brock knew. He already knew who she was. And her Uncle John knew. They had to have known. Why else would her family send her along with Brock?

How had they figured it out? After pacing her room, thoughts rotating in her brain, she grabbed the letter from beneath her pillow and slipped through the door. She felt her way down the stairs in the dark, turning right at the bottom. At Brock's closed door she paused. Never, even when she awakened in the Rankins' guest bedroom, burnt and feverish, had she experienced such a yearning for a particular person's presence.

She wrapped her arms about her, wishing for Brock's comforting arms. But, more importantly, she had to confront him.

Jenna inhaled a long breath. What a ninny. She had no business here.

Yes, you do. You are his wife.

Suddenly the door opened. She gasped and clutched her hands across her abdomen. He stood in pajama pants, naked from the waist up.

His eyes raked her form. "What do you need, Jerrica?"

His voice was clipped. *I'm Jenna, your wife.* Yet she couldn't push the words from her mouth, so she clamped her tongue tight to the bottom of her mouth. Her face flamed beneath his scrutiny. Her voice reappeared in a breathy version. "I failed to give you this letter that arrived today."

His eyes narrowed. "Jerrica, go to bed. I'll read it tomorrow."

Brock's eyes sparkled dangerously, his voice husky. She stepped past him, brushing against his chest, and advanced into the room, her pulse speeding. "It's from the Indiana State Police."

A nerve throbbed near his left eye. "And?"

"You need to read it." She shoved the envelope against the hair of his torso. He made no move to take it. She let her hand fall to her side.

His jaw worked as he drew in a deep breath. "Perhaps you could fill me in on the highlights."

She flicked her eyes towards his bed with the lamp lit on the nightstand. "I don't know a lot of things, Brock. Like the woman I saw today. I'm unsure of where I came from, and what I did before the last three years."

He closed his eyes and parked his hands on his hips.

"I don't know where these scars came from or—"

Brock bowed his head, his voice hoarse. "Forget the scars. What did you find out?"

"I am Jenna Price Langston, your wife." She paused and turned to square up in front of him. "But I think you already knew that, didn't you?"

His jaw clenched and he nodded. "Robert had a dental mold done. We all knew before you and I left the Smokies."

"Why didn't you tell me?" A sob worked its way up her throat.

He groaned and rubbed the nape of his neck. "We knew you weren't ready to know."

Well, she couldn't argue that. "Maybe that's true. I wasn't ready for a lot of things when I first met you. I shut everyone out and constructed my safe little shelter to stay away from anything or anyone that challenged me. Look."

She held up her left hand where the diamond ring gleamed. "You gave this to me, didn't you?"

"On one knee, in the moonlight. At the park by the pond." A slight smile tugged at the corners of his mouth as he knelt before her. She caught her breath. "I'd marry you all over again. We can start once more, Jenna. Fresh."

A fuzzy recollection lit inside her brain while she studied his face. Tears washed down her cheeks and she smiled. "You were the one person I let in. I *know* the reason I allow you near is because I love you. Somehow, I must have always loved you."

He took an uneven breath and rose, a flame of desire leaping from his dark eyes. His hands brushed up her back. "I've never stopped loving you, Jenna. Never."

He eased her body towards his and his hungry mouth sought hers. Her breath stopped as she returned his fervor, her hands running through his hair and across his taut back. The letter floated to the floor.

He held her suffocatingly tight and yet, it wasn't close enough. The passionate tide swept them away, and he carried her to the bed. This time, there was no reason to stop; no reason to deny. They were husband and wife in every way. And what God has joined, no man could put asunder.

The following day Mr. and Mrs. Langston cancelled all appointments and screened all calls through the answering machine and voicemail. The lovely blue nightie remained on the floor for most of the day while the Langstons reveled in their rediscovered love. And although many questions loomed yet, for now, Jenna put them on hold to celebrate the questions that had been answered.

Early the following morning Brock awoke when his wife stirred. He smiled down at her sleepy, relaxed face. He'd found her, and yet the smile faded. There were so many new questions. Why had she left immediately after the wedding? Where had she been going? Why had he been told she'd perished in the plane wreck when in fact she'd survived, walked away, and ended up some one hundred miles from the wreckage?

He massaged the back of his neck before laying his head on the pillow and looked at the ceiling. His biggest challenge ahead of him? Being patient while Jenna sorted out her life.

As he lay there, Jenna rose and stretched her arms wide.

"I could get used to waking up this way," he kidded sleepily.

She nodded her head, but said nothing.

He sat up and wrapped his arm around her rigid form. "Hey, you awake?"

She turned to him then, her eyes anguished. "Something's wrong."

He jerked his head in confusion. "What do you mean?"

She spread her hands wide. "I can't remember something."

Brock's eyebrows rose. "Listen, babe, there's a lot you can't remember. I for one—"

She pushed his arm from her, grabbed her robe, and sprang from the bed. "I have to talk to her."

He got out of bed a bit more leisurely before asking, "Talk to whom?"

She pivoted and set her hands on her hips. "You know. *Her.*"

"Jenna, it's only," he glanced at the clock on his bedside table, "five twenty-three. We can't drive down there now. Come back to bed, and we'll go as soon as they'll allow us to visit."

"No. We've gotta go now." She rushed from the room and rumbled up the stairs.

"Jenna," Brock called as he followed her. He paused at the bottom of the steps. Man, it felt good to call her by her real name.

He lowered himself on the third step from the bottom, thanking God for his wife. He prayed for guidance, prayed for God to open her memory. Was it always going to be like this? Herky jerky, new revelation?

He had to visualize Jenna's side of it. The poor woman couldn't remember half the things that made her the person she was. Although it thrilled him to have her back as his wife, she wasn't yet whole.

When he stood he found Jenna a few steps above him, fully dressed. He pivoted toward her. Tears sparkled in her eyes. He rushed up the stairs. "What is it?"

She shrugged. "I don't know."

With a cry she wrapped her arms around his neck. He picked her up and carried her to their bed. He held her in his arms while she mourned about something she couldn't understand herself.

At eight o'clock they arrived at the Auberry Center. They waited almost an hour and a half for Dr. Oxby. Brock explained the new discoveries to the physician while Jenna remained silent. The doctor had Margaret Price brought to the visitation room. Only then did she realize the implications of her task. Her stomach rocketed, and she clung to Brock's arm.

"Jenna, you said you needed to talk with her, but we can do this another day. We can slow down."

She shook her head. "No, it has to be now."

The first step is always the hardest. The worn phrase rolled in her mind like a dilapidated jalopy with four flat tires. Fear reared like a prancing stallion with thunderous hooves about to stomp her tattered tenacity into the ground.

She put her hand into her pocket and gripped Katie's smooth stone. *Roll the window down!* If a child could figure out how to free herself from fear, she could too. God was a God of faith, not fear. *Faith, not fear.* God was her Rock, and He *would* liberate her.

She gazed through the window to the woman in the chair. A cigarette dangled from her hand, and she tilted her head back to blow smoke. She wore red slacks and a red tank top at least two sizes too big. Her arms, brown and wrinkled, hung like laundry caught in a downpour.

One leg crossed over the other. She looked haggard, the deep circles under her eyes darker than the last time. With teeth tugging at the top skin layer of her lip, Jenna cracked the door open and slid inside.

The woman gave a sideward glance before reaching down to flick ashes onto the floor. She turned and looked at Jenna and gave a mocking smile.

"I knew you'd come around." Her husky tone was deep, like a man's voice.

Jenna crossed her arms over her nauseous stomach.

"You did good, Jenna." She grabbed the cigarette and took a drag before blowing a stream of smoke out the side of her mouth. She motioned with her hand toward the one-way window. "Got your man, didn't you?"

The gaunt woman laughed gruffly and brushed a hand against her scraggily hair. "Our worries are over. I knew you'd honor our deal."

Bile scaled her throat. "What deal?"

The woman smiled broader, showing stained teeth, doubling the leathered wrinkles around her face. She stood, circled the table, dragging on the cigarette as she went. Jenna caught her breath as the woman walked closer.

"Stay back," Jenna whispered.

"Oh, my dear." She rubbed a speck of tobacco from her lip. "I'm sure she hasn't forgotten you by now. It's been a shade longer than I expected, but look at the rewards."

Her face came within inches of Jenna's, and her stale cigarette breath filled the atmosphere. The frightening look-alike's face stretched into a Grinch-like grin. To avoid her glare, Jenna fixed her eyes on the ever growing ashes at the end of her cigarette.

"Look at me, you brat," the woman hissed.

Something hot exploded in Jenna's brain and spread into a pool inside her head. It numbed her brain, and a haze of gray descended across her vision. The words reverberated in her mind.

You brat. You brat. Jenna blinked and wobbled at the familiar echoes in her brain. She *knew* this woman.

"You're lucky they've got good drugs in here, otherwise, I'd have been gone." She glanced at the window and took a drag on the cigarette. Everything decelerated to slow motion as the cigarette ashes floated to the tile and burst into crumbles.

"Where is she?" Jenna asked. Everything twisted out of focus as if she were staring through a hotel peephole. She gripped the door handle.

The woman grinned.

"Suddenly not so stupid, eh?" The Grinch shrugged and cursed. "What do you care? You got old moneybags out there."

Memories swelled.

The old hag indicated the window. "Fact is, you owe me big."

She reached out and caressed Jenna's arm. Then clamped her hand that morphed into a pinching vice. "*Big.*"

No more. She'd stolen everything. This evil woman would hurt her no more. Jenna leaped upon the woman, knocking them both to the floor.

"I don't owe you anything," Jenna screamed. "Tell me where my sister is!"

The door behind them exploded open. Big hands pulled Jenna from the woman while white-coated assistants wrestled the she-devil. Jenna saw nothing but Brock's body, blocking her, as he wrested her away.

Jenna's face burned white hot, leaning around Brock. "Where's my sister? Where is she?"

Three male orderlies subdued the look-alike, her eyes were still filled with hatred. She threw her head back in laughter. The same laughter that had filled her nightmares.

The skeleton woman in the red dress!

More attendants clustered about. Brock nearly carried Jenna outside to the waiting area, and the woman shrieked and cursed, swinging at the aides until she broke away to beat on the window. The attendants subdued her, plunged a needle in her arm, and dragged her from the room.

Dr. Oxby directed them to his private office, and she crumpled into a chair and bawled. Brock wrapped her in his arms, and the physician left the room.

At least thirty minutes passed before she could calm herself enough to talk. The doctor slipped back into the room and settled in a nearby chair. Brock took a seat next to her, his hands still wrapped in hers.

A nurse entered and held out a small yellow pill and a glass of water. "Here, Jenna. The doctor says this will help calm your nerves."

She pushed her hands away. "I don't want any medication. I need to think clearly."

The doctor settled behind the desk as the nurse left. Dr. Oxby's shrewd eyes scanned her. "Jenna, tell us about your sister. Margaret has alluded to another child, but she never elaborates on her, or who she might be."

She cleared her throat to gain control of her voice. "Her name isn't M...M...Margaret. It's Marcene—Marcy. My mother's name was Margaret."

Dr. Oxby leaned back in his chair and shot Brock a questioning glance.

Brock shrugged. "Dr. Oxby, she knows exactly where her mother and father are buried."

"Who then is she?" Dr. Oxby's brows dropped. "All of our records indicated she's your mother."

"That horrible woman is my aunt, my mom's identical twin. After Mother died Aunt Marcy—" she almost gagged on the name, "exchanged documents to keep us from going to a foster home. She knew someone who could hack the computer files and change the information. I was only fifteen at the time, and I thought it was best to keep us together. But my mother and Aunt—Marcene were very different. She was crazy. And abusive." She looked at Brock. "We have to change my mother's headstone and get my...Marcene's real identification."

Brock nodded. "We will. But I still don't understand. What about all these debts? Is this why you left?"

Jenna's head swiveled to his. She pulled her hands away, folded her arms around herself, and rocked. "Oh, Brock, I'm so sorry. I didn't want to leave you. But I couldn't bear it any longer. She had all these outstanding debts and said if I married well, they'd be taken care of. I just couldn't do that to you."

"But why did you leave?"

"She hid my sister and said I wouldn't see her until the debts were paid in full. She planned it all. Your cousin's wedding? We crashed it to get at you. She bought me an expensive gown as an 'investment.' And she wore that horrid red dress."

Brock's face pinched in thought. "That nightmare you have. Is she the woman in the red dress?"

Chapter Twenty–Four

"Yes." Tears drained down her face. Memories crashed upon her. The baby must have represented her sister. "Once I married you, my aunt revealed where she'd stashed her. I left in the plane to retrieve her. Only, I don't remember where. How am I ever going to find her now?"

"We have a number of things in your aunt's file. But nothing that would indicate where she might be." Dr. Oxby reached for a thick file folder and rifled through it. "She's mentioned a number of places throughout the years of counseling. But most of the time she refers to Chicago. Do you know anyone who lives in Chicago?"

Jenna racked her brain. Chicago? "I'm not sure. My memory is extremely sketchy at best."

"Well, I can continue to question her, but I'm afraid I can't give you much hope. A lot of what she says is merely her imagination. And if she's been strong enough to keep this from us this long, I doubt it will spring from her lips anytime soon."

She nodded, a strange sort of peace settling on her. "I shouldn't have jumped on her. I hope I didn't hurt her."

The doctor gave a chuckle. "We'll check her over. Although she appears feeble, she's really quite physically strong. But you did seem to bring out the worst in her."

"I have to persuade her to tell me." She snatched a few more tissues from the doctor's desk. "Somehow."

Brock settled in the chair next to her. "Jenna, listen. I stored several boxes in the attic that belong to your mother—sorry, aunt. Maybe we should start there."

Her eyes widened and she jumped up. "Yes. Let's hurry."

The doctor rose and came around his desk. "As much as you'd like to, please hear me. This process may take some time."

Brock stood. His arm about her shoulder sent a surge of strength through her.

Jenna straightened her back and nodded. "You're right. But if you knew the obstacles I've endured over these last few months, you would know that nothing is impossible. I will find her, Dr. Oxby. With God's help, I know I will."

Brock stopped at a restaurant halfway home, and they sat in a quiet booth near the window. Jenna peeled an edge of crispy chicken and nibbled it. Was it tasteless because it had no flavor or because she had no appetite?

Finally, she put down her fork and lifted her swollen eyes. "Tell me about my aunt's debts."

Brock crumpled his napkin in his fist. "She was in hock over two hundred thousand dollars."

She groaned and grimaced. "You paid them, didn't you?"

"Yes." He took a swig from his drink. "I paid them all."

She grimaced and planted her gaze out the window. "Oh, Brock. How could you possibly afford that?"

His molars clamped. "Well, your aunt had certainly done her homework. My grandfather left me well-cared for."

"But not anymore?"

Brock pulled a weathered smile. "We're fine."

Tears pricked her eyes.

"It's just money, Jenna."

She huffed. "Just money. *Right*. This was more than just money. It was extortion."

He reached across the table, pushed aside her plate, and clasped her hands, drawing her gaze. "Why did you marry me?"

She stared at him and sniffed. "Because I loved you, Brock."

"Not because your aunt wanted you to? Not because of some elaborate plan?"

"Never."

A smile creased his face. "That's all I needed to hear. Let's head home and sort through those boxes."

Jenna stood near the dining room table with four boxes spread about the room. Two contained random files of bills, expenditures, and the like. Another cascaded with pictures that she longed to go through. A fourth had a plethora of childhood trinkets that made her head swim trying to place them, and a strong box without a key.

She turned her eyes upon Brock, who sat patiently flicking through the first box of files. "What am I ever going to do? It'll take months to go through all this information, and my brain's fried already. Literally fried."

With a cry, she collapsed into the nearest chair and hid her face in the crook of her arm. Brock's footsteps echoed to her ears and when he pulled her arm away, he knelt before her. "It's okay. We'll figure this out."

"I don't have time to sort pictures and file water bills, Brock. I want to find my sister."

He nodded, a note of helplessness entering his voice. "So let's just cut through all of it and concentrate on what's most important."

"But it's all important." She grabbed a picture from the top of the stack. A young family stood there. A husband and wife and a young daughter holding a suitcase. She flipped it over. Jenna's trip to Camp Bethany. "See, this is me. And my parents. How can I not go through all of this?"

"True. But what we're looking for is some lead as to where your sister is." He snatched a photo of a baby wrapped in a white blanket. "For instance, who is this?"

She took the photo and read the back. Her brow knitted. "It says Jerrica, three months old. Grrr, I'm so confused."

Brock sorted through the stack until he located a young girl holding the same baby. "Here we go. It says, Jenna, fifteen, holding Jerrica, six months."

She caught her breath and pulled the photo from his hands. "Let me see that."

The doorbell rang. Brock headed toward the door. "Must be the pizza I ordered."

She continued to stare at the photo while he paid for the pizza and then trailed him into the kitchen to prop herself on a stool. "Yeah, that's it."

She slapped the picture in her hand, and a realization washed over her. "My *sister's* name is Jerrica."

Brock set a plate in front of her and then one for himself. "Well, in a way, that makes sense. Your brain would have had distorted fragments of your earlier life. Maybe it was your way of holding on to her."

"Maybe."

He blessed the food and took a bite while she continued to contemplate. "We could discover a lot of maybe's in the next several months. So let's try to cut to the chase. I say we pry open that lock box and see what's in there."

She picked up a piece of pizza and nodded. "That sounds better than piecing together hundreds of photos and attempting to construct a paper trail from bills. I'm in."

~ ····· ~

Brock collected several tools from the garage. When he returned to the kitchen, Jenna was shaking the lockbox. Something rattled within.

"It feels empty." She sighed.

He laid a kiss on her head. "Obviously, not empty."

Brock laid the metal box on a pile of newspapers and grabbed the screwdriver to wedge it into the crack under the lid and twisted. It held fast.

"I'm going to check through some more pictures. Holler if you manage to get the thing open."

Brock laughed. "Oh, I'll get it open, my dear. Even if I have to drill a hole through it."

She left the room, and he continued to pry at it. Whoever had bought the confounded thing had gotten their money's worth. He picked up the hammer and beat the stew out of the lock, but it didn't give. Fine. He flung the screwdriver down. Time to get some serious tools.

He carried the box to the garage and pulled out his reciprocating saw. Once fitted with a metal-cutting blade, he angled it against the lock. Slowly but surely, he cut through the metal, and the box flew open. He grabbed it up and hurried to the kitchen. "Jenna, I got it open."

She came rushing through the door, sliding across the wood floor in her stockings. "What's in it, what's in it?"

Brock picked up the only item from the dented box. "A key."

Jenna slumped onto the counter. "That's no help. We haven't a clue what that fits."

He turned it in his hands. "Do you know what this is?"

She stood. "Not really."

"It's a bank lock box key." He gave a small grin. "And where there's a key, there could be a way."

The next morning Jenna followed Brock from bank to bank until they located the correct one. It took a couple of hours to convince the bespeckled manager that she had a right to open the box. They produced all their paperwork, including a fax from the doctor declaring Marcene Price incapable of attending to her own affairs. The man became much easier to work with once Brock paid the overdue rental fee.

She latched onto Brock's arm as the clerk escorted them to the correct box in the small, jail-like room. The container, a small one, indicated that whatever it was, wasn't much. With the turn of two keys, the door opened and inside, a simple white paper with three names, addresses, and phone numbers. Loretta Garvey, Evansville, Denny and Carla Hawking, Chicago, and finally, Haywood McCoy with his Tennessee address.

Jenna's jaw dropped open. "Haywood McCoy?"

Brock's face grew stiff. "I think it's time to call Robert."

"So what did you find out?" Jenna knifed the mayo onto the long hoagie bun then piled on the ham. "Did Uncle Robert find out anything?"

Brock paced a moment before settling, eyeing the notes he'd scratched on a notepad. "He's looking into it quietly for now. As for the Evansville police, they said since there's no warrant for this woman, they have no reason to question her. So it looks like we're back to square one."

"But would the hospital know her? My aunt obviously must be acquainted with her to keep her address locked up like some valuable piece of jewelry."

He nodded. "It smells fishy, I'll admit."

Jenna flung the knife to the counter. "It's all taking so long. How are we ever going to solve this? I need to find my sister, and I need to find her pronto."

Brock sidled up to her and took her in his arms. She swiped at the tears that squeezed between her lids.

"Let me get another appointment with—"

"No. No more appointments." She pushed away and pointed to the list of names they'd recovered from the lock box. "Let's go find this Evansville lady."

He nodded and linked his fingers with hers. "You got it."

Brock pulled into a modest retirement condominium on the north side of town and glanced around. Well, whoever it was, didn't live too high off the hog. But in a community like this, there would be no hiding their visit. Curtains opened on several of the residents' windows as they drove slowly through.

"Here," Jenna's voice gave away a tinge of excitement. "It's on the end."

He parked across the lot and grabbed her hand when she attempted to leap from the vehicle. "Hold on."

"What? We can't hesitate, Brock. My sister could be in there."

With a shake of his head he cupped her hand in his. "Jenna. That's highly unlikely. You know that, right?"

Her shrug and glance away told him she did.

"We have to go about this methodically, step by step. We're going to find her. We will. But we need to stay cool and discreet. You got it?"

She turned a resigned face to him and nodded. "I'll try."

It was too hot in the car to ask much more than that, so he stepped out, checking his wife over the hood of the car to see if she still remained calm. They met near the trunk and made their way to the white door, lush red geraniums bloomed in a pot nearby to welcome a visitor. Jenna exhaled slowly as he pushed the doorbell.

Several minutes passed. The PTAC unit under the window blocked out most noise, and Brock wiped away the sweat that collected at his temple. Finally, the storm door rattled as the solid door behind it opened. A white-haired lady peaked through the small opening.

"Loretta Garvey?" Brock raised his voice above the air conditioner's whirl.

Her white brows collected in the center of her forehead. "Yes?"

"Marcene Price sent us to—"

The woman's wrinkled face grew long in surprise, and her bright blue eyes bugged. The door shut in their faces, but Brock sent up a stiff arm which bounced it right back open. Without so much as an apology, he dragged Jenna into the small unit as the woman hurried toward the back.

"Stop right there." Brock shut the door behind them.

Loretta disappeared through a white door across the room.

"If you call the police, Loretta Garvey, it will definitely speed up the process. I've already informed them of who you are."

Brock waited. The elderly woman had about two minutes to make up her mind before he barged into the next room. The door cracked open. She tottered out, fear written across her face.

Jenna seemed to find her voice. "We're not here to hurt you."

"I know who you are. Marcy promised you'd never find out." Her face contorted into a scowl before she eased herself into a soft rose-colored rocker.

"Find out what?" Brock stared her down, but she didn't seem too perturbed about it, although her gnarled hands tremored in her lap.

The old woman narrowed her eyes. "Nothing. I don't know nothing."

That stuck in his craw. "I beg to differ—"

"Please, Loretta." Jenna stepped forward and perched on the loveseat near the bullheaded woman. "I have to find my sister."

The woman raised her chin and puckered her lips like a pouting child. "You two ain't got no business in my house."

Brock took a wide stance and crossed his arms. "You're right. We'll head on out and summon the police and see if they have any business here."

His wife swung her gaze to his, pleading with her eyes. But Brock kept his face stiff and stared at the old woman to see if she'd take the bait. When she hesitated, he took one last plunge.

"That blackmail money set you up pretty well, didn't it?"

The elder woman's face went limp like a spilled bowl of mashed potatoes, and her hands flew up to clench the rocker's arms. "I..."

"Brock, I don't know about this," Jenna whispered.

He ignored his wife and leveled his gaze on the trembling lady who scooched to the end of the chair and huddled as if cold. "Mrs. Garvey?"

Her head rose slowly. "I don't know where she is."

Brock strolled over to a small lace-covered table on the far side of the loveseat and picked up a photo of a young family with several boys. He held it up and peered at it. All the intimidating words he'd been forming disappeared. The oldest boy looked familiar.

"Put that down," Loretta barked as she rose.

"Jenna, come here."

"Unhand my picture."

His wife stumbled forward, tears on her cheeks. Jenna caught her breath and swung to stare at the woman. "Why do you have a picture of the Hawks?"

The woman collapsed in the rocker once more. Brock pulled his phone from his pocket and quickly snapped a picture of the photo and of her scowling in her chair.

Jenna grabbed his hand. "Brock, this woman knows the Rankins' neighbors."

His wife stood immobilized for a full minute, peering at the older woman who avoided her eyes.

Brock set a comforting arm around his trembling wife. "From the way our friend here is behaving, I believe you might have something there."

He thumbed through the contacts on his phone until he reached the Evansville Police Department. "Mrs. Garvey, I think you're about to have more visitors than you want."

Jenna paced beneath the line of Bartlett pears outside of Loretta Garvey's condo. Her muscles wanted to lock up, but she kept moving and pressed down the fear that seemed to halo her like a haze. She dabbed her face with the worn tissue in her hand. When would Brock reappear? The police had been in there for over an hour. What was going on?

Her husband emerged from the door, and she hurried over to link up with him in the middle of the blacktop lot.

"What did they say? Did they find out where my sister is?"

"No. They told us to go home."

"Go home? Are they crazy? That woman knows where she is." Jenna could barely keep her voice from climbing into hysteria.

He turned her toward the car and urged her across the lot. "They haven't found out anything yet. They'll have to go through her documents, pictures, phone records, everything. It could take several weeks."

Her body went stiff. "That's too long!"

A muffled wail escaped Jenna's lips, and his arms wrapped around her. His voice mumbled lowly into her ear. "Let's get in the car. We'll boil on this blacktop."

Reluctantly she turned and allowed him to steer her to the passenger side of the vehicle. He helped belt her in, circled the vehicle, and climbed in the driver's side to start the car. She covered her face with her hands when he reversed and backed out of the parking spot.

With a groan, she slapped her hands to her lap. "We have to tell Uncle Robert about everything. Maybe he—"

"Already did. There's no proof she's involved. There's nothing to do but wait."

Jenna let her head slide to rest against the window and let the air-conditioning blow through the vent onto her hot tear-streaked face. *Now what, God?* Had He brought them so far just to wait in agony? Brock's hand reached over and clasped hers in his, and more tears washed down her face. At least she wouldn't have to endure it alone.

⟅ ⋯⋯ ⟆

The phone vibrated on the dresser across the room, bringing Brock out of a dead sleep. After a long evening of racking his brain for answers, he'd finally fallen asleep while Jenna whispered prayers in his arms. He tugged a deep hiss of oxygen into his lungs to rouse himself and disengaged his limbs from the sheets. Jenna stirred to wakefulness, and he snatched the phone up and growled a greeting into the phone.

"What's up, Robert?"

"Katie is missing."

Brock's brain startled to full alert. He glanced at the clock which revealed the morning had rolled past nine a.m. "What?"

"I went to investigate the Hawks this morning. They've disappeared."

He walked into the hallway when his wife's sleepy eyes widened with hope. By the time he'd reached the living room, she had caught up to him and circled him, to watch his face. He held up his arm to ward her off and paced to the windows. "Now what do we do?"

Robert replied. "I have no option but to head up the mountain and question McCoy."

Brock gripped the phone. "We're waiting to hear from the police up here, so we'll sit tight and see what you find out."

Jenna wandered to the table and snatched up the safe deposit envelope and pored over the contents. He glanced down to concentrate on Robert's words, but her leap and two double steps toward him caught his attention. Then she froze. Her gaze went from him to the missive in her hand. Her face grew pale, and the paper trembled as she clenched it.

"Hold on, Robert." Brock gripped the phone in his hand. "You okay, Jenna?"

"Denny and Carla Hawking? How obvious! I know who they are. Katie's parents are Lenny and Marla Hawk. They altered their names. Katie is my sister, Jerrica!"

A bolt of realization nearly knocked him from his feet. "Don't do anything until we get there, Robert."

Chapter Twenty–Five

Never had a trip taken so long. Brock talked on his car phone for the first half of the trip, first calling Uncle John, Robert, and the Washington Police Department about the turn of events. Jenna kneaded the white quartz rock in her hand that Katie had given her, mentally reviewing the many conversations she'd had with the girl over the last couple of years.

Had she ever told her she wasn't really part of the Hawk family? Had she ever given any indication her name wasn't Katie? Her mind focused on her blue eyes and blond hair. Now that she thought about it, she and Jerrica looked so much alike. Why hadn't anyone noticed?

Jenna gnawed her lip. Katelyn Jerrica Price. She'd been named after her grandmother, and they called her Jerrica. Brock had located the birth certificate in the boxes after much searching.

But if the Hawks were in on the scheme with Aunt Marcene, Loretta, and possibly McCoy, it would have been easy to adjust her common name. Jerrica would've been only three. What could a toddler really remember?

The conversation she'd overheard at Katie's house suddenly made sense. A shiver of fury shot through her, knowing the Hawks had known all along who she was and chose not to disclose it. She'd spent three years in fear groping for her identity, missing out on knowing Jerrica for who she was.

She glanced at her companion. They'd let Brock grope through a funeral, grief, and years of sorrow. Her midriff seized up, and she let out a long breath from pursed lips. No use following that trail. Agony was written all over that history.

Brock hung up the phone.

"Robert's got the Sevier County Sheriff's Department involved. They're going in tonight." He fixed his eyes on the road. "He's also managed to obtain a court order to search and detain the Hawks and Haywood McCoy on suspicion of kidnapping. If they can find them."

He paused a moment and glanced at the digital clock on the dash. "Your Aunt Ellen started their church's prayer chain. She wanted you to know."

Jenna smiled, took a quivering breath, and tried to relax into the seat. Aunt Ellen was right. All her worrying and struggling had done little good. And why was she fighting God? He held everything in His hands. She had to give it all to Him.

Her gaze took in the man next to her, jaw tight, hands firmly planted on the steering wheel. Oh, the fear she'd had when he first arrived on her doorstep. And here they were, reconciled, growing together, rediscovering their love and life together. The two of them were better than one.

As she peered at him, the familiar set of verses bubbled from her soul that had buoyed her hope when terror surrounded her in the throes of panic. Tears moistened the corners of her eyes. "'Cease striving and know that I am God.' 'He will never desert me, nor will He ever forsake me.'"

Brock turned and locked gazes with her. A small smile tugged at his mouth.

Her voice continued stronger, "'Be anxious for nothing; but in everything by prayer and supplication with thanksgiving let your requests be made known to God. And the peace of God, which surpasses all comprehension, will guard your hearts and your minds in Christ Jesus.'"

He cleared his throat before answering. "'We are afflicted in every way, but not crushed; perplexed, but not despairing; persecuted, but not forsaken; struck down, but not destroyed'"

He squeezed her hand. Jenna allowed a small quirk to tug at her mouth as tears made a trail down her face. Truly, if God were for them, who could be against them?

They arrived at Uncle John and Aunt Ellen's house as the mist descended on the mountains at dusk. The Rankin home seemed relatively quiet when they pulled up. Normally the odd stillness would've made Brock quite nervous, considering a major sting operation would commence mere hours from now. But he knew they had set up headquarters in the workshop.

The family ushered them in at the door with a hush and faces red with tears. Aunt Ellen and Beth embraced Jenna with whispers of love and comfort. Brock gave a firm handshake first to John and then Robert. The marshal wasted no time as the ladies drew Jenna into the kitchen.

He slapped a file into Brock's hand. "This was faxed to us about an hour ago."

He scanned the top sheet inside. "So, there is a family connection between Loretta and the Hawks."

Robert grimaced. "And to Jenna."

"What?"

Jenna appeared at the door, swiping tears.

"A distant cousin of Marcene's."

His wife rushed forward and took the paper. She quickly scanned the contents and her mouth opened.

"Someone with superior computer hacking skills changed the paperwork but left a trail nonetheless."

"I was right. Katie is Jerrica," she said in awe.

"Yes," Robert nodded. "But we need to find the person responsible for changing these records. I have a feeling it's the third person on your lockbox list."

"Haywood McCoy." Brock's face tightened.

"Here," Robert tugged at Brock's shirt pocket and slid a metal disk in place. "You're my official temporary deputy. Let's head to the workshop and get in on the plans."

"Uncle Robert!" Jenna's voice wailed.

The big man groaned. "No, Jerrica. Sorry, Jenna. You're too involved."

She stepped forward, eyes blazing. "If you don't take me, I'll go anyway. I know these hills like the back of my hand."

The room snipped into silence while Robert's face twitched.

Brock stepped forward and linked his hand with hers. "She has a point. No one knows these mountains like she does."

"Fine. But if you impede the investigation, I'll cuff you to a tree. You got it?"

She nodded, chin trembling.

Robert growled lowly, rolled his eyes, and handed her a silver deputy's badge. "Can't say I'm shocked. Now, let's go."

❧ ······ ❧

Seeing the black clad figures cluttered with weaponry standing about the workshop with stern, guarded expressions sent a chill through Jenna. Brock had relayed that Haywood McCoy's lair proved a dangerous place to visit even on a hi-howdy day, but to charge up there in darkness demanding answers seemed pure lunacy. She swallowed, shocked that, instead of terror, only determination rose up within her.

Robert joined right in the melee at her painting counter, covered with papers—invasion and capture plans. Once he'd studied them and nodded a few times at the clean-shaven man in charge, he strode back to her and Brock.

"All right. So, you two will stay back, approximately at the tree where Haywood shot at us the first time."

Brock nodded. She clenched her hands around Katie's rock, slipped it in her pocket, and leaned in.

"They're going up in three sections on the mountain to keep any escape route closed."

What if they aren't up there?" Jenna couldn't repress the question.

Robert shrugged. I've got everyone on high alert for miles around. If they spot their vehicles, they'll be stopped with great caution."

She nodded.

Her uncle's eyes burned into hers. "We won't be taking in vehicles. So you will be the one to direct everyone to their cover until we reveal ourselves. Can you do that?"

What a question. Of course she could. Did her Uncle not remember how she had trod this area while seeking solace for the last three years? A gasp worked its way up her throat, drawing Brock's gaze.

God had worked it out. He'd conditioned Jenna for this very day. The day Jerrica would be rescued. The realization drove the last of the fear from her heart. "I know every leaf out there, Uncle Robert. I can, and *I will*."

It took nearly two hours to set the first two groups of police officers in place around the mountain. In her excitement, Jenna had set a stiff pace, and even the conditioned men had lagged behind. Now, her calves, thighs, and hips were screaming. The steep slope was an unforgiving master.

"Is this our area?" one of the officers behind her huffed.

Even though she couldn't get a fix on his expression in the dark, she recognized weariness in his voice.

They stopped, and the two police officers who followed them paused too, breathing hard. Another thirty seconds brought Robert to their group.

"These mountains ain't made for old joints," he groused. He stood and planted his thick paws on his hips to breathe a moment. "I believe this is close to where we were, Brock."

D.J., one of the county police officers, slid down the night vision goggles from his head to his eyes and scanned the area. "It's clear."

Robert let out a whoosh of air from his lungs. "Good. Hunker down. We've got a few minutes before we approach."

Jenna squatted on the ground. Now that she was idle, sweat poured from her brow. Gnats swarmed her face and she swatted at them. Mosquitoes buzzed. But she barely acknowledged them over her own heartbeat. Minutes ticked by, and she squinted at Brock through the dark. He seemed a statue. Suddenly she felt his fingers upon her arm.

His lips pressed against her ear. "It's going to be all right."

"I know," she whispered back.

"We're moving out. Stay put."

Robert rose silently, and Jenna could barely make out his wave to the other two officers. Even though they moved slowly and cautiously, scanning the area with goggles, the noises of their boots snapped through the air. She let the air rush from her lungs. How would they ever sneak up on old McCoy?

An ominous feeling clutched her heart. "They're not going to be there."

Brock leaned forward. "Why do you say that?"

She tried to slow her breathing and stood up. Brock pulled her back down.

"Jenna, how do you know?"

"It doesn't make sense, Brock. This is the first place to look. Why would you hole up in your own backyard?"

He whispered back. "Where would they go?"

She shrugged against him. "Just not here."

Silence surrounded them for another fifteen minutes until voices drifted down through the mist. Then shouts. Jenna held her breath. Then nothing. Finally, she could stand it no more. "Didn't you say the cave led to Haywood's?"

"Well, yeah, but—"

"What if that's where they are?"

Brock rose, pulling her with him. "Nice observation. Let's go."

"What about Uncle Robert?"

"He's a big boy. He'll call if he's curious. You'd better lead the way. It would be safest to start at the original entrance that you showed me. If that's closest."

Maybe leaving Uncle Robert wasn't wise. But then, he'd led the trek up when he and Brock visited McCoy. Besides, her sister needed her.

"Okay." She stepped out and then accelerated to a sliding jog, thankful to be going downhill for once.

Owl hoots drifted through the trees. Fog had fallen thick on this side of the mountain. A couple of times, she had to double think her location. Then a familiar tree or copse of brush would set her straight. Twenty minutes of walking on the steep slope had her feet aching.

As they grew near, she hesitated. A particular group of shrubbery and its accomplice, the eerie mist, did its best to veil the low opening.

"What's wrong?"

Fiddlesticks. Not having wandered in this area for a while made it hard to decipher the new growth. "I'm looking."

"You don't know where it is?" His voice rang out a little louder in the chorus of insects.

She beamed the flashlight from bush to bush. "Just...hold on."

Ah, the huge, old, fir tree. The only one this far from the higher elevations. Like a lighthouse beacon and she could have kissed its sticky branches. She shoved aside the eager new plants shielding the entrance. She flashed the beam from the fir to a mound of periwinkle some thirty feet downhill. Bingo.

Eager to reach the cave opening, she picked up speed and slid down the last few feet.

"This is it?"

"Yup." She parted the eager flowering plant, flattening the stiff shoots to reveal the low hole.

Brock murmured behind her. "Well, tallyho."

They were both winded and stood to catch their breath. The beam flickered weakly by the time they ducked their heads to enter the claustrophobic opening.

Going, going, gone. Her flashlight rendered itself useless mid-crawl.

"Perfect." Brock muttered behind her.

No problem. She'd done this without light for a long time. After a pause, she continued to crawl, Brock moving behind, brushing her feet with his arms.

Jenna heard the cavern rise before she bothered to feel for it. She had to clear Brock out of the tunnel. Here no growing plants changed the lay of the path.

"Stay there." Her echoed command froze his movements.

She rose slowly, closing her eyes and visualizing the cavern in her mind. With her hand against the cold stone wall, she trailed to her flashlight storage area. Those batteries better still be good.

Inside the dank cave, her movements and their breathing reverberated from the stone walls. She reached behind the rock and felt for the flashlights.

She flicked on a light, and a weak beam sliced through the darkness. Then another. Dead. The next was the same. The last one was dimmer than the first. It was all they had.

"Give me the dimmest one. You're the guide here." Brock's whispered words sounded like a yell. With the room lit, he rose and approached.

She shoved one into Brock's hand. "Let's just use mine for now."

A low humorless laugh spilled from his chest. "Yes, conserving energy might not be a bad idea. Sure would hate to get stuck in here without a light to guide us out. Hey."

She froze, and he pulled her close, laying a warm kiss on her mouth. "What was that for?"

"Just because."

Her fingers clutched at his collar, and she pressed her forehead to his. "Pray, Brock. Pray."

"Lord, we need your guidance and protection. Amen."

Jenna turned and fastened the weak light on the space ahead. She couldn't repress the whisper. "Amen and amen."

Chapter Twenty–Six

Brock could hardly think it possible, but the cave appeared darker than ever. They had hardly gone forty feet when Jenna's light flickered and grew dimmer.

She tapped the end against the palm of her hand, and it brightened. "We need to hurry. We don't have much juice."

They picked up the pace and made it to the thin corridor of columns as Jenna's light grew weaker. Brock motioned to the right and took the lead veering off her familiar route. The light waned before they had gone far.

They reached the s-curve, and Brock kept the light low to avoid alerting anyone who might be ahead. He grabbed her hand and flicked the flashlight off. A blackness so dark engulfed the cave. Either no one occupied the subterranean rock tunnel, or they were huddled somewhere in hiding.

He flicked on the light once more, and Jenna let go of it, urging with her hands for him to lead the way. Brock stepped down into a drier part of the cave, and he reached back for her to navigate the lower section in safety.

The pathway turned into a narrow channel with the chin-high shelves on either side. To the left, under a thousand white soda straws, he made out where the path doubled up on itself and he peered between the rock formations.

Oomph. Jenna's face came into contact with his back. "Oh, sor—"

"Listen." Brock stood stock still as he grazed the feeble beam around the enclosed passage.

"What?"

"Shhh."

He edged forward. They were nearly to the stairs. He paused for a moment, his ears searching for a human voice. But all he heard were drips. Evenly spaced. Everything was so incredibly dark. If anyone were nearby, wouldn't there be some kind of light?

He raised the flashlight and dipped his head behind the wall. Rows of the handmade pottery still lined the steps. Would they have taken—

"Oh, my. What is all that?" She leaned around him, gripped fast to his shirt.

"McCoy's products."

"Hmmm."

"Yeah, exactly what I was thinking. Would he leave those?"

He felt her shrug next to him. "If he's extorting big money, those pots are just change."

Disappointment pooled in his gut. "You're right. And we wasted about ninety minutes finding out we're at a dead end.

"I really thought they'd be here." Discouragement hung thick in her voice. "Come on. We better get back and meet up with Uncle Robert."

The flashlight played out as they reached the other side of the soda-straw shelf, and they both paused. Brock flicked on his extra one and handed it to her. They needed to get back to the crossroads. If necessary, Jenna could feel her way from there to the exit. Even with his limited experience, he knew going towards the church was shorter, so—

Jenna froze for a moment, flicking the light around. "Do you hear that?"

Brock stepped ahead of her. "What?"

"I'm not sure." She urged him forward. Yes, there was something. It grew louder. A distinct ticking.

"Do you hear it? I think it's a—"

Brock spun and shoved her ahead of him. "Run, Jenna. Run!"

Jenna's legs seemed without batteries. When she didn't move quickly enough, Brock wedged past her and grabbed her hand to yank her behind him. Her flashlight jerked wildly around the walls, and she stumbled on uneven stone. By the time they'd reached the turn off, Brock shoved her down the path toward the church.

"Head back. Go!" He punched a number into his phone. "Robert, if you're still at Haywood's, stay away from the mouth of the cave."

Jenna stuttered to a stop and pivoted, shining the light on his chest. His eyes shone red, and he screamed at her to run, bellowing into the phone again. "Get away from the cave entrance."

Before she could think, he'd grabbed her hand again and began to sprint. Suddenly the air sucked from the tunnel, and an explosion lit the air behind them, rocking the cavern. The pressure sent them airborne, the noise deafening Jenna's ears to the point she could no longer hear her own screams. Rocks and debris flew about them as she landed on her side and rolled over and over.

She groaned, curled up in a fetal position, and gripped her skull to protect it from falling rock. The echo rumbled beyond them and the cave became quiet. Pitch black once more. Aches and bruises covered her body, but on the whole, she was relatively unscathed. A horrible ringing continued in her ears, and she wasn't able to decipher her own moans.

Painfully, she pushed to a seated position, stretching parts of her body to assure herself everything still worked. "Brock?"

Had she said the word? She clapped her hands over her ears. Thankfully she could still hear over the tinnitus. She tried again much louder. With a sigh, she realized she might not be able to hear his reply. The flashlight had scatted somewhere on the floor of the cavern. She had to locate it and find Brock.

She rose to her hands and knees and began to do blind sweeps at a slow crawl. Her hand reached to the right, dipped down into a hole, and she pulled it back with a gasp. Where was she? How far had they been thrown? Was this her old familiar path?

Her heart drummed a painful tattoo in her chest. "God, oh God, help me."

A moan. She froze. It had to be Brock. With her ears still ringing from the blast, she couldn't distinguish much audio. She crept back left and continued sweeping.

Her hand smacked against cold metal. She stilled and returned to the object. The flashlight. With a prayer on her lips, she clicked the button. A weak light poured out and Jenna cried with relief.

She circulated it around the area and found Brock propped against the wall of the cave, his head in his hands. He lifted his face to her when she focused the beam on the floor in front of him.

"Are you all right?" She knew she was screaming, but couldn't hear herself otherwise.

He nodded, but the look on his face registered pain. She helped him to his feet, and together they worked their way to the mouth of the cave. After crawling through the low tunnel, Jenna sucked in the misty night air and crumpled on the dew-covered ground. "Oh, thank you, Jesus, thank you."

Brock also collapsed beside her, the moon like a beacon filtering through the sky next to the pure blackness of the cave.

She wiped the tears from her face. "What happened?"

"Not sure." Brock rubbed a spot on the back of his head. "You okay?"

She nodded and then raised her hand to investigate the area he probed. A doughy knot met her fingers. "You're hurt."

"I'll be fine. We gotta get back to Robert. I lost the phone inside the cave."

Jenna bit her lip. He didn't need to be trekking across the mountain with a bump on the head. "Let's go to the church. You can call him from there."

"We won't be able to get in."

She rose and clasped his big hand in both of hers and eased him from the ground. "I know how to break in. I've done it several times."

The look he gave her, even in the dim moonlight said it all. She shrugged. "I know. But it was one of my hiding places."

She led him down the mountain and across the next until they came up the upward slope of the connecting hill. A shameful thing to break into a church, she supposed, but it had helped her survive the last three years. She desperately hoped the trustees hadn't replaced the unlockable window she'd always shimmied through.

Insect noises were still indecipherable, but she managed to pick out something else. Sounds of the running stream sent thankful trickles amongst the sweat rolling down her spine. It wouldn't be long before they would be there.

Going more lateral now made the pace a tad slower. She flicked the flashlight beam toward the thick brush. The leafy cover made the trek even slower. She paused to grab a quick breath.

"What's up?"

"Nothing. Just wishing for a machete to clear this mess." She whispered. The oppressive, humid air rode her shoulders like a heavy rucksack.

"While we're wishing, let's go for a flame thrower. We could clear a huge swath in no time."

A nervous laugh popped out of her throat. "That had better come with two complimentary fire suits."

He spoke no more when she set the pace. The rushing water echoed louder. Navigating the stream in the dark might prove tricky. Her lips tightened in a repressed smile. Memories of Brock, thigh deep in the icy water. Sock first aid. Intro of sock puppets. Her cheeks tightened in droll humor.

A rustling noise from the left both froze the fond memory and her feet.

Brock came to a standstill. "Wha?"

She flicked the flashlight up and down.

Brock set his hand on her shoulder and leaned close. "What are we looking for?"

"I don't know. I heard something."

The leafed undergrowth gave no indication anything was afoot. Besides, with the rushing of the stream, it could have been her imagination.

"I think we're clear." Brock muttered.

Still, she hesitated. Even a fox or a bobcat could prove dangerous. Or Haywood McCoy.

Just for comfort, she veered down the mountain a bit, avoiding the area her impaired ears had managed to pinpoint.

Now the stream blocked any noise. Brock stepped forward to sweep the final bush barrier aside, and she clambered to the edge.

Her flashlight revealed a shallow area, crisscrossed with footstones, perfectly set for a traveler to pussyfoot right across. *Thank you, God.* She swept the stream down with her light, hunting for any signs of other visitors.

She turned the beam behind her, shielded part of the light, and checked Brock's face. He was pale but looked alert.

"You okay to cross?"

"Yes." He grabbed the flashlight from her hand and directed the beam upstream. "Oh, shoot."

His arm whipped around her waist and tugged her into the brush, flicking the weak light off. He came to a fast stop and held her hands down.

"What? What are you doing?" Impatience lanced her hiss.

His warm lips pressed to her ear. "Bear. Upstream."

She caught her breath. They needed to get downstream and put as much distance between the third-shift bear and them. She grabbed his arm. This wouldn't be easy in the heavy shrubbery.

Brock pressed the flashlight back in her hand and grabbed her other one. She backed away from the stream and then picked her way down the slope, ever alert for any variation in sound from the teeming H_2O.

When she sensed the sloped path evening out, she turned toward the stream once more. Here goes nothing.

With twice-shy trepidation, they peeked from their vigil on the side of the creek. The pitiful beam searched up and down as well as across. Great. Not much power left. She bumped it against her hand and it brightened slightly. She turned her attention to the crossing. More difficult here. Wider. Deeper. More below-surface steps.

But black bear free. Hopefully.

She double tugged on Brock's dark t-shirt, and he squeezed her hand. Ignoring her new tennis shoes, she took the first step in, steadied herself against Brock's strength, and moved forward. He followed behind.

The water permeated her socks and filled her shoes. The flow splashed high against her knee, and she turned sideways to take the pressure with a little more flex. No repeats of a semi-dunking. Not now.

She gratefully slipped into the bushes on the other side, ducking to miss the wild hydrangea's branched arms, tipped with a ball of white blooms. A grunt from behind her notified her that Brock hadn't been so lucky. She glanced behind her, bringing up the dimming light.

He flinched, eyes closed, and swiped at his nose. Then his hand went wide. "Keep that out of my eyes."

"Sorry."

She started to pull away, and he held back on her hand. "How far?"

"Close."

He sneezed behind her. Best to get them both on the trail, before Smokey the Bear trailed down to the owner of that sneeze. Despite his snuffling, he dogged her quick steps, following her and her weak flashlight. Thankfully, it was pretty uncomplicated from here.

They broke from the trees into the surrounding yard, and she climbed up, skirting the north side cemetery and past the former steps of Solomon Oliver's era. She paused at the southeast corner where the basement window lay flush against the blocks.

Her fingers sought to find the missing rubber insulation on the bottom of the casing to get her bearings. She slid her fingers between the casing and the pane and gave a shove. "It's okay. Put your foot against the bank, and fasten your other foot into that depression in that block. See it?"

He nodded. "What happens when I get inside?"

"No worries. If no one's moved it, I even had a chair to slide onto."

Without much effort, she zigzagged into the opening, flipped over while hanging onto the sill and eased her feet down. Ah. The old folding wooden chair. Just where she'd left it. She shot a thumbs-up at Brock before sliding completely into the building.

She stepped down and watched a larger shadow fight through the tiny opening. Several minutes ticked by as the dark form shimmied and struggled through the window. Finally, he managed to get both legs inside. She rushed forward to help align his feet onto the small chair.

The only light came from the moon behind them. Two feet in front of them stood the squirrel cage of the huge ac unit. It whirled like a rock concert drum solo.

Again, noise and darkness proved no barrier to Jenna. Multiple visits had etched the map to this room into her memory. She stepped left to go towards the louvered door. The light switch was on the left as was the handle. Too easy.

Brock snatched her close and whispered in her ear. "Why didn't you just go open the front door for me?"

"I don't know, I—" Had she heard voices?

Muted light suddenly streamed through the door slats in front of them. She pointed, bugged her eyes at him, and then set a finger to her lips for silence. He nodded, his jaw growing tense.

Both of them tiptoed to the door and pressed their heads against the wood. Who could be here this time of night? It had to be after midnight.

Brock's head pounded. He'd been struck on the back of the head by a flying rock, but right now, he wasn't too worried about that, for he swore he'd heard Haywood's voice through the door. But it was hard to tell with that blamed fan running behind them. Then a young child began to cry.

"Shut up and lay down," a gruff voice countered.

Jenna's eyes grew large and fastened on him. She motioned to the door and mouthed, "Katie."

Great. Now, how to get out of here and alert Robert. He glanced back to the small window. No way was he ever going through that small opening from six feet down. Jenna yanked on his sleeve and pointed forward then diagonally up. He shook his head. What was she saying?

She pressed him back and gripped the doorknob. He laid his hand on hers to stop her. She thumbed to the right, indicating the stairs. Did she think she could exit the room and head up the stairs without any of them seeing or hearing?

The light in the outer room flicked off. The furnace room lighting nudged to zero. She tugged him toward the fan motor whirling and pulled him down to whisper in his ear.

"I can get upstairs and use the phone."

"No."

"Yes. Please, Brock. I know Jerrica is here in the basement."

With some reluctance, he nodded. "I'll follow you up."

The AC flicked off. Everything but the whistle in his ears grew still. Both of them froze. With some concentration, he could make out muffled sobs. They stood for several minutes and finally the AC kicked back on, providing a white background noise that might just hide their exit from the room.

Jenna slid her shoes from her feet and stepped to the door to twist the knob. She rotated the smooth cylinder with tortoise slowness and eased the door open. If his calculations were correct, fellowship room to the left, stairs to the right.

She stepped from the room. He yanked off his shoes and slinked through the opening behind her. Her form elevated up the stairway to the right, and he felt his way through the dark passage and soon arrived at the top of the stairs. Jenna stood in front of the pastor's study, outlined in pure fear from a dim light.

The door swung open.

"Well, looky here." Haywood McCoy stepped from the room, shotgun outlined in his hand. "Just the two I want to see. Get in."

Brock held his hands up in surrender and entered the office. The room, previously lit by only computer backlight, brightened into full light when he flipped on the switch. He flinched at its brightness. Jenna stood next to him, the fluorescent bulb outlining the fear on her face.

He shut the door. "Don't think we'll be disturbed. Have a seat."

His wife eased into a chair ahead of him, never taking her eyes from the hairy woodsman. Brock sank into another next to her.

Haywood plopped in the chair, and it bounced a tad. In rhythm, he set the gun barrel on the desk.

The man appeared right at home. Brock's thoughts raced to the night he and Jenna had returned to get her aunt's purse. The monitor. The phone. McCoy had definitely been here before. Something burned deep in Brock's stomach.

Haywood grinned, displaying an overlapped set of yellowed teeth. "Right glad to meet up with ya. We got business to settle."

Jenna clenched her hands in her lap, and Brock could tell she trembled from the corner of his eye. Probably suppressed anger. Dead calm enveloped him. He sat back in his chair and crossed his arms.

Brock frowned. "What do you mean, McCoy?"

The whiskered man parked his dirty boots on the gleaming cherry wood. "I got her. You want her. It'll take money. Just like it did before."

A dawning made Brock raise his head. "So the money I paid for debts went to you."

A squawk of laughter came from the man. "Some of it. Not enough. Finally ended up bleeding Auberry. Marcy locked in the looney bin for three years has proved quite a windfall for me."

Brock lowered his brows. Why would he risk telling them? Unless..."So you blackmailing us or killing us?"

The man's feet dropped to the floor, and he pulled his chair in, folding his hands on the surface of the desk. He raised a finger to point at them. "You tell me."

"Dead dries up your profits."

The yellowed teeth appeared again through the man's wiry salt and pepper beard. "Point taken. But there's still Marcy."

"Medicaid's much stingier."

Haywood McCoy saluted him with two fingers and a wink. "Ya got that right. A tad harder to touch, too. So let's talk money."

"How much?"

Another guffaw from the country bumpkin with a brain like a razor. Brock knew when he'd interviewed the man that something didn't ring quite true. His keen eyes belied a genius mentality wrapped in a warped character.

"Well, I blew up the evidence. So, I'll take less with silence."

"Meaning I just keep feeding you money?"

The older man rose and leaned forward, his hands propped on the desk. The gun went diagonal towards the door as his body brushed it. Good. Point blank off Jenna.

Haywood's eyes glittered like a rabid dog. "Indirectly. You keep Marcy in that funny farm, and I'll bleed it. Simple."

"What about Katie?"

The old man winked. "You can have her. Off ya go into the sunset. Unless...you squeal."

"And if I don't keep quiet?"

He reached for the shotgun and cradled it in his hairy arms. "Option two."

Chapter Twenty-Seven

"You swine!" Jenna leaped from the chair and fastened her hands around the man's bony neck. A red heat boiled within her, knocking all sense of self-preservation from her mind. The wizened hippie's face registered shock before they tumbled backwards and hit the floor with a flurry of limbs.

Jenna became a hellcat, biting, kicking, screaming, kneeing, slapping, punching, inflicting pain like a collapsing rogue windmill with little use for form or technique. His stronger arms pushed at her, and he elevated the shotgun.

Sobs and gasps ripped from her body, "Three years! I've lost three years of my life. Of my sister's life!"

The gun in the man's hand fired, the huge blast filling the entire room.

The ceiling tumbled down onto them, white particles spiraling down. Then Jenna felt herself being lifted. She fought it off until she comprehended it was Brock who held her. Only then did she realize the room had filled with black-clad police officers, guns drawn on the felled man behind the desk.

"Stay on the floor, sir. Put your hands up. Don't move." All the terse commands were delivered in rapid fire, and Haywood closed his eyes and acquiesced.

In the background, Jenna heard more police personnel storming the basement. Her ears, now able to hear completely, latched on to a young girl's cry, and she broke from Brock's arms to run down the stairs.

There sat Katie, or rather, Jerrica, ensconced in a ragged blanket among the bedraggled Hawk family bawling her eyes out. Jenna rushed over and embraced her sister, her tears matching the child's. It had been so long. So horribly long. But at long last, she'd found her sister.

Haywood McCoy and the Hawks were taken into custody. The Tennessee Bureau of Investigations had swarmed in during the night to dig for evidence in the church's computer and recover the damaged documents in the cave explosion. Foster workers recovered the exhausted boys while Jenna latched on to her sister. After much finagling, they were allowed to take Jerrica, a.k.a. Katie, to the Rankins' home.

The poor girl fell asleep before they'd reached their destination. Brock carried her in and laid her on the couch where Jenna set up vigil. She wouldn't be parted from her sister again. And there was no way Katie would awake in terror. She would be there, ready to explain everything.

The next morning after showers and fresh clothes, Jenna quickly made her way back to the living room, in case her sister had awakened. There she sat, wide-eyed with fear mixed with determination. Uncle Robert sat across from her while Aunt Ellen, still in her robe, perched on the arm of Uncle John's wing chair. Brock came in, showered and dressed.

Jenna locked eyes with her sister. "I'm sorry I wasn't here when you woke."

"They said I got a sister. And I don't know who she is." Her face puckered and tears spilled from the corners of her eyes. "I don't need nobody to take care of me. I can take care of myself."

Jenna gave a laugh as she seated herself next to the little girl. She swiped away the moisture on the small child's face. Her throat closed. "You are pretty tough, all right. Remember this?"

She pulled the rock from her pocket, and Katie took it in her hands and nodded. Jenna picked her up and set her on her lap. The morning sunshine streamed in through the blinds, and Jenna wrapped her arms around the ragamuffin while she gripped the white rock in her hand.

"Remember how you told me you were afraid of being in that car when you were little?" At her nod, Jenna continued. "Well, you found out there was nothing to worry about, didn't you?"

"Yes," she said in a small voice.

"You and I have always had conversations about how God always takes care of us, right?"

The child's watery eyes searched hers, and her bottom lip quivered. "Yeah. But I had to stay here. By myself."

Jenna took a deep breath, trying to not let the tears flow. "You weren't alone. I was here. And so was God."

Her eyes, blue and wide, so much like Jenna's own, widened. "Huh come?"

She bit her lip. There was nothing like the truth. "The Hawks took you away from your real family, did you know that?"

Her brows knitted. "They did?"

"And your real family misses you very much."

The child turned her eyes back to Jenna. "But who is my family?"

Jenna smiled, unable to keep the tears from toppling over her eyelids. "I am. I'm your sister."

The little girl's mouth formed an O. After a moment's hesitation, a smile crept across her face. "We look a lot alike."

A laugh popped from her, and she wiped her eyes. "Yes, we do."

Her face puckered. "Why didn't you tell me before?"

Jenna looked at Brock who handed her a wad of tissues.

"You know all the times I couldn't remember things?"

The imp nodded and added with a grin, "Yeah, and how you were afraid even though you were a grown-up?"

"Exactly." Jenna chuckled and squeezed her. "Well, I couldn't remember who I was, and I didn't know who you were. But maybe, in a way, I knew all along."

The girl's smile faded. "They said I have a different name."

"Not really. Your name is Katelynn Jerrica Price."

Katie caught her breath. "I have your name."

A happy sob broke from Jenna's throat, and she managed a smile.

"Well, if I'm Jerrica, who are you?"

"I'm Jenna Loralynn Price Langston." She reached for Brock's hand and pulled him forward. "I'm married to him."

"Whoa. He's hot!" Jerrica giggled.

"Yes, he certainly is." Jenna laughed.

Robert rose and Jerrica wrapped her arms around Jenna's neck. "Wait, cop-man, I don't want to leave my sister."

Robert grinned as he stooped in front of them. "Well, lucky for you, little Katie, you don't have to. After we do some paperwork, you'll be free to go with your sister."

Jerrica gave a hundred-watt smile, and turned to put both hands on either side of Jenna's face. "Did ya hear that? I'm gonna go with you. And," she turned to face Robert, "I'm Jerrica, not Katie."

The room filled with laughter, and Jenna hugged her little sister tightly and whispered around the huge lump of tears in her throat. "Thank you, Lord. Thank you so much."

Jenna eased back into the patio swing, her eyes going to the window, her old room in the big Victorian house, where Kat— Jerrica lay sleeping. Wow, that was going to take some getting used to. Brock settled next to her under the Indiana moonlight, and she rested her head on his shoulder.

"You think she's really asleep this time?" Brock chuckled lowly.

Laughter bubbled up Jenna's throat. "I hope so. I'm kinda feeling sorry for you. Not only did you have to make room for a wife, you have to make room for a child."

He reached and threaded his fingers into hers. "As long as I'm with you, I don't care if there are ten kids."

"Yikes. Let's work on one kid at a time." The corners of her mouth tilted upward, and she turned her head to him. He dipped his head for a sweet, lingering kiss.

"You know what I'm thinking?" he murmured, his head tipped back to take in the stars on a black velvet canvas.

"Sock puppets?" She giggled, her eyes on his profile.

His soft baritone laughter tickled a happy shiver through her. "Uh, no. I'm thinking this patio would make a great place for a second wedding."

She caught her breath. Surely he could see stars in her eyes, too. "That's a fabulous idea. Jerrica could be in it. Oh, my. That child will be over the moon with excitement. Perhaps we should keep it as our secret, at least for now."

He pulled her close and pressed his forehead against hers. "If you don't mind, Mrs. Langston, I've had enough secrets to keep me a long time."

She leaned forward with a conspiring chuckle and whispered into his ear. "Not all secrets are bad, Brock. Like...the color of my underwear, for example."

His arms tightened about her and his eyes flamed.

She laughed, pulled from his embrace, and pranced toward the house. Tingles of joy and expectation raced through her as he

strode to meet her at the door. Her eyes flicked to the stars one last time, a murmur of praise to God for a second chance at life and love. She closed her eyes as Brock wrapped his arms around her. Together, with God's guidance, they had a whole new lifetime to discover.

Peggy Trotter loves to hear from her readers. You can find her at:

peggytrotter.com

peggytrotter.blogspot.com

diamondsinfiction.blogspot.com

Twitter: https://twitter.com/Peggy_Trotter

Facebook: https://www.facebook.com/PeggyTrotterAuthor

Goodreads: https://www.goodreads.com/book/show/25294770-year-of-jubilee

Amazon Author's Profile Page: http://www.amazon.com/Peggy-Trotter/e/B00V15P2LU/ref=ntt_dp_epwbk_0

Don't miss the second installment from the **Unchained Souls Series** by Peggy Trotter, coming this summer, 2017! From *Unchained Souls Book 2~**The Secret Storm***

Chapter 1

"What are you doing in there? Get out. I need to use the john."

"Forty-three." The clank of the metal stud clinked against the side of the glass jar. *Don't dump it.* Smallest vanity ever. And grungiest.

Eyebrow studs were history. Nose, top lip, and ear studs gone too. Stormi Zorbroski ignored the voice at the door and gripped the next stud in her tongue. Bingo. Face cleared.

The door rattled. "You hear me?"

"I need a couple of minutes." She lifted her torn tank and made quick work of removing the three remaining studs beneath her clothing. Several hundred dollars were represented in the mound of metal in the jar.

Finished. Stud naked.

Her lips twitched as she met her own eyes in the mirror. Those green/blue/gray eyes seemed to have such an issue picking one color or another. She always despised the color of her eyes. Blue the color of a June sky would have been so much better. Or violet, maybe a deep iris purple, so captivating. Nope. She had…tealish muck.

Focus on the task.

She rubbed the stubble above her ear and stroked the jagged rainbow Mohawk that had become her signature look. Blue, red, yellow. Clown hair. Not washed in six months. At one time she'd been proud of that.

The dread locks resisted the wide-tooth plastic comb like a toddler in a muscle-seized fit. Moisture collected in her transfixed eyes as she forced the knots from her hair. *You will submit.* Strands stretched and popped, creating a multi-colored ball in the dirty sink.

When the locks freed, she parted it and combed it straight down. She grabbed the dye box on the back of the toilet beside her and examined the color. It was as close as she could get to her natural blond.

Next she grabbed the scissors, and one by one she lopped off all the stringing ends, ending with hair about 3 inches long. More needed to come off, but she wanted to hide the shaved sections above her ears. So this is where she started.

The dye covered all vestiges of her multi-colored mop. Slicked it down short. Now to wait. She hardly recognized the creature in the mirror. Loud banging shook the door.

"Hey, selfish brat. Open up."

Stormi pulled the door open.

Her mother's face pulled back, eyes raking Stormi's face and hair. "Finally got rid of all that git-up. About time. Get out. I'm about to pee my pants."

Better not to confront. Flee. *Flee.* Stormi walked into her mother's bedroom.

"You better not get that stuff all over this bathroom." The door slammed.

"Yes, Mother."

The door whipped open. "And if you think I'm buying that subservient sass, think again."

Stormi clenched her jaw and kept walking. She gained the living room and turned right and marched across the dipping floor of the kitchen, through the back porch, and then into her small sanctuary. Nothing more than a shed linked to the house as an afterthought. She shut the oversized door.

Why had she come home? She glanced around at two twin beds and the two clothes rods filled with clothes. Nothing was hers anymore. Mother hadn't wasted much time getting rid of her stuff. True she'd been officially gone six years, four to college and two on her own. Still, shouldn't there be something left?

She rubbed her chilled hands together and headed straight for her phone. No message from Alan, and she refused to text him till the deed was done. The outside door slammed, and Stormi breathed a sigh of relief. Mom, flouncing to her next card party.

The car door sounded the final evidence that she was alone, and Stormi rose to return to the bathroom to complete her task. Out the kitchen door window, mother's sky blue car pulled away. The tenseness in her body eased. Hallelujah chorus reverberated in her brain. After a good shower, she emerged and looked full on her reflection.

That same old insecure, rebellious teenager stared her straight in the eye. Only older and less rebellious. And wiser. Much wiser. Her fingers probed the pierced knobs, wondering how long before they disappeared. She flipped up the hair and assessed the stubble. Nothing but time could repair that.

She applied a little gel and dried her hair, the hot air burning the bald spots. Well, not necessarily pretty, but better. Back at her phone she sent Allen a text.

"Well, it's done." She played with what was left of her hair, trying to get a good look of herself in the small rectangular mirror of her make-up case. Her phone flashed.

"Done what?"

She sank onto the bed, typing with her thumbs. "Hair-blond, metal-gone."

"Not what it's about." He returned. Alan, ever the pastor.

"4 me it was."

"Then—congrats. But study."

Stormi's eyes went to the Bible lying on the other bed. "Have been. And will. No going back."

She tossed the phone on the pilled brown blanket that served as a bedspread and stepped over to the other bed to grab her Bible. The wind blew through the narrow window between the two beds, sending the navy, satin curtain dancing into the air. The one thing she loved about this room. Two windows exactly opposite of each other in the rectangular room. Perfect crosswind.

She settled beneath the sill and looked out on the neighbor's big house with its long porch. A charming church pew rested against the wall, inviting one to rest. The window's low position allowed her to set her chin on the wooden sill. Memories rushed in. Not all good. Most not. She reached back and grabbed the phone.

"Trust God to lead you."

Stormi smiled. Long distance Facebook conversion. Someday she hoped to meet up with her old high school classmate again. Oh, how she'd tortured him in the old days. Meanness, just plain meanness. He, a straight-laced Christian all the way. Never wavered. Now he pastored and she...a new creature.

The Bible flopped open in her lap where the bookmark lay. Second Corinthians chapter four. Her finger whisked down the column to verse seventeen. Therefore if anyone is in Christ, he is a new creature; the old things passed away; behold, new things have come.

The breeze wafted in sending the gauzy curtain across her cheek. She swiped it aside smoothly from her unstudded face.

Indeed the old had passed away.

References

All Bible verses are from the New American Standard Bible. (NASB)
Bible verses used in *The Secret Things:*

"Cease striving and know that I am God." Psalm 46:10a

"Even though I walk through the valley of the shadow of death." Psalm 23:4a

"Be anxious for nothing; but in everything by prayer and supplication with thanksgiving let your requests be made known to God. And the peace of God, which surpasses all comprehension, will guard your hearts and your minds in Christ Jesus." Philippians 4:6-7

"When I am afraid, I will put my trust in You." Psalm 56:3

"Cease striving and know that He is God." A paraphrase of "Cease striving and know that I am God." Psalm 46:10a

"He will never desert me, nor will He ever forsake me." A paraphrase of "I will never desert you, nor will I ever forsake you." Hebrews 13:5b

"And we know all things work together for the good to them that love God, to them who are the called according to his purpose." Romans 8:28

"We are afflicted in every way, but not crushed; perplexed, but not despairing; persecuted, but not forsaken; struck down, but not destroyed." 2 Corinthians 4:8-9

"No temptation has overtaken you but such as is common to man. For God is faithful, who will not allow you to be tempted beyond what you are able, but with the temptation will provide the way of escape also, so that you will be able to endure it." 1 Corinthians 10:13

"The Lord is my shepherd, I shall not want. He makes me to lie down in green pastures; He leads me beside quiet waters, He restores my soul." Psalm 23:1-3a

"Two are better than one because they have good return for their labor." Ecclesiastes 4:9

Quotations used in *The Secret Things*:

"I also found being called sir rather silly." Harold Pinter

"My most brilliant achievement was my ability to be able to persuade my wife to marry me." Winston Churchill

"Coincidences are spiritual puns." G. K. Chesterton

"A man works from sun to sun, but a woman's work is never done." Author Unknown

"It takes less time to do a thing right, than it does to explain why you did it wrong." Henry Wadsworth Longfellow

"Forgetfulness is a form of freedom." Kahlil Gibran

"Early to bed and early to rise, makes a man healthy, wealthy and wise." Benjamin Franklin

Films mentioned or referenced in *The Secret Things*:
Frankenstein (1931)
Sayonara (1957)
Roman Holiday 1953)
On Golden Pond (1981)

www.ingramcontent.com/pod-product-compliance
Lightning Source LLC
Chambersburg PA
CBHW032207190626
46810CB00019B/2173